NOWHERE WILD

NOWHERE WILD

Joe Beernink

HarperCollins*PublishersLtd*

Nowhere Wild
Copyright © 2015 by Joseph Beernink
All rights reserved.

Published by HarperCollins Publishers Ltd

First edition

No part of this book may be used or reproduced in any manner whatsoever
without the prior written permission of the publisher, except in the case
of brief quotations embodied in reviews.

HarperCollins books may be purchased for educational, business,
or sales promotional use through our Special Markets Department.

HarperCollins Publishers Ltd
2 Bloor Street East, 20th Floor
Toronto, Ontario, Canada
M4W 1A8

www.harpercollins.ca

Library and Archives Canada Cataloguing in Publication
information is available upon request.

ISBN 978-1-44342-243-7

Printed and bound in the United States of America
RRD 9 8 7 6 5 4 3 2 1

For Lisa

PART I

CHAPTER 1

Izzy

(Winter)

In the cold light of morning, Izzy Chamberlain began to tremble. Three strangers blocked the bottom step of the ransacked house. From behind her sister, Izzy eyed the knives in their hands, their sallow cheeks, and their long, uncombed hair. Broken pieces of wooden furniture fell from her arms and clattered onto the concrete porch.

One of the men lurched toward them. Angie tossed her load of firewood at his chest. She pulled at the strap of the shotgun looped over her shoulder with one hand, while shoving Izzy back into the house with the other.

"Run, Izzy!" Angie yelled.

Izzy ran—through the house, and away from those men. Away from Angie.

The screen door slammed behind Izzy as she vaulted down the three steps and into the backyard. She leaped through the neighbor's stripped-down fence. Her malnourished legs could still run fast when necessary. Less than a year ago, shortly after her thirteenth birthday, she had run 10K races with her mother for fun. Now fear drove her legs.

She paused only to see if Angie had followed. The door to the house she had just escaped opened with a squeal, and, for an instant, a mat of tangled hair appeared to be Angie's long auburn locks. But from within the house, the voice of her older sister screamed again, before abruptly falling silent. Izzy's illusion vanished, replaced by a weasel-faced man in a camouflage parka. The blade of a long hunting knife glinted in his right hand.

Izzy bolted. She hopped a split-rail fence, turned north, and looped around the next block. Her legs found their own way to the two-story apartment building within sight of their home base, where Angie and Rick had told her to wait if they were separated or threatened.

She wriggled through the broken front door of a town house, then tiptoed up carpeted stairs to the back windows from which she could watch the house she had fled moments before. Shapes moved by darkened windows. Cackles of terrifying laughter broke the silence of the neighborhood. Izzy could do nothing but wait. Warm vapors from her lungs fogged the frigid air as the relentless cold seeped into her muscles.

She, Angie, and Rick had swept this apartment block two days before for food and supplies. There was nothing to eat here—there was never anything to eat. There had, however, been clothes in the closets that would fit her, and at that moment, she needed a new jacket. She had removed her old one when they began breaking the furniture for kindling. It remained on the counter of the house where Angie was trapped. Izzy raided a pile of clothes, grabbing a coat two sizes too big and a mismatched pair of mittens. She zipped up the coat, pulled on the gloves, and flexed her fingers. No frostbite. Not this time anyway. An hour without protection from this cold and this wind, and she wouldn't just have frostbite; she'd be dead.

She crept from one bedroom to another, then raised her eyes above the windowsill. The rear entrance to the house they had been looting loomed tantalizingly close. She waited and she watched and she listened. The numbing realization that Angie might not make it out rose like the northern-winter sun: cold and distant.

Not even a glimmer of heat came from the hot-air register in front of her feet. She wiped her nose on her new sleeve. The smell of musty fabric made her cough. She'd find a better coat later. There were lots of clothes her size available. Few teenagers had survived long enough to see the winter. She had seen others in the early days, but eventually they had either succumbed to starvation or had vanished to the roads and the bush like everyone else.

Clothes were easy to find now.

People were not.

Izzy searched the room for something, anything, she could use as a weapon. The men had knives, and there were three of them. Nothing here would help her overcome those odds. Angie had a gun, but she hadn't fired it—oh, why hadn't she fired it? The men's faces wore that desperate look that Izzy had seen before on others they had met on the road: the look of men who had lost touch with what made them human. Not quite animals. Animals had fear, and for the most part, animals did reasonable, rational things. These men had abandoned rationality.

To her right, across the parking lot behind the apartment complex and four houses down from where Angie was—*captive? fighting for her life?*—the door on a different house opened and a figure emerged. He was taller than the three men who had attacked Izzy and Angie. Izzy recognized his ice-studded beard instantly. Rick had returned early from his hunt. He looked up and down the narrow stretch of open yards, apparently unaware of the threat just a few doors over, then disappeared back inside.

Izzy flew out of the apartment and sprinted around the block to the house they had called home for the past week.

"Rick!" Izzy's voice cracked with fear as she careened through the back door. "Rick! They got Angie!" The warmer air from the kitchen, liquid and luxurious after her time in the freezing-cold apartment, weighed heavy in her throat.

"What?" Rick's gruff voice practically rattled the plates in the cabinets. "Goddamn it!" He slammed a mug down on the counter. Four months of near starvation had changed his weight, but not the way he carried himself. He still towered over her like he always had. He pulled the Glock from the pocket of his coat. Izzy took an involuntary step back.

"Where?" His boots fell like pile drivers onto the hardwood floor as he paced the room.

"Four houses down. Three of them. We were getting firewood, and—"

"Stay here." Rick pushed her aside and stepped out the door.

Izzy choked down a sob as she watched him leave. Three against one—three against two if she helped him. *I should help him.* Her feet refused to move. The tears began then, hot and burning against her frozen cheeks, like cinders from a campfire falling into fresh snow, sizzling all the way down to her chest. The first weeks after this had all started had seen her cry often. When Angie had been there, she would help stem the flow. Now the tears ran freely, and alone, Izzy could not stop them.

It was only then that Izzy noticed the dead deer lying on the kitchen table: a young doe, skinny, most likely born too late the previous spring to have put on enough fat to survive the winter. Izzy could count its ribs. In the old days, no hunter of any repute would have wasted a bullet on it.

She rested her hand on the side of the animal. Food. Real food. The creature was cold but not quite frozen—the kind of cold that creeps into something that was alive and moving just a few hours before. The house grew quiet, save for the rumbling of her empty stomach. The floor floated away. The tiny kitchen spun as if the walls had flown outward, filling the air with swirling snow. The deer began to feel warmer—almost alive. The faintest beat of a pulse nudged her fingertips. Izzy tried to pull her hand back, but it stuck firm.

The deer's nostrils flared.

Run, Izzy. Run now.

Izzy sprang back from the deer. It lay there as before, still cold and still dead.

The crack of Rick's handgun made her jump again. Then three more shots. She pulled a knife out of the butcher block—a chef's knife with a short, sharp blade. A tang of cold steel ran through the wooden grip, sucking heat from her hand like a vein of ice. She adjusted her grip to prevent her fingers from touching the metal.

A fifth shot.

The window over the kitchen sink provided a partial view of their backyard and the neighbor's. Her eyes darted back and forth across the snow to the drifts clustered around trees and shrubs. The ground had been scalloped by the same gusts that had driven them out of the bush and back into town. Crisp brown grass showed through the thin white crust. The frozen blades rustled in the breeze.

Another shot and Izzy ducked, the grip on her knife tighter still. The deer's hollow voice echoed in her mind.

Run, Izzy. Run now.

Hunched low, she moved toward the back door, ready to flee, but as she reached for the door handle, an unseen force ripped it from her grasp. She tumbled onto the patio, dropping the knife to the concrete. A rough hand grabbed the back of her coat and lifted her up.

"Get your stuff, Iz. We have to go." Rick set Angie's shotgun on the table, patted the stock once, then turned his eyes toward the sink. Izzy caught a glimmer of a tear sliding down his cheek. She gazed at the gun. Her eyes flicked to the door, then back to the gun.

"Where's Angie?"

"She's dead, honey. She's . . . dead." He left the room before she could ask anything else.

Dead? Izzy grabbed the counter to steady herself. The blood in her veins stopped moving, packed hard by a single word, like the wind had packed the snow outside.

Dead?

Rick returned a minute later, his backpack in hand. The pack was always ready to go with essentials, but he searched the kitchen for more things to stuff into it. A box of table salt. A pepper grinder. A dishcloth. He pulled the Glock from his pocket and began feeding fresh cartridges into the magazine.

"I need you to get your stuff, Iz. Now."

"I need to see my sister," she said after a moment.

A glimmer of pity crossed Rick's face. "No, darling. You don't want to see her like that."

He grabbed Izzy before she collapsed and brushed his hand over her blond hair as he hugged her close.

"We're going back into the bush. It's not safe here."

Rick lifted the deer from the table and threw it over his shoulder. He gave Izzy a gentle push toward the room where she kept her pack.

Izzy did as ordered, in a daze, her thoughts swirling around the horrible, impossible idea of never seeing Angie again. As her mind spun, the deer's words—imagined, surely, but imprinted in her brain nonetheless—returned: *Run, Izzy. Run now.* But she had nowhere to run, nowhere safe to go. Angie was gone. Everyone she loved was gone.

She looked back at Rick as she shouldered her pack. He bent low outside the door, picked up the knife she had dropped, studied it for a moment, and then held it out to her. It looked ridiculously small in his huge hands.

Rick was all she had left now. He would protect her. She took the knife from him, pocketed it, and followed him out the door.

CHAPTER 2

◄○►

Izzy

(Winter)

Rick led Izzy northwest through Thompson. An invisible rope pulled her reluctant feet across wind-drifted snow, down streets that had once been familiar. There were some footprints in the white, but they were far too rare. Ice crusted over a body-shaped lump in the alley between two houses. Izzy looked away. Her sister was now one of the countless dead, and she didn't want to imagine Angie like that.

Rick slowed as they turned past a park. Swings on rusty chains swayed in the breeze. A low groan crawled across the open ground with each oscillation. Izzy kept her eyes to the street. She knew these places too well. She had grown up three doors down from the park. She wanted to tell Rick not to turn onto that street, but she knew where he was going, and it wasn't a coincidence they had ended up back here.

"Nineteen years, Iz," he said as they stopped in front of a white-sided bungalow beside the two-story house she had called home for most of her life. He moved off the center of the street, toward a tree at the edge of the sidewalk. His gloved hand stroked the maple as if it were a favorite pet.

"I planted this tree nineteen years ago—the day Lois and I brought Brian home from the hospital."

Brian had taught Izzy how to spit and how to skate; how to play cards and how to shoot a basketball; how to get into—and out of—trouble on a routine basis. Though more than five years separated them, they had bonded. He became the big brother she never had.

Their families had been close, too. Before Rick and Lois divorced, Rick and Izzy's father had spent evenings on the screened-in porch talking fishing during the summer and watching hockey in the winter. In the backyard they built an ice rink that covered both properties. All the neighborhood kids hung out there when the ice was set. Rick kept the rink smooth and fast for months. Everyone in the area knew Big Rick.

They wouldn't recognize him now.

"That was a long time ago," Izzy said. She focused her eyes on her boots, denying the temptation to look at her old home. Without Angie, there would be no one to pick up the pieces if she broke down.

Her heart burned. Three hours ago, Angie had been alive. Three hours had changed everything. Izzy turned back in the direction they had come. The wind had already blown granular snow into their tracks. Soon, there would be no trail left for anyone to follow. Once they left the town and hit the edge of the woods, the world would be the same in every direction: cold and white.

"You remember that party we had a few years ago? When he turned sixteen?" Rick wiped his face with his glove. Izzy nodded but stayed quiet. The urge to look for Angie one last time swelled. She shuffled a step and stopped.

Angie was dead.

"We got him that old Chevy half-ton. Put that big bow on it. You remember that, Iz?" She remembered it. She had helped put the bow on. It looked ridiculous and lopsided, but they had laughed the whole time. When Brian saw it, he jumped off the porch with such pure joy. He picked up Izzy and tossed her into the air. Izzy, then just eleven years old, had squealed with delight. Brian was almost as big as his father, and she had been as light as a feather to him. She was nearly lighter now than she had been then.

Two years after that party—just over a year ago—Brian headed to British Columbia for college. She hadn't seen him since. Before the storm that knocked the power out in Thompson for good, he had been trying to return home. Three months—a lifetime—had passed since the phones last rang. Rick held out hope that Brian was still alive somewhere, but Izzy knew that he was probably dead. They were all dead now. Her father. Her mother. Rick's ex-wife, Lois. *Angie.* Everyone except her and Rick. Two families. Two survivors.

A patch of compacted snow crossed part of the sidewalk by the front porch. Izzy wondered how many times in the past week Rick had come here while he claimed to be out hunting. He stopped just short of the patch.

"I miss them, Iz," he said in a low voice.

Izzy nodded and fought back more tears. It had been four months since her parents died. Four months? When had the count gone from days to months? She looked up, finally, at the white house with the blue trim to her left, and remembered "that day." The flu hit the town like an F5 tornado. Her father died first. Her mother, less than twenty-four hours later. Angie had taken Izzy outside, and they sat on the steps, huddled together, scared and shaking from fever. Lois had seen them and taken them in. She had been healthy then. Forty-eight hours later, she was dead. Rick stumbled back to his ex-wife's house the next day, sick with it, too. Then it was just the three of them, weak and dehydrated, but spared by an immune response that graced a precious few. The girls hadn't been apart for more than an hour since. Angie had always been there.

Now she was gone.

Izzy couldn't hold back the sobs. Rick turned and caught her as her knees gave way.

"It's okay, darling," he said, holding her close. "We've made it this long. We'll make it through the winter. I know where we can go. We'll be safe there. You'll be safe with me." He rubbed her back.

"You want to come in? I need to grab the skis."

Izzy shook her head. "I'll be fine right here." She glanced back over her shoulder. Going into the house where her parents had died was not an option. Not today. Not ever. Even though Rick had hauled their bodies away—he wouldn't say where they were now—she had not been able to cross that threshold since the day they died.

"I'll be right back. Holler if you see anything." Rick patted her head, checked up and down the street, then disappeared around the side of his old house. Izzy leaned up against the tree and watched the snow swirl through the air. Rick returned a few minutes later, his arms loaded with supplies.

"You remember how to use these?" he asked as he held up two pairs of cross-country skis and poles.

"Sure."

"Good." He handed her the smaller set, and a pair of boots. The boots fit, but just barely. Her feet had grown since last winter. Rick ran back to the house and returned with two sets of aluminum snowshoes. "We'll carry these, just in case."

He strapped one set of snowshoes to the outside of his pack, atop the carcass of the deer, then tied the other set to her pack. Rick was standing and clipped into his skis before she finished with her final buckle.

Izzy glanced at the house she had grown up in one last time. Wherever they were going had to be safer than this place. Of course, they had thought that last house was safe. And now . . .

"Come on, honey. We need to get out of town before dark." He nudged her shoulder and led her down the street: down the street, into the woods, and away from the dead city.

CHAPTER 3

Jake

(Spring)

Jake Clarke put down the battered frying pan and stopped digging. The hole didn't even reach his knees. From the pile of gravel he had already excavated, he grabbed the ax, hefted it one more time, and wearily banged it against the permafrost. A few bits of ice and rock flew off in odd directions, but not enough to even bother picking up the pan again to scrape them up.

Behind him, to the southeast, the sun began its arc through the northern sky. He had been standing in this shallow trench for what seemed like hours. His calloused hands, equipped with only the crudest of tools, had torn away the leaves and the grass, and burrowed into the gravel shore of the lake. Jake tossed the ax aside and stepped out of the hole. Dirt covered his face. His black hair had worked its way free from the rawhide tie securing his ponytail. It fell against his sweat-and-tear-marked cheeks. He pushed the loose strands back from his face. His grandfather had told him not to cry. That was like telling the rivers not to run, or the wind not to blow.

Jake stumbled back to the cabin. He hesitated at the door, staring out at the dock and the lake beyond. In a perfect world, now would be the moment the plane would finally arrive and save him from this next horrible step, but the sky remained silent and empty, as it had been for the past eleven months. And his father, who had left the cabin all those months ago with a promise to return in three weeks, was still nowhere to be seen.

Inside, on the cot to Jake's right, sat his backpack, fully loaded and ready to go. On the cot to the left, beside the now-cold stove, lay the body of his grandfather. Jake bent close to the old man's face, paused, and kissed him on the forehead. Jake smoothed strands of Amos's gray hair back into place, then zipped the sleeping bag closed, till only his grandfather's face remained exposed to the light.

Jake slid his arms under Amos's shoulders and legs. A year ago, Jake wouldn't even have tried to lift Amos. But after months of wasting away, giving whatever extra food there was to Jake to keep him strong, Amos had been reduced to a shell of the proud Cree warrior he had once been.

Jake maneuvered through the narrow door, then across the ground back to the grave. He didn't look at the discolored ground a few paces to the south. His mother, Emily, lay buried under that mound.

Jake stepped down into the shallow hole and, as carefully as he could, set his grandfather into place. Despite his labors, the grave was too short. Jake struggled to bend Amos's knees, but they were as frozen by rigor mortis as the ground was by the winter not so long past. Jake picked up the pan and extended the trench until his grandfather's feet finally slid below the surface. Before exiting the hole for the last time, Jake bent low and straightened the cowl of the mummy bag around Amos's head.

Amos deserved more than this, Jake knew. He deserved to be buried like a warrior: with a celebration of his life, his trials and his victories. He had overcome so much. Certainly, dying out here was better than dying in some hospital bed and being buried in some city cemetery. He had told Jake as much a dozen times. Jake was to bury him here—to return him to the ground so he could meet his ancestors who had roamed this frozen land for centuries before the white man had even dreamed such a place existed. Amos's memories and lessons would live on through Jake. And that, Amos had said, would make his people happy to welcome him into the spirit-world.

But no matter how hard he tried, Jake could not pick up the pan and drop that first scoop of dirt onto Amos's body. Though the spirit was gone—and no doubt in a better place—Jake could not mar the flesh like that. He set the pan down and ran back to the cabin, returning a moment later. In his arms was the fur of a black bear— one he and Amos had killed the previous fall. The bear meat had kept them alive for months, and the fur had kept Jake warm through the bitterest of nights. Jake couldn't take it with him—it was far too heavy for him to carry—but it could protect Amos and make the next task possible. Jake gently laid the skin over his grandfather, covering him from head to toe, then picked up the pan and began pushing the dirt back into the grave.

An hour later, with the job completed, Jake carved his grandfather's name into a crude wooden cross, and pounded the cross into the earth. He stepped back, wiping his eyes. There would be no more tears, he vowed then and there.

Back in the cabin, Jake surveyed the single room. The contents of his pack had been planned and re-planned a hundred times. *Only the essentials*, Amos had said. Amos had vetoed every extra ounce: the ax that was bigger than the little hatchet strapped to his pack; the camp stove with its empty tank that could be refilled if he could just find another cabin with a supply of propane; the spare blankets that would keep him warm if he could keep them dry. He couldn't carry all of that.

The pack was ideally suited for his lanky frame. Inside were a few extra clothes, cooking supplies, a first-aid kit, a sleeping bag, and his tent. Buckled to the right side was his prized possession: a

.308 Remington 700 rifle in its padded case. On the other side were a dismantled fishing pole and a long bush machete. Stuffed into side pockets were coils of wire for traps, and extra ammunition. To the top of his pack frame, he had strapped a large food canister containing smoked venison and fish—enough for three weeks if he rationed them. A compass dangled from the webbing of his harness, next to a can of bear spray. Both would remain close at hand while hiking.

On the wall, hanging from a hook, was Amos's old Colt pistol, a remnant of his time as a young man in the Canadian Army. Five of the .45 caliber rounds remained for it. The gun weighed a ton, and with over a hundred and fifty kilometers to go to reach Laroque, that weight would be felt with every step. Jake knew he should leave it, but it was the only tangible memory he would have of his grandfather. He couldn't leave it behind. Jake wrapped the gun in an old dishcloth, shoved it deep into his pack, and rolled the bag closed. It bulged with the extra item. He hefted the pack and headed for the dock, pulling the cabin door shut behind him.

• ◆ •

Eleven months before, when Jake was fifteen and before everything had gone to hell, he had sat on the end of that same wooden dock, looping his toes through the cold water of the northern Manitoba lake, waiting for a fish to take the bait on the end of his line. A mosquito buzzed about his ears. He absently shooed it away, as he had done a thousand times on that trip. In early summer, the bugs were always horrible up here.

To Jake's right, on the strip of gravel that edged the water in front of their cabin, his father, Leland, and his mother, Emily, had stood together. They swayed, as if dancing a slow dance, and spoke in hushed voices. Sound, however, carried well over the short stretch of calm water.

"Bridger should have been here by now," his father said. Even from a few dozen yards away, the concern in his voice had been obvious.

They had been at the cabin nine days—two days longer than planned. The calendar had rolled from June to July. Overhead, a large flock of geese raced north against a broken sky. Jake's hunter eyes followed the flock and calculated the odds of reaching one of the birds with a shot from the 12-gauge in the cabin. Too far.

"He must have had problems with the plane, Leland. Every time we see him, he complains about how that engine is always costing him money. Might be waiting on a part. Or maybe he's socked in."

Emily wound her arms around Leland's waist. Leland's right arm clung to her shoulder. He brushed a strand of blond hair away from her pale cheek. Jim Bridger piloted the bush plane that had dropped them off at the start of their trip. He was normally reliable, but always at the mercy of the weather. A day or two's delay due to a storm wasn't unheard of.

"And the radio?" Leland's head dipped toward the water as a small wave rolled up onto the shore. The radio had been strangely silent. That was possible up at this latitude—for a while at least—but not likely for three straight days, and not at the beginning of the summer busy season. That had not happened before.

"Sunspots?" Emily asked with a touch of hope in her voice.

"Maybe . . . but it'd have to be one hell of a storm, and the lights don't seem much bigger this year than normal. Barely anything last night," Leland said. Jake looked toward the horizon. Some days, when the solar storms were big, you could see the northern lights from dusk to dawn. Last night's glow had barely been bright enough to see.

Leland glanced over at Jake, who swirled his toes in the water, careful not to create any noise that might interfere with his hearing.

"We'll keep trying," Emily offered in a worried voice.

Jake knew that voice. In the middle of every winter, when the money from the guiding trips of the previous summer began to run out, that same voice crept into every conversation between his parents. Emily's meager salary as a part-time teacher's assistant at one of Thompson's elementary schools barely covered the rent and the heat.

"We should have bought that satellite phone last winter when it was on sale." Jake's father bent over and picked up a rock, then skimmed it across the water. It skipped twice before it sank into the depths.

"We'll get one as soon as we get back. The credit cards can take it. Or maybe we can borrow one from Bill?" Bill Six Rivers operated another local outfitter and had helped Leland launch his own business years earlier. He had lent a hand before. He'd do it again, and not ask for anything in return.

They tried the radio until the batteries ran dead, broadcasting an SOS every few hours during daylight. They tried again in the evenings, when the radio waves traveled farther. The planes had always come. This time, no one replied and no one came.

They rationed the gasoline for their generator all the way into August. Theirs wasn't a permanent camp meant for months of occupation without resupply. By the time they realized no one was coming to rescue them, it was too late.

A simple mistake with a fillet knife turned their situation desperate at the end of August. Emily's knife slipped while she was cleaning a fish. The gash in her left palm didn't seem bad at first. They stemmed the bleeding, wrapping her hand in gauze from their first-aid kit. Leland even tried to stitch the wound closed with fishing line. Emily gutted out the pain of the surgery and said everything was fine, hiding her true state until it was too late—not that they could have done anything for her. The infection started in the

wound, and spread through her bloodstream. The fever that followed had her shaking and nauseated a few days later.

"*Sepsis*," Leland whispered to Amos and Jake while Emily lay
curled up in her cot. "She needs a doctor . . . antibiotics." The nearest
doctor was hundreds of kilometers away.

The next day Jake's father left to go for help. A cool breeze blew
out of a gray September sky, ruffling the water next to the dock as
Amos and Jake helped Leland load one of their two canoes with
supplies. Leland traveled light. It didn't take long to transfer his gear.

"Three weeks, tops. I'll be back in three weeks." He had never
done the hundred-and-fifty-kilometer trip from their camp all the
way back to Laroque by canoe. They had always flown in. Three
weeks was an estimate, but his father had been venturing around
this part of Manitoba going on twenty years.

"You sure I shouldn't come with you?" Jake asked.

"You need to stay and take care of your mother."

Leland looked Jake straight in the eye, his weathered face framed
by a military-surplus jungle hat, then he glanced at Amos, and his
grip on Jake's shoulders tightened. Amos was eighty years old. This
was to have been his last trip to the cabin. Years of hard living had
taken a toll on the old man's body. Jake knew his grandfather could
not care for Emily alone, not with her fever raging. Some days he
could barely care for himself.

"Dad—" Jake's voice cracked.

"Do me proud, Jake. Listen to your grandfather. Do what needs
to be done. Okay? I'll be back in three weeks."

Jake nodded, gave him a hug, and stepped aside to let Amos have
his chance for good-byes.

Leland leaned down slightly to wrap his arms around his frail
father. "Take care of him, Pop," he whispered into his ear. "I love
you."

"Love you, too." Amos's eyes glistened as they separated. "Be careful."

"I will." Leland stepped down into the canoe and took the paddle in his large hands. "I'll be back in three weeks," he said one last time.

With a single sweep of the blade, he turned the canoe and straightened its path.

Now, Jake stood at the end of that same weathered dock and gazed out over the lake he had called home for the past eleven months. He shuffled his feet on the gray wood and kicked a splinter into the water.

Common sense told him that his father would have done everything possible to return to the cabin. But Leland had been gone nearly nine months, and Jake knew what that could mean. Jake's only choice was to find his own way back to civilization—to leave this cabin and all its memories—before he, too, succumbed.

No one remained to dig his grave.

Jake glanced back at the cabin as he stepped carefully into his canoe and inspected his gear, making sure he hadn't left anything behind. Then he released the line holding the canoe to the dock. He picked up the worn paddle and tested its weight. With the paddle in his hands, he had a goal and a sense of purpose. There was comfort in that.

He pushed away from the dock, swung the bow toward the center of the lake, made a quick steering stroke, and adjusted his posture. With a lean in one direction, then back to the other, he checked the balance of the craft. Satisfied that all was well, he gripped the top of the paddle with his left hand and the shaft with his right. He stuck the blade deep into the cold water and pulled.

It was time to go.

CHAPTER 4
―◄○►―

Izzy

(Winter)

Izzy trudged through knee-deep snow, struggling to keep up with the hooded figure ahead of her. Her legs balked with exhaustion. Her feet, frozen inside her boots, felt like blocks of wood tied to the end of rubber-band legs. They were nine days out of Thompson now, headed straight north according to Rick. At yesterday's breakfast they had finished the last of the venison. Twenty-four hours had lapsed since anything but hot water or pine-needle tea had passed her lips. The snow here was too deep to ski through, and walking with snowshoes required a level of concentration she could no longer muster. The skis, strapped to her back like a giant cross, snagged every low-hanging branch. Rick set the pace. He wasn't going to slow down. They couldn't afford to be caught outside if the weather really turned bad.

Angie had been caught in a different type of storm, and now Angie was dead.

Fuzzy images of her parents flitted across her memory, their faces torqued as if the light bent to the gravity of the situation. Angie was—*had been*—her only sister, and as hard as her parents' deaths had been, losing her sister hurt more. She was alone now, except for Rick. She stumbled in the snow, distracted by her thoughts.

"Damn it—" Rick yelled. Izzy glanced up.

The deer, thirty meters ahead of them, jumped and disappeared before Rick could raise the gun to his shoulder. Thick pine trees prevented any attempt at a trailing shot. The deep snow halted Rick's chase after a few short strides. His snowshoe-clad feet were no match for the leaping, prancing deer. It vanished so quickly that Izzy thought it might have been a hallucination.

Izzy struggled to her feet. The brief thought of food—for that's what the deer represented—set her stomach growling. Her mouth felt as if it were stuffed with dried leaves and sharp twigs. She pulled her water bottle from the inside of her coat, where it wouldn't freeze, and took small sips, just like Rick had taught her.

"Should we follow it?" She coughed as she asked.

"No use. Not with the racket you're making back there," Rick snapped.

Izzy resisted the urge to respond in kind. Angie had been able to stand up to him when he got like this. Izzy wasn't Angie.

"I could carry the rifle," Izzy offered. "Then we could both try to—"

"Hell no," Rick said.

"I can shoot," she said defiantly. "I'm a good shot. I got that buck—"

That buck, huge compared to the doe Rick had killed on the day Angie died, had kept the three of them alive through September and the beginning of October. Only when the meat had run out had they come back to town. If they had been able to kill one more, they might have been able to stay out a little longer... *and Angie might still be alive.*

"We lucked out there," Rick replied. He turned from her and surveyed the forest ahead.

But it hadn't been luck. Sure, the buck had wandered into their camp while Angie and Rick were down by the river. Izzy, despite being starved and then suddenly faced with a feast, had sat perfectly still for over five minutes. When it started to move off, she grabbed the rifle from the tent, carefully stalked the deer, waited until she had the perfect shot, and took it. It hadn't died right away. Later, Rick explained that a .22 wasn't a big enough caliber to bring down an adult buck in a single shot, but it didn't stumble far before he found it and finished it off with the pistol.

"It wasn't luck," she muttered.

"That deer was just plain stupid, wandering into the camp like that. There's a big difference between hunting and being served dinner on a plate." He shook his head. "We've only got the one rifle. We lose it, or wreck it, and we're dead." He motioned with his hand. "Come on, Isabelle. We need to make some more distance before dark."

"Don't call me that—call me Izzy. My name is Izzy."

Her mother had only called her Isabelle when she was in trouble. Angie had called her Iz-Kid when she was younger. Her father had called her Izzy from the start. That was who she was, and who she always would be.

Rick softened his voice. "Izzy's a little girl's name. Isabelle is a much better name for a young woman."

"Oh." Despite the cold, an ember of warmth flared in her chest. A short smile formed on her lips. If Rick saw her as more of an adult, maybe he would listen to her ideas. She let her eyes drift away from his face.

"You okay, darlin'?" His voice cracked as if he were too tired to even finish his sentence.

"Just tired." In every direction, bright white snow covered everything.

"Once we get to the cabin, we can rest. And maybe I'll teach you the right way to handle the guns. I suppose you're gettin' old enough to learn." He tipped his head northward. "We gotta keep moving." He adjusted the straps on his pack and started forward again.

Izzy shifted her backpack. Despite being completely empty of food, it still weighed a ton. She waited for him to get farther ahead of her so she wouldn't get slapped by branches as he moved, then resumed her march. She focused on her feet, simply following Rick's trail. It saved her the effort of looking where she was going.

She seemed to have been following Rick like this for years. It had only been months, though, she corrected herself. She and Angie had fled Thompson with Rick in July when the food ran out in the city. Along with a few dozen other survivors, they followed the road south in a convoy of vehicles, hoping that Winnipeg still had food in the stores. They met the first trickle of survivors from the south less than halfway to the city. They told horror stories of how bad things were down there. At first, no one wanted to believe those tales. But as they came upon more survivors—every one of them emaciated and running for their lives—the reality began to sink in.

Then they encountered the first of the large gangs. Rick dumped their car and took Angie and Izzy off the main road and into the bush, where they watched in terror as a gang from the city descended onto the rest of their unprepared group from Thompson like a pack of wolves. Rick didn't let them hang around to see what happened next. He led them deeper and deeper into the bush, along a peaceful river filled with fish. There they remained for the rest of the summer. Rick kept them alive through what they had thought was the worst of it.

But their luck peaked with Izzy's killing of the deer. The river ran low and the fish moved to deeper water. The geese and the ducks winged their way south. Angie and Rick began to bicker about the littlest things, like camp duty and fishing techniques. One morning in mid-September, they awoke to a thin layer of ice on the water. A flurry of snow drifted through the air to confirm their fears.

When the deer meat ran out shortly thereafter, and their sleeping bags were no longer warm enough to keep them comfortable in their thin tents, they headed back to Thompson, where they had hoped to keep a low profile while surviving the winter. It should have been easy in an empty town where the few who remained were too scared of strangers to make contact. Somehow, though, after only three weeks, they had been noticed, and the consequences had been beyond terrible.

Now, as Izzy marched northward with Rick, she was sure that wherever they were going, there would be no more gangs and no more attacks. With each step, however, she grew more despondent, certain their stomachs would never be full again, and that, when all was said and done, they would still be dead, just for different reasons.

The tips of her skis grabbed a low-hanging branch like a grappling hook and stopped her dead in her tracks. She fell to her knees to break its grasp.

Rick heard her cry out and turned. He waited for her to regain her feet, an exhausted look on his own face.

"Fine. We'll stop here. Set up the tent." He pointed to a shallow depression to the left of a cedar tree.

Izzy didn't wait for him to change his mind. She set her pack down and, by shuffling with her snowshoes in small circles that gradually got larger, tamped down the snow to build a better platform. This routine she now knew by heart. She set up the tent and gathered firewood. He set the traps and lit the fire. If they were lucky they'd have rabbit or squirrel or something for breakfast.

They ate nothing for dinner, settling their stomachs with more hot water. The small fire did little to keep Izzy warm. As the cold of the subarctic night set in, they climbed into the tent and sank into their sleeping bags. Rick lay motionless, zipped deep into his mummy bag, asleep within seconds.

Izzy's body ached from her head to her toes. She had been tired before, but never this tired. After long training runs with her mother, she had routinely slept twelve hours straight. Those sleeps had been in her bed, where she didn't have to worry about the cold or where her next meal was coming from. She had never gone to bed hungry. She had taken her safety for granted. Out here, so far from anywhere, she took nothing for granted: not the next meal, not a fire to warm herself by, not even whether she would see the sun rise the next day. The snoring figure next to her was all that kept the fire burning and food in her stomach. Today, there had been no food, and the fire had barely warmed her hands. And whether she would be alive to see the sun rise in the morning remained to be seen.

The nylon walls of the tent, pitched beneath sullen skies, rattled in the breeze like bones in a tomb. She sensed Rick more by smell and sound than by sight. Before her mind drifted to tumultuous, hunger-fed dreams, she rolled away from him and pulled her sleeping bag tight around her head. She covered her mouth with her hands and forced herself not to cry.

CHAPTER 5

Jake

(Spring)

Jake set an aggressive pace southward, his brown eyes shaded by a sweat-stained camouflage cap. His grandfather had cautioned him a dozen times about overexertion, but he needed to put some distance between himself and the cabin with its graves. He focused on his paddling and on his breathing, pushing the memory of the previous night's heartrending chores out of his thoughts. But forgetting his grandfather altogether was not possible.

"Jake, you'll need to be smart about this," his grandfather had warned one night. Notches cut into boards on the western wall of the cabin told them February had arrived. The only light came from a small candle of bear fat, its wick made of cloth from a tattered old shirt. Their potbellied stove provided enough heat to keep one corner of the shack comfortable. Ice and snow glazed the window overlooking the frozen lake. The darkness of the middle of winter swallowed up the rest of the North. The brief daily episode of daylight had already come and gone. A desperate chill had taken hold of the land back in late October and never released its grip.

"If you go out too fast, you'll burn up like a firecracker. Set a comfortable pace and stick to it. You'll last longer." Amos made a paddling motion with his arms. The words had made sense back then. Despite the warning, Jake reached the first portage before lunch, cutting a full hour off his best solo time. The distance didn't help with how he felt, though—his heart still ached with every beat.

The portage trail zigzagged between impassable bogs, bypassing the rocky riverbed in favor of more even footing. In most years the trailhead would have been obvious to untrained eyes, but now, two seasons' worth of weeds hid the entrance.

"It's the portages, Jake," Amos had said that night. "Those are the tough parts. A lot of the lakes here, they don't feed rivers, not big enough to paddle, anyways. They're potholes. Some are no bigger than this cabin. Some are the size of Winnipeg."

He waggled a thin finger at the map spread on the table and traced the route they had marked in pencil a month before. They had just two maps: a local topographic map that covered about forty square kilometers around the cabin, and a Manitoba road map bought at a gas station in Thompson years ago. They had been over this route nearly every day since the ice had set in on the lake and the darkness had fallen. Jake had grown weary of hearing the same warnings day after day.

"All the rivers around here flow north or northeast. See?" Amos traced his finger along a series of thin, unnamed blue lines that joined one small lake to another, eventually emptying into Hudson Bay. He didn't wait for Jake to look.

"You get out into the Land of Little Sticks without food—without someone to watch your back—and it's trouble. That's polar bear country, Jake. Not like the little blacks we got here. Big ones, the size of your mama's Toyota. You'd be about the size of a snack for them. And a pitifully small one at that." He flashed a grin short two more teeth since the end of the summer. Soon he would have no teeth left at all.

"And north isn't the way you want to go anyway. Once the rivers start turning that way, you need to hump it overland and connect up here," he continued after giving Jake a moment to worry about polar bears. He tapped his finger next to a small lake near Sand Lakes Provincial Park. The lakes north of this lake drained into the Seal River. The lakes to the south followed a line down to the Churchill River.

"You'll have to take your time on those portages. Short hauls. Scout the line. Always keep your pack with you. You leave it alone for half an hour, and you'll have company. Blackie can smell you ten miles away, but he'll stay away as long as you're making noise."

Jake had nodded as if this were new information to him, but he knew the black bear. The cover on his bed was the skin from a black that had harassed their cabin in the fall. They had, for a while, eaten relatively well.

Before setting out down the trail, he took a moment to chew a mouthful of dried venison, then washed it down with a swig from his canteen. The water had been boiled the night before. He would have to boil more each night to be safe. His father had drilled that lesson into him years before, but it only took one round of *giardiasis* as a child to reinforce it. The water here, even as clear as it was to the naked eye, could be as deadly as the polar bears his grandfather had warned him about.

He tightened the straps on his pack, slid his paddle between the thwarts of the canoe, and tipped the canoe onto its side. With a single, practiced motion, starting from his knees, he flipped the canoe up over his head and heaved himself to a standing position. After a deep, bracing breath, he marched into the woods.

In the shade of the jack pines, the cool, pine-scented air wrapped around him like an old blanket. Jake's long-sleeve shirt kept the ever-present bugs off his skin. The light fabric prevented overheating in the early-summer temperatures. Summer was short but could be pleasant here, two hundred and sixty kilometers north of

Thompson and nine hundred kilometers south of the Arctic Circle. Bad weather always lurked close on the horizon though—never more than a couple of days away at best. Once, Jake had seen it snow here in July. Today, however, the skies were blue and the temperatures comfortable.

Nettles ripped at his hiking pants as he walked. He knew better than to wear shorts or jeans on a trip like this. When jeans got wet, they stayed wet. Here, everything got wet, eventually. His father didn't even let him bring anything denim into the woods. "Urban trash. Great for cowboys, but useless in the bush." Jake grinned as he did his best imitation of his father's deep voice.

His father had surely hiked this same portage nine months before, but as Jake made his way down the crude path, he found no sign of his passage. The weeds and bushes obscured any hint of recent travelers. The weather had washed away the footprints.

"You head south, Jake," his grandfather had told him. "Always south. Take your time. You need to get into the Churchill watershed. Laroque is small, but you'll find it. Once you hit the big lakes, get your bearings, figure out exactly where you are, and head for town as quick as you can. If the river starts turning north, you're too far east. And don't even think about trying to run the Churchill. It'll ruin you. Even if you somehow made it down there, you'd have to paddle on the bay, and no canoe we got is going to handle those waves. They'll swamp you before you get far enough out to not see bottom. You'll be hypothermic in seconds." He snapped his fingers.

"If you end up west of the lakes, you'll eventually run into roads, but you'd have to be off course by hundreds of kilometers to reach them. But if you're that far off course, you've got other issues. The Churchill drains half the damn province. Hard to miss. And I know you're a better navigator than that, anyways. You won't get that lost."

Jake had smiled at the compliment until Amos coughed. The cabin's cold air came back out in clouds of vapor and spittle. Amos wiped his mouth with his sleeve again, then looked at the cuff. Jake pretended not to see the worried glance, just like he had pretended not to see the blood on the fabric when he was scrubbing their clothes during the last laundry cycle. He knew it couldn't have been from their last kill; Jake had dressed and butchered that buck himself.

Amos had scratched the back of his hand. Dark liver spots covered it as reminders of a different life, a long time ago. He looked at his hand in the pale light of the fat candle, and then covered the arm back up. He cleared his throat and licked his lips. Jake watched him for a moment, waiting for his grandfather to continue. Amos said no more. He simply folded up the map, placed it back onto its spot on the shelf, then curled up into his bed for another nap.

Jake had been relieved that day that the lecture had been cut short. Now, with his grandfather gone, he wished he could have heard it a hundred times more.

After only a few minutes of walking, the reality of portaging alone began to set in. Sweat poured down Jake's face, chest, and back. The mosquitoes hounded him, buzzing around his face and flying into his mouth whenever he inhaled. His shoulders burned with the weight of the pack and the yoke of the canoe. His legs ached with the combination of it all. He focused on taking each step, picking a tree he could see ten meters in front of him, reaching that point, then picking the next goal.

Just keep walking, he reminded himself.

His grandfather had done a lot of marching in the army. Forty miles in two days while peacekeeping in the Sudan, he'd told Jake many times, and a hell of a lot more than that while doing cold-weather training around Cold Lake, Alberta. "Wasn't much of a challenge for the Eskimo, they'd say," Amos recounted. "I kept telling them I wasn't no Eskimo—that I was Cree—but those guys, those guys don't know the difference. Don't care neither."

Jake covered nearly a kilometer and a half before a raspberry vine seized his ankle. The canoe tipped to the right as he went down, jolting to a stop with a dull thud. The yoke drove Jake's face into the brambles. He yelped in pain and muttered things he would never have said in front of his mother.

Jake lay still for a moment while he inventoried his aches and pains. The weight of his pack glued him to the ground. Forcing back a groan of self-pity, he rolled onto his side before pushing himself into a sitting position.

A flip of a clasp loosened his pack straps and released the plastic hip buckle. He sucked in a lungful of air, then took a long drink of water from his canteen.

He stood slowly and stretched his aching muscles. Ahead, the trail sloped downward to the next lake, passing through a thick line of pines. He checked his pack. Everything remained secure. A survey of damage to the canoe showed only a small, fresh scratch on the bow. He ran his finger over the new scar and tested the hull with his knuckle. It held.

With the detailed map from the pocket on his pack, he verified his position and direction. He'd been reading maps since before he could read books. He'd been so good at it that his father had started letting him lead trips at each one of the outfitter's camps. He had picked his way through dense forest, paddled hundreds of kilometers of backwaters on private tours, and navigated thick swamp while hunting moose—all with just a compass and a topographic map. They called it orienteering in school. His father called it survival.

It would be weeks before the raspberries would be in season, but there were other berries, other plants around at this time of year he could eat. Amos had shown him the leaves of the pigweed and the shoots from the cattail and the leaves of the dandelion. Even the roots of stinging nettles could be eaten if he boiled them first. Those plants, however, did not compare to the taste of the fresh berries these bushes would hold late in the summer. His mother used to come out to the camps while his father guided a hunting trip and pick them by the bucketful. She filled their deep freezer to the top by October. Jake, Leland, and Amos emptied it, without fail, by the next season. Jake smiled as he thought about his mother without breaking down. That, a few months ago, would have been impossible.

The trip down the hill left him next to a trickling, spring-fed stream. The roots of willows and more raspberry bushes fought for the extra water the spring provided. It took Jake two hours to go half a kilometer through the thick brush, forcing him to set the canoe down to hack his way through the growth with his machete.

The ground softened and the stream widened into a small delta as he approached the lake. Centuries' worth of dead vegetation stacked up to form a thick, stinking bog. The trail disappeared completely. Glimpses of open water appeared a few hundred meters ahead, tantalizingly close.

He towed the canoe to the water with a short rope tied to the bow, grunting and straining with each step. Swarms of giant mosquitoes and tiny gnats lined up to take their turns harassing him. The muck pulled at his boots, making every step a gargantuan effort. Jake pushed on through the knee-deep bog, stirring up rank odors of decaying plants and rotting fish, burning energy and time he didn't have.

The water deepened until he was finally able to pull the canoe beside him and hoist himself in. A gentle breeze rippled the open water ahead. When he cleared the reeds, the mosquitoes returned home, leaving him puffy and caked with dried blood. He removed his boots and socks, gave them a rinse in the lake, and set them forward in the canoe to dry.

On the shore to his right, a small clearing came into view. A piece of metal nailed to a nearby tree marked a trailhead. His trailhead. Jake's chin dropped to his chest. Somehow he had missed a turn in the portage and cost himself time and energy he didn't have. There were no small mistakes out here—only big ones. He vowed to do better. He pulled the map out of his pack to verify his bearings. Satisfied that this time he had his heading correct, he set off down the lake at an easy pace.

CHAPTER 6

Izzy

(Winter)

Izzy's internal clock warned her that afternoon was already well under way even before they emerged from the forest on the southern shore of the lake. Obscured by an impenetrable layer of clouds, the sun barely brightened the sky. A vast expanse of flat, featureless ice stood between Rick and Izzy and their goal—a cabin Rick promised was tucked into a protected bay on the northern shore.

Above them, the clouds threated to dump another squall. Every muscle in Izzy's starved body protested further exertion. It had been four days since they'd eaten anything substantial. As soon as she saw the wind-ripped frozen lake before her, Izzy knew that they should make camp and wait until morning to cross it.

And yet Rick barely paused to check his bearings before sliding down the berg of ice pushed up against the shore, and out onto the lake proper. Izzy mustered a brief objection, but it was lost to the wind.

On the ice, there were no branches to duck under or deadfalls to step over. There were no hills to climb or deep snow to push through. On the ice, the skis ran fast across the compacted snow. A single push on her poles allowed Izzy to glide the length of a tennis court.

Here, there were also no trees to block the incessant wind and no landmarks to measure their progress against, especially when the snow squalls dropped out of the sky like curtains. There was nowhere to stop if the weather got even worse. On the ice, the constant headwind pushed them in an eastward arc, requiring frequent checks of the compass to fix their direction.

They had scooted along the edges of dozens of lakes on the way up, staying in the shelter of the shoreline as much as they possibly could. Compared to the bushwhacking required on land, that was almost pleasant. On this last lake, however, they had no choice but to cross the center.

Ahead of her, Rick tipped his head into the wind. Izzy raced to keep up. If she could stay close enough to him, he would break some of the wind for her. Rick's pace quickened. The farther they went, the longer his strides grew, the harder his arms pumped on the poles. Her short legs could not keep up the pace. She hollered for him to slow down. The wind tore the words from her mouth. A ski slid sideways beneath her. She screamed again as she fell down hard onto the ice. By the time she pulled herself back to her feet, Rick had disappeared into the blizzard. His thin tracks vanished like letters wiped from a chalkboard.

Izzy screamed again. The wind whistled back at her, mocking her panic, driving her backward. She spiked the tip of her pole into the ice to stop sliding and leaned on it. The sky had darkened. If night arrived before she found her way off this lake, she wouldn't be alive come morning. She pulled the plastic emergency whistle from the clip on her jacket and blew into it as hard as she could. The chirp of the frozen plastic barely resonated above the howl of the storm.

She fought back the panic threatening to overwhelm her. Rick had their only compass. But the wind had been steady from the north-northwest all day. If she could keep it on her left cheek, maybe she could find her way to the other shore. Once back in the protection of the trees, she might be able to see Rick . . . or find his tracks. Perhaps he had realized she had fallen off the pace, and was waiting just ahead. She held the whistle between her cracked lips and blew it every few seconds, hoping that sooner or later it would pierce the rattling din of the snow on the ice.

How far had they come? How big was this damn lake? Was the wind really as steady as she thought it was? Her heart raced. It had been like this the first time she and her mother ran a half marathon. Her mother had taught her to set smaller goals—to break the run into manageable fragments and focus on the progress of each segment, not on the entirety of what lay ahead. On the run, she had picked visible landmarks and worked on reaching them. Each telephone pole was a battle won, each mile marker a victory unto itself.

But here, every bit of ice looked the same, the horizon bleak and white, so instead of choosing landmarks, she counted her ski strides. Twenty, then thirty, checking after each milestone, both for the wind direction and for what lay ahead. Five meters per stride on the ice where her skis ran fast, a little less on the packed snow, she calculated. She guessed they had been perhaps halfway across when she lost sight of Rick. How much farther? Fifteen hundred meters, give or take, maybe, to the shore. Three hundred more strides. She ducked her head to cut into the wind and jammed the tips of her poles into the ice with each push. Two hundred. The gusts shifted slightly. She adjusted her heading to compensate. One hundred. Ninety. The numbers wound down. At sixty, the wind began to slacken. At forty, a dark shadow emerged from the white. A triumphant smile crept onto her face. The snow began to deepen, dumped by the wind before it traversed the lake. A few meters to her right, the snowbank looked disturbed. *Tracks!* She altered her path and blew her whistle again. The faint chirp grew louder with her hope.

"Isabelle!" Rick's voice boomed across the snow.

"Here!" Izzy screamed.

"Over here! Follow my tracks!" Izzy pushed through the snow.

Ahead, by the very edge of the ice, Rick waved his arms. Izzy powered through the last few strides.

"I thought you were right behind me!" Rick grabbed her as she slid beside him and wrapped her in a bear hug.

Izzy shook her head, gasping for air. "Couldn't keep up." Rick released his hold. Izzy dropped to one knee, still panting. Rick beamed from ear to ear.

"I'm so sorry, Isabelle. I thought you were right behind me. But look! We made it! We're here!"

Izzy lifted her head. At first she couldn't see anything but trees, snow, and more trees. Then a shape emerged, tucked into the forest a short walk from the shore: an impossibly small, perfectly square cabin built of cut logs and lifted off of the ground on short stilts. Rick turned on his skis and headed for it. Izzy caught her breath, then followed him.

It wasn't much to look at from outside or in. Plywood covered the floor—thick enough to stop most rodents from chewing through it, but soft and rotted in a half dozen places by water that percolated through the tin roof. Drooping moss and mud caulking filled the gaps between the logs in the walls. Animal scat clustered in small piles in every corner. A year ago, Izzy would never even have set foot in such a place. At that moment, however, after all the nights in the cramped, unheated tent, this cabin felt like a palace.

"There should be wood around back, Isabelle."

Rick dropped his pack in the middle of the floor, pulled a stubby candle from a pocket, lit it, and held it up for a better view. Izzy set her pack down next to his and retreated out the door. She kept one hand on the cabin, working her way around the rough-walled structure. The woodpile wasn't large, but it would last for a few days. She picked up an armful of sticks and trooped back to the door.

The inside was brighter now. A rusted kerosene lamp flickered and glowed on a small table in the center of the room.

"This was my grandpa's lamp. He used to come up here to trap beavers, way back, when there was still a market for them." Rick turned down the brightness as the wick sucked more fuel from the canister below.

"Oh? Really?" Izzy feigned interest in the history lesson. A single cot sat in one corner, a solid wood frame with no mattress. In Thompson, she and Angie had shared a soft, comfortable, queen-sized bed. This bed presented no such luxury. All they had brought with them were their two sleeping bags and two spare blankets.

Izzy dropped the load of sticks by the hearth, marched over to her pack, and pulled her sleeping bag out of its protective pocket. Rick fed twigs into the kettle stove while watching her.

"You take the bed, Rick. I'll sleep by the stove." She unfurled her bag close enough to the stove to be warm, and far enough from the cot to be out of his way. Satisfied that her spot was claimed, she ducked back out the door for additional wood for the fire. The night would be as hard as the floor, but as long as the stove generated heat, she'd be fine.

"Sure you don't want the bed?" he asked when she returned. He pulled a few sticks from her grasp and slid them into the stove. The snow on the wood hissed and sputtered in the new flames.

"No, I'll be fine."

"We'll make up another bed for you in the morning."

"Whatever. I've slept in worse places." In the tent, they had slept side by side because there was no other choice. At least here she had a little space to herself.

She looked around the cabin. Two plastic five-gallon pails stood by the door. "Are those water pails?"

"Yeah. Clean 'em out good first. Who knows what's been living in them the last few months."

"Yep." She disappeared back out the door, wiped her brow with her sleeve, and stretched her shoulders as she walked. She scrubbed the pails with snow from a deep bank to the south. As she worked, she gazed out over the lake they had just crossed. Luck, she decided, had been on her side those last few kilometers. And now they were . . . where? How far had they come? Seventy kilometers? A hundred? A hundred and fifty? Which direction? North, mainly, but Rick had the compass, and as good as she had become in the outdoors, navigating this land required more than a vague sense of direction.

Another flurry settled in over the lake, turning it even whiter than it had been just a moment before. The features disappeared till all that remained were the few trees between her and the shore.

A vague sense of direction had nearly gotten her killed.

By the time she returned, the air in the cabin had warmed enough that she could barely see her breath. She placed the pails, filled with clean snow, between the stove and the back of the hearth. By morning there would be water to drink and to wash with. She took a long look at Rick as he prepared his bed. His clothes were rank, as were hers, but his . . . his she could smell from across the room. She would have to scrub them soon. That wasn't even a question. If she didn't do it, it wouldn't be done. Eventually, he would notice she hadn't been doing her part and then he would grow surly. Once, Izzy had accidentally hit a rock with the ax while chopping wood. Rick had ripped into both sisters that day. The ax, he said, was vital to their survival, and they couldn't afford to lose it. After that, Angie had taught her to avoid doing things that would set him off.

Tomorrow, Rick would go out hunting for food and Izzy would be left in the cabin. It would be up to her to make it habitable. Cooking and cleaning, that was her role now. Angie had played that part a short two weeks before. Izzy had been there to help Angie. Angie helped Rick. Now there was no buffer between her and Rick—no one to tell her what needed to be done. It was her responsibility to figure it out, and to do it without being asked.

A year ago, she had still been the baby of the family. Her mother, always busy at the hospital with one emergency or another, had leaned heavily on Angie and on their father. No one ever expected much out of Izzy. Only in the few months after her thirteenth birthday had her parents' expectations changed, and she had been given more responsibility for getting herself organized and ready on a daily basis. At the time, she had resented that. Now, she longed for those simpler days. This was a whole new level of responsibility and it weighed heavy on her shoulders.

"What's wrong?" Rick asked. His bed was made, such as it was, and he stood by it, watching her intently.

"Um, nothing." She wondered how long she had been standing there, drifting. "Just thinking about how much cleaning this place needs."

"Plenty of time for that tomorrow. Get some sleep, darling."

He crawled into his sleeping bag, testing the strength of the cot with one knee, then the other. The frame creaked, but did not splinter or crack. A few months ago, Rick might have weighed double what he weighed now. It would never have held *that* Rick.

"Good night, Rick."

She ducked into her bag, zipping it up tight. Her pack was her pillow, and the edge of the hearth was her headboard. She waited until he was snoring before she dozed off. She filled the time with memories of Angie and her parents, and thoughts of a life that was now far behind.

CHAPTER 7

Jake

(Spring)

As the sun slid across the horizon, Jake searched for a place to spend the night. He chose a clearing on the eastern shore of the lake near its southern tip, and pulled the canoe up onto the grass. A splash of cold water on the mosquito bites covering his face did little to calm the intense desire to scratch.

He emptied the canoe, inspecting the bottom for any fresh gouges or cracks; only a single new scratch from the fall marred the surface. Jake gave the hull an appreciative tap for getting him through the day.

Next, he turned his attention to setting up camp. He removed a pair of worn sneakers from a strap on the outside of his pack to save his bare feet while his sodden boots dried on top of the canoe. He re-rinsed his socks and draped them over the bow. Debris from the marsh stuck to the fabric, and no amount of washing would remove the smell. Regardless of how bad they looked or smelled, he wasn't carrying enough extra clothes to discard anything. At some point, these would become the cleanest, and the driest, socks he would have.

Other travelers had used this clearing in the past. A small stack of leftover wood remained next to a fire pit dug into the gravel near the water. An area picked clean of large rocks made an ideal place for a tent. Jake wondered if his father had used this site on his trip through, the previous fall. *Unlikely*, he thought. His dad was a much stronger paddler and in much more of a hurry. He had probably made many more kilometers that first day out and had surely, at the very least, waited until the end of the next portage to stop and rest.

It took Jake only a few minutes to set up and stake down the tent. He added the fly as an extra layer of protection, just in case. The sky showed no signs of bad weather, but it was prone to changing in a hurry in the middle of the night. *No more mistakes,* he reminded himself.

His father's survival checklist ran through Jake's head: *Shelter. Fire. Water. Food.* In that order. Those were the essentials. He had the first. His stomach tried to convince him to jump forward to number four. His father's warning trumped his desire. He needed a fire and he hadn't consumed enough water during the day. Dehydration was as much of a killer as starvation, even this far north. He gathered some kindling, lit a fire in the pit, and hung a pot of water over it to boil.

The exertion of the past twenty-four hours had his stomach growling. A look at the dried meat in his canister made him pause. The menu had been a constant conversation during the previous winter, when the fresh food had long run out and all that remained was what they had killed and preserved before the weather turned. Jake had never been a picky eater, but there were days when Amos had been less than patient with Jake's grumbling.

"Just eat it, son," Amos said as he dropped a small piece of cold venison onto Jake's plate. A three-day-long storm roiled outside. Their traplines were hidden under deep, windblown snow. Jake's frozen fingers fumbled with his utensils. Wet gloves steamed by the stove from a trip to the lake to force a hole open in the ice to retrieve a bucket of water. There had been no time to fish. The fresh meat of the last hunt had been rationed a week before.

"I'd kill for some pizza."

"Boy, there's no use talking of such nonsense." Amos placed a portion of dried meat, no bigger than the size of his palm, on his own plate. He cut it into tiny pieces and pushed a morsel into his mouth. His teeth—never that good to begin with and long in need of a good dentist—couldn't chew large pieces of the tough jerky. His jaw stopped and started as he tested each tooth. He winced in discomfort twice on the first piece.

"How about pasta? With some of Mom's sauce. Or scrambled eggs? With salt and pepper." Visions of a table set with orange juice and bacon made Jake swallow.

"Enough. Eat." Amos shook his head. "Cripes, boy, it's the same thing every night. It's not like I don't have the same thoughts. Talking about it just makes it worse."

Jake looked at the shelf that had once contained their flown-in supplies. The few resealable bags they had, had been used and reused multiple times. A dozen lengths of clear plastic wrap were constantly recycled as well. A large tub of dried meat, broken into pieces like the ones they now ate, represented the only food remaining.

"Don't you miss it, Grandpa?"

"Of course I do. Don't be daft." Amos placed another piece of meat into his mouth, mashed it with two of his good teeth, and swallowed. "But there's nothing we can do about it. Not right now. If the weather breaks, maybe we go out and get another deer, or a moose or another bear. Then we can shish kebab it, fry it, stew it, whatever you want. Right now, this here is what we got."

"I'm just so tired of meat. I want something green. Some beans. Peas. Lettuce. Tomatoes. Carrots. Corn on the cob."

Amos stopped his chewing. "This from the boy your mother practically had to beg to eat the broccoli off his plate."

"I didn't say I wanted broccoli," Jake said, straight-faced. Amos shook his head in frustration and chuckled.

There were only a few days when they didn't laugh at least a little during the long, hard winter. The memory evoked a pang of loneliness that Jake swallowed now with a small piece of the venison. It added a bitter seasoning.

Amos made it through the winter and the first half of the spring but struggled to even drink weak tea those last few days and hours. He hadn't been able to eat any meat the last week, and because of that, Jake's pack was slightly fuller than it might have been.

Every extra ounce weighed heavy on his heart.

• ◆ •

Jake slowed his rhythm with the paddle as he set out the next morning. His arms and back ached from the exertions of the previous day. It took a while for his muscles to loosen up and even longer for the pain to subside.

To the east, beyond a ridge, thin clouds danced as a breeze swept in from Hudson Bay. Cool air from the north usually met warm air from the south where the prairies ended and made even odds that the day would have some rain. On this day, the dice rolled in Jake's favor and he reveled in the warm sun.

The lake flew by in less than two hours. Jake crossed a small bay, and let the canoe drift just beyond the grasp of the current pulling water down the next river as he worked out his position with his compass. Reckoning wasn't as good as GPS, but in his hands, it was close.

The river that flowed out of this lake turned northward, drained northeast into Hudson Bay through the Knife River—four hundred kilometers from where he needed to be. To the south, a chain of lakes and small rivers would eventually dump him into the Churchill River, his next goal.

To get to the Churchill, though, he first had to endure twenty kilometers of pine forest, swamp, and smaller lakes.

Heading south, Jake traced the path he and his grandfather had worked out the previous winter. The next lake lay a short distance ahead, on the other side of a steep-faced ridge. The topographical map showed a navigable path to the west that wasn't too much longer. Jake backtracked the canoe to a small creek, paddling upstream until the flow reduced to a trickle of water over jagged rock.

His boots, still damp from the previous day's fight with the bog, felt heavy and stiff. He tightened the straps on his pack and started up the streambed with the canoe balanced precariously on his shoulders.

A few times on the climb he wondered if it wouldn't be faster just to leave the canoe and hike the whole way, but he knew better. In good weather, a paddler in a canoe could make two or three times the distance of a hiker on flat land. A paddler could go around kilometers of tangled underbrush. A hiker would be forced to ford rivers and circumnavigate large lakes. A paddler used them for additional speed. No hiker could keep up to the pace of a canoe in the hands of an experienced paddler on a downriver run. Saving a day or two on the rivers could mean the difference between starvation and salvation.

The streambed disappeared into a cluster of bushes and vines. A thin line of blue sky hovered over the top of the ridge. Prickly bushes carpeted the remaining climb. He set the canoe down and, with machete in hand, began hacking his way up the hill. By the time he arrived at the top, sweat soaked his shirt.

The top of the ridgeline provided a grand view of the lake he had just paddled, and a view of the next valley and next lake. The shallow lake grew tight with grass, reeds, and lily pads, leaving only a narrow channel of open water glistening as it wound its way through the cattails. After that, another ridge, much like this one, blocked his view. Beyond that, more ridges, and more small lakes.

Amos had called the area the Land of a Million Aches. Every step would be painful.

Once through that, however, he would return to an area of larger lakes, fewer portages, more navigable rivers moving in the correct direction, and a greater chance of discovering humanity. If the trip had consisted of a hundred and fifty kilometers of downriver runs, Jake could have completed it in a week of hard paddling. But paddling one klick, then portaging one or two or more, was a much, much slower way to go—a much more difficult way to go. These portages—and these climbs in particular—had prevented the elderly Amos and the ill Emily from making the trip with Jake's father.

The climb up the ridge was easier the second time. He gave himself a break at the top by setting the canoe on a log. Then he grabbed his pack so as not to chance losing it and used the machete to slice a path clear down the back side of the hill. It took half an hour to reach the water. Then he went back up to the ridge to retrieve the canoe. It took fifteen minutes to drag the canoe down the cleared path to the water. An hour later, he arrived at the southernmost point on the next lake and began chopping his way up the next ridge. By midmorning, he stopped taking inventory of what hurt and began searching for something that didn't.

He ate lunch stretched out on a rock halfway up another ridge while the canoe rested on a tree branch just below him. Shiny red abrasions marked the spots on his hands where the handle of the machete had rubbed the skin raw. The beginnings of a blister arched the webbing between his thumb and index finger. His hands had long ago developed thick calluses where they came into contact with the paddle or the ax during the time at the cabin, but the machete was a different tool, abrading different parts of his hands. He gently rubbed them together, willing the skin not to blister.

From the rock, he watched an eagle work its way upward into

the sky on a hidden thermal. The rising warm air pushed it higher and higher with seemingly no effort from the raptor. Jake wished, as he had many times before, for a plane to spot him, to rescue him, and to take him home.

Despite his wishes and his prayers, the sky remained as empty as it had been for the past eleven months, except for that one regal bird. A few minutes later, the bird, too, disappeared from sight, leaving Jake once again alone with his thoughts.

CHAPTER 8

Izzy

(Winter)

Izzy spent two days cleaning the cabin and gathering firewood. It kept her mind off other things—mainly her stomach, which grumbled incessantly. Her energy dwindled every hour, until all she wanted to do was to curl up next to the stove and go to sleep. There was no stopping. The work had to be done, and Rick had high expectations. He hunted and set traps from dawn to dusk. But the sun disappeared with alarming quickness each day after its brief stint in the sky. Somehow Rick always found his way back to the cabin just as Izzy began to fear he was lost.

Despite his sometimes harsh demeanor, she did fear something would happen to him. He had the skills and the knowledge to survive—to keep them *both* alive. He also had the guns and the maps. He left her with only her knife, the chef's knife she had picked up at their former home base while he had attempted to rescue Angie. Rick didn't trust her with the spare hunting knife in his kit. With just that single, pitiful implement, she scraped rot from the floors, cut frozen moss from nearby trees to fit gaps in the walls, and chipped icicles from the lone cabin window to allow a measure of natural light into their dingy shack.

On the second night at the cabin, Rick brought home their first substantial food in six days: a rabbit caught with one of his traps, and a white fox shot with his .22.

"Lots of tracks out there, Isabelle. Lots of tracks," Rick said as he gobbled down his meal. Izzy took her time, savoring each bite.

"What kind of tracks?"

"Lots of rabbit. More fox. Ptarmigan by the bunches. A wolverine, too. And a whole herd of deer." He smiled, raised his eyebrows, and cocked his head.

"Deer?" Izzy's head bounced up.

"A whole bunch of them. Looks like they might be hiding out in a hollow to the northwest. Found their tracks on my way back, but my hands were full and it was getting dark. You know what they say. A bird in the hand . . ."

Izzy nodded. Despite the food on her plate, she salivated at the thought of another deer. A full-sized buck would provide them with three meals a day for a month, and that hadn't happened since . . . a lifetime ago.

"We get ourselves a deer or two, and we'll be all set. We'll be living high on the hog, you and me. I told you this place was perfect, didn't I?"

"Uh-huh. If you get a big one . . . like the one I got last summer. That'll last us a month at least. Maybe longer since there's just the two of us now—" She nearly choked on her food. *Forgive me, Angie! I didn't mean it.* She dropped her fork onto her metal plate with a clatter and covered her mouth. Rick's head dipped slightly.

"It's okay, darling. I know how much you miss her. I miss her, too." He dabbed at the corner of his eye with his fingertip. He shook his head and cleared his throat.

"We'll get this place set up nice, Isabelle. Real nice. There's some other cabins around here that might have stuff we can use. Laroque is just a few klicks—" He stopped, stuffed another piece of meat into his mouth, and continued as he chewed. "We've got a good place here. Me and you are going to be real happy here for a long time. If

I can find a hand pump and some pipe somewhere, we can even have running water. Well, in the summer at least—too cold for that now."

"The summer? We're not going back?"

"Go back to what? More gangs? No food? Looking over our shoulders all the time?" He stopped eating mid-bite. "I don't want some bastard doing to you what they did to your sister." He wiped his mouth with the back of his hand. "That wasn't right, Isabelle. They spoiled her. She was so beautiful." His voice cracked. He reached across the small table and put his hand on Izzy's. "But don't you worry, I'm not going to let anyone hurt you." He rubbed her hand, and in the dim light of the oil lamp, his eyes misted.

Izzy coughed. Rick's hand jumped.

"You okay?"

"Just cold. A bit cold."

"I'll get some more wood. You stay put and finish your dinner."

"Thanks, Rick," she said as he stood.

"No problem, darling."

He threw on his coat and disappeared out the door. She sat for a moment, staring at the thin blade of the knife next to her plate. The grease from the rabbit had dulled the steel to a reddish brown. Bits of charred meat clung to the metal. She wiped the knife slowly on the tip of her finger, and then licked the grease from that. She ate another bite. The carcass of the fox hung on a rack over the stove, the heat turning it into a slow-cooked jerky. Breakfast. Rick had skinned it while she fried the rabbit. The two skins hung on another rack away from the stove, drying slowly. She pictured what the pile would look like by the end of the winter: a mound of skins and furs big enough to fill the cabin. She envisioned a thick winter coat, and new fur-lined boots keeping her feet warm. She stood and ran her hand over the fox pelt, letting the individual hairs slide between her fingers.

"We get a few more of those and we can make a nice big

bedspread," Rick said when he returned, loaded with pieces of wood large enough to get them through the night. "No more getting up every hour to stoke the fire. A few of those and we'll stay nice and toasty all night." He pushed a big piece of wood into the stove, closed the lid, and tightened down the dampers.

Izzy ran her hand over the fur again, drifting off into her memories. She imagined herself back in her bedroom, before the flu. A pile of stuffed animals—remnants of a childhood now long gone—sat in a corner. She had often fallen asleep among them when she was little, protected by a lion named Simba and stuffed cat named Kiya. Every night, her father would pick her up and put her back into her bed, tucking the blankets tight around her. Sometimes she would wake and talk to him. Even when she slept through his visit, she always knew he had checked on her, and that made her feel safe.

"We're going to have a nice home here, Isabelle, you and me. In a couple of months, all that back in town will seem like a bad dream. Lois and I used to bring Brian up here when he was younger. He always loved it. You will, too." He stepped forward and put his hand on her shoulder.

"I'm sure I will."

His hand lingered and then touched her hair. Claustrophobia tightened her throat. She ducked around him and returned to her seat. A little bit of rabbit remained on her plate. She picked at the lean meat.

"Save the bones, Isabelle. Put them in the soup pot for tomorrow. It won't be much, but it'll help until we get a deer."

"Sure. Good idea."

She fetched the pot from the counter, dropped the rabbit carcass into it, and added water from the melt pail. The rabbit floated for a moment and slowly sank. She thought again of her father.

Daddy, I miss you so much.

CHAPTER 9

◄○►

Izzy

(Winter)

Rick killed a deer on the third day at the cabin, and they did eat well. Izzy reveled in the sight of the rack overflowing with drying jerky. Outside, strung up high in a tree, the rest of the deer had frozen solid while awaiting room on the rack. With a large kill, however, there came an unexpected problem: Rick stayed close to the cabin. And the closer he stayed, the smaller it became.

After helping her to patch some of the holes in the walls, he dragged a few large pieces of wood into the cabin, all of which were too long to fit into the stove.

"What are those for?" Izzy asked.

"We can't have you sleeping on the floor all winter." He pushed their little table to the side to give himself room to work.

"Oh. Okay." She watched him for a moment as he laid out a rough frame with the larger pieces. Having a bed to keep her off the hard floor, and its pools of cold air, was a good thing. Except something tickled the back of her mind like an itch she couldn't reach. She watched him as he trimmed back a few branches with a hatchet. He worked quickly, apparently following a plan.

"We're going to need some hot water so I can bend some of these pieces, hon. How about you get some for me?" He looked up briefly to smile at her.

Izzy nodded, grabbed one of the buckets, zipped up her coat, and ducked out the door. The fresh air offered some relief, despite the cold temperature. The smell of drying meat inside overwhelmed her senses. The crisp air rinsed her lungs. A day ago, the smell of cooking meat would have driven her mad with hunger. Today, with a stomach so full that it bulged out from her rail-thin frame, the smell was almost sickening in its sweetness.

Outside, gusts drove the smoke from the chimney out over the water. She dug a path through the snow to the ice, where every scoop allowed her to take another step farther from the cabin.

They had butchered the deer until late into the night and collapsed into their sleeping bags. Izzy hadn't forgotten about the previous evening—the memory of Rick's hand on her clung to her thoughts like a spider web, wrapping around her and refusing to let her move on. She missed having Angie to talk to more than ever. Keeping herself busy around the cabin helped as a distraction, but Rick's presence made it harder to focus on her work. Earlier, while she was slicing meat for jerky, he had "assisted" her by showing her a better way to hold the knife. The tip was useful, and the knife did work better when she followed his instructions, but during the minute he stood by her, his free hand had returned to that spot on her shoulder and guided her arm. The smell of him was so close and so tight that she had to fight her gag reflex.

When she returned to the cabin, she knew immediately what was wrong.

Rick had set the outline of the new frame right beside the existing cot, and the way he had put the pieces together didn't seem like he had plans to move it. "Wouldn't it be better to put that over in the other corner?" Izzy asked.

"We've got the fur racks and wood pile over there, Isabelle. And we'd have to burn a ton of wood all winter long to keep this whole place warm. We've only got the two bags, those ratty blankets, and that deer hide out there. When the cold really sets in, it'll be better for us to be bunked together."

"Together?"

"Much easier to keep warm that way, darlin'." He shaved down a stick and fit it into a gap in the existing bed. Izzy searched for an objection that would make sense to him.

"I snore pretty loud. You may not want to hear that all night," she said. That was true. Her sister had complained about it a dozen times.

"Ain't bothered me so far, hon. Kinda cute, if you ask me. Lois used to say I snored like a chain saw, but I guess that was when I was a little heavier. Seem to have starved the snoring right out of me. I'm probably in better shape now than I was back in high school. Maybe not as fast as I was back then, but probably a lot wiser."

He rammed another stick into the frame. It came together more quickly than Izzy could think of excuses. She stood there, watching him for another minute. Her stomach rumbled and she felt slightly ill. Rick had warned her about overeating, but she had not listened. Now a cramp tore across her abdomen.

"I'm going to use the bathroom," Izzy said.

"Fine. I should be done here soon. Then we can gather up some pine boughs to make a bit of a mattress so it's nice and soft. A pine-bough bed can be just as comfortable as a feather bed if you know what you're doin'."

"Right," she said as she left.

The outhouse squatted a dozen meters to the south. Even compared to the cabin, the outhouse was dark and cold and small. Cobwebs hung in the upper reaches. It hadn't been moved from its pit in years. Rick said he would dig a new one as soon as the ground wasn't frozen solid. He had checked before they used it the first time to make sure no animals called it home—they would have been dinner the first night. It had been empty, except for the smell.

Sewer stink escaped from the wood with every creak of the boards. The pit, filled with dirt and debris and the frozen refuse of occupants now long gone, was barely deep enough for its purpose.

Even still, given a choice, she would have stayed out there all night rather than spend even one minute in a bed with Rick. It was bad enough to have had to sleep in the same tent with him since leaving Thompson. He was always sweaty despite the subzero temps, and his clothes smelled like old gym shoes. The idea of spending the night that much closer to him made her stomach roil even more. As she sat there and relieved her cramps, she tried to think of a way out. She could continue to sleep on the floor near the stove. Sure, it had been cold the first two nights, but with a little work, she could make it warmer. Her confidence in that plan faded as a gust of wind shook the loose boards of the outhouse. They barely had enough blankets to keep one person warm now, and it wasn't even officially winter yet. She had lived in the North her whole life, and in the wild now for months, but even as rough as the summer had been, the cold of the earliest part of winter had still been a shock.

Rick had been right a hundred times. He knew what it would take for them to survive out here. If he said bunking together was their best chance to make it through the worst of the winter, when temperatures in this area were known to drop to eighty below, then that was probably the case. She and Angie had shared a queen-sized bed in Thompson, and half the time she had had no idea whether or not Angie was there. Still, the idea of being that close to Rick caused shivers that the cold could never match.

When she returned, the frame was nearly complete. Rick greeted her with a proud smile. Izzy stared at what he had built.

"It ain't much to look at right now, darling, but I think we'll be pretty comfy. Should do us for a long time." He tapped the frame with his hand and shook the bed to show how sturdy it was.

Izzy clasped her hand over her mouth. This was no queen-sized mattress. The bed, as it now stood, would be barely wide enough for the two of them lying side by side. Her cramps returned, and she bolted for the outhouse once again.

CHAPTER 10

Jake

(Summer)

With each ridge and each valley, the isolation of the wild pressed more heavily onto Jake's shoulders. Here, in the thick of it, Jake felt more alone than he had ever been in his whole life.

A single airplane was all they had needed. A single plane could have saved them all.

His mother had died just three days after Jake's father left. She had been convulsing one moment and screaming in delirium and pain the next. Jake held her down as Amos forced water between her lips, past a swollen tongue that dangled from her mouth like a dead snake. Her pulse beat like a snare drum—fast and weak. Her abdomen had bloated, becoming rigid and discolored.

Amos whispered as he mopped her brow with a cloth, "Shhh, child. It'll be okay."

By that point, they all knew that was a lie.

Her face matched the color of the thick layer of fog draped over the lake. She shook continuously, despite being perched on a cot next to a stove pumping out enough heat to melt the arctic ice pack. Her eyes jolted wide open for a brief, terrifying moment. She looked at Jake and gave Amos a look of fear and worry. A final, gut-wrenching scream, and she was gone. The shaking stopped; her agony ended as if a switch had been thrown.

It took Jake days to get out of bed, to make his own food again.

His dreams—when he did sleep—were nightmares. During the day, he sat by the radio, dead as it was, waiting for it to miraculously chirp to life. He watched the lake from their single window, praying for a plane to land. Not even the formerly omnipresent contrails of intercontinental jets appeared in the stratosphere.

Three weeks after Jake's mother died, Amos sat down on the bed next to Jake. "Jake . . . " Amos started. Jake lay on his cot, his back to Amos. He pretended not to hear.

"Jake . . . I need you to listen to me for a bit." Amos put his weathered hand on the covers hiding Jake's shoulder. "We need to talk.

"I know . . . I know you think we've talked enough, and you're probably tired of me telling you to get off your ass, but that's not what we need to discuss. Not right now." His voice lowered and steadied. Jake stared at a line of browned insulation stuffed into a gap in the plywood wall of the cabin and gritted his teeth.

Talk. Talk was not what he wanted. He wanted to yell—to scream. Anger, bitter and raw, snuck up his throat like bile. It coated everything and burned. *My mother is dead.* He had stayed for no reason. His father was out there, *doing* something. Jake squeezed a fold of the blanket in his fist. He closed his eyes and willed Amos away. He didn't want his grandfather so near. He didn't want the old man to become a target for his rage. He needed time. Couldn't Amos understand that?

"Your grandmother Beth was the love of my life, Jake. She was the kindest, most gentle creature that ever graced my eyes. She was everything to me. But I was always second in her life after your father was born. She loved your father—doted on him. She would have walked through fire for him. Much like your mother would have for you." The bed moved as Amos changed position and sniffled.

"My Beth died way too young. Like your mom. Way too damn young. Both senseless deaths, Jake. God-awful and senseless. We haven't talked much about your grandmother, Jake. Not in a long time. It's always been too hard. God knows we're no good at talking about that kind of stuff. There's too much history in this family, and too much tragedy. We keep it covered up like some disease, like we'll all catch it if we talk about it. But you need to know. You need to understand . . ." Jake adjusted his position. The old man's hand lay heavy on his shoulder, and it shook just a little.

"When your father was a few years older than you are now, he left the rez—went out on his own. The house got awfully empty once he left. It wasn't a big place, but Beth and I seemed to rattle around in it. Empty nest, they say. There was so much we hadn't done in our lives. So I lived it up, sometimes too hard. I never worried about it. I knew that Beth was always ready to pick me up and drive me home when I did.

"She was on her way to pick me up when she got hit. She never had a chance. That Chev pushed the driver's-side door on her little Dodge nearly out the passenger side."

Jake pulled his knees up to his chest. Pain radiated from Amos's words and cut into Jake's heart like a hunting knife.

"My world got a lot smaller that night, Jake. My Beth. Gone. Quick as that.

"I thought up a thousand other ways to end it all—to take the easy way out—but I couldn't do it. I didn't want to take the chance that the preacher was right, and that there is no heaven for those who kill themselves. I was scared I'd end up looking through those gates at her, but never able to be with her. She was everything to me, Jake. Everything."

He paused, and took a sip of water from a cup before continuing his story.

"I've never told anyone all of this. Not even your father. But you need to know . . . you need to understand." He coughed again.

"I couldn't stay on the rez after that, so I ran. From one crappy town to another, looking for jobs that weren't there. Not for me. I had the wrong color skin. Didn't matter though. I wasn't in any kind of mind to settle down. I ran from the spirits of my ancestors, and from my family. But you can't outrun your memories, Jake. They follow you. Wherever you go.

"Then your father got this idea into his head to start up this outfitting company, and whether it was foolish or not, he decided he wanted me part of it. We fought like alley cats, but he made it work. I never understood how your father could forgive me for what I did. I wanted to run a dozen times, but he held on tight. He wouldn't let me go. Your father is a strong one. Stronger than me, that's for sure. And then he met your mother, and she took me in, too. I didn't know why. But when you were born, and I saw you for the first time and saw those eyes, I knew . . . I knew why we had to make it work. Why I had to stay . . . You have your grandmother's eyes, Jake. When I saw those eyes, I knew . . ."

Amos took a long pause to catch his breath.

"I'm not going to be able to hang on much longer. Not without your help, and even then, I'm not sure how much longer I've got. My body just isn't what it used to be."

Jake turned over in the bed, his hair falling about his eyes. It had been days since it had seen a comb or been washed. Tangles covered half his face and forced him to push the mess aside.

"Grandpa, you can't . . ." He couldn't bring himself to say it.

"It's not going to happen today, or this week. But it is going to happen, and probably before we get out of here. The doc said spring if I was lucky."

"Spring?" Jake tried to calculate the impact. He'd lost track of the days. He had no idea how far off Christmas was, let alone spring.

"It don't matter about me, but there's a lot of things I have to teach you, things you're going to have to learn, so that at least one of us gets out of here. We're going to make sure that once the ice breaks next spring, you can get your ass home."

"I'm not leaving you, Grandpa. Not a chance."

Jake sat up in bed and grabbed his grandfather's hand. Amos looked at the boy and smiled.

"You have your father's hands, Jake. Your grandmother's eyes, your father's hands, and your mother's heart. I've never known a boy to have been dealt those kinds of cards."

"You're coming with me, Grandpa."

"Maybe so, Jake. Maybe so."

But that wasn't to be. The doctor had been right, and by spring, Amos was dead.

Now, Jake attempted to trace the same route as his father had taken. Tracks would be hard to find unless his dad had left tell-tales such as stone cairns, or perhaps markers tied high in trees. He wouldn't have done that though, Jake reasoned. His father had expected to be back from Laroque within three weeks with a rescue party in tow. Jake could think of no *good* reason why his father hadn't returned within a month. There were only bad ones—night-mare scenarios that curled him up in his sleeping bag, night after night, imagining the worst.

Amos had, however, made good on his promise. He taught Jake everything he knew about living in the wild. Now it was Jake's turn to find a way out, to find his father, and then to pick up the pieces of his life and live. The memories of generations gone before had been stuffed into his head during the long winter. That had been his grandfather's gift to him.

Jake would honor those memories by doing the one thing they had all trained him to do: survive.

CHAPTER 11

Izzy

(Winter)

The thin buffer of trees and scrub barely held back the roaring wind. As the temperature dropped, Izzy and Rick had filled the cabin with firewood. The snow-covered wood left puddles on the floor as meltwater dripped in the relative warmth of the cabin—puddles that formed ice under the pile every night. They foraged for more firewood any time the snow let up for even a few minutes. The cold drove them back inside before frostbite set in.

"Seems like this storm's never going to end." Izzy pulled her coat tighter and gazed out the frosted window. It should have been daylight out, but heavy flurries had turned the sky dark. The tinkle of snow pellets hitting the roof nearly covered up her words.

"It'll pass," Rick said. "Go back to sleep. There's a reason bears hibernate in the winter up here." The bed frame creaked as he rolled over.

Izzy checked the meat on the drying rack. Two days before the storm blew in, Rick had killed another buck. Blood-soaked drapes of drying meat hung over the stove. A nine-point set of antlers crowned the door. That had been Rick's project the previous day. Izzy thought the antlers were slightly gruesome, but wasn't bothered by the meat.

She wiggled her toes in her new rabbit-fur slippers. Next to the bed, a set of mittens made with deerskin and lined with more fur awaited final stitching. A half dozen failed attempts at creating leg warmers lay in a discard pile next to bed. Even her latest creations weren't elegant, but they were getting better, and definitely warmer than the thin gloves she had brought with her from town. Her original gloves, layered with high-tech materials and warm to minus forty, remained on the counter in the house where Angie had been killed. She flexed her fingers and closed her eyes, trying to shake off a memory dulled little by the passage of time.

Time. How long had they been here? Izzy stepped back to the window. A gust of wind shook the cabin. She caught her reflection in the glass and pushed her hair back from her face. She would have to cut it soon. Angie had cut it for her last. Months ago, it seemed. September? She swallowed and counted the days. She'd lost track after they left Thompson. She could only guess that it was late November. Her birthday was November 11. *Fourteen.* She had turned fourteen without even noticing. She ran her hand over her cheeks, wiping them dry. Dates meant little out here. Survival was the only thing that mattered.

"You're gonna freeze if you keep standing around," Rick said with a deep grumble. "Throw a stick into the stove and put out the light. We ain't got enough fuel to let it burn all day."

Izzy nodded, pulled two short, thick pieces of wood from the pile, and dropped them into the stove. On her route from the stove to the bed, she passed a draft that roared across the floor like a frozen locomotive. She set the lamp down beside the wall and pushed more moss into the offending gap between the logs. The brief exposure to the colder air made her teeth chatter. She hesitated only slightly before pulling off her coat and slippers and crawling back under the covers. The bed was now toasty warm, with its thick layer of pine boughs covered in deerskin, two sleeping bags, and blankets over the top of them. She shivered as it sucked the cold from her bones.

"Slide over here, hon. You're freezing." Rick lifted the covers slightly. Warm air trapped between the layers looped around her. She slid slightly closer to the center of the bed. She had worn a groove along the outermost edge of the mattress, as far away from Rick as possible, but the cot was barely wide enough for two to begin with. With her tiny shift, the heat from his body extended warming tentacles around her.

Rick moved, his arm pushing up against her side. It seemed innocent enough, but Izzy knew better. A half dozen times he had done that since she had moved from the floor to the bed. The last time he had done it, his hand had worked its way onto her stomach. A few times during the night, she had awoken from a deep sleep with a start, as if something had been crawling on her. Rick had quickly turned over and away from her, feigning sleep.

Izzy hesitated before slowly rolling onto her side, facing away from him. The pine boughs under the deerskin dug into her, especially on her thin shoulders and hips. She could deal with the discomfort. It gave her an extra bit of space.

"You know, back when Lois and I and Brian used to come up here, we all crammed into this little shack. It was so peaceful and we had so much fun," he said wistfully. "Brian used to fish from dawn to dusk. That lake is just chock-full of fish, Isabelle. By the second day, we'd always have our limit and be dumping them back. Wasn't no better place than here."

"Must have been crowded with the three of you in here," Izzy said. Her eyes slowly adjusted to the dim room. The ghosted outlines of the stove and woodpile formed monsters in the dark.

"Didn't seem that way, not when Brian was young. By the time he got older, he'd put up a tent by the shore and Lois and I would snuggle up in here."

"You weren't here in the winter then," Izzy said.

"Naw, we never made it up here in the winter. Lois wasn't much on really roughing it. She'd do it, but if the weather turned, she'd be tellin' me to get on the radio to have the plane come back and pick us up," Rick said with a chuckle.

"Smart woman," Izzy said.

"She always thought so. Said a vacation shouldn't be something you have to come back and recover from. She always wanted to go to Mexico or Jamaica or somewhere. That was her idea of a good vacation." Rick moved and the distance between them shrank a bit more.

"Did you ever do it?" Izzy asked. She coughed as cold air bubbled up from another draft. Her hand moved forward to see how much room she had to the edge of the bed.

"Nope. Never went. Never had the money. Should have done it though. Should have figured it out." He moved again. His leg touched her curled-up feet. She pushed it back with her heel. Sliding any farther forward would pitch her onto the floor.

"Angie always wanted to go to Europe," Izzy said, trying to ignore the movement behind her. Sometimes, when she talked like this, Rick would grow bored and go to sleep. Brian had said she could talk the ears off a stalk of corn when she wanted to. "Paris and Barcelona," she continued. "She used to talk about touring the museums and eating bread and cheese under the Eiffel Tower. Wanted to see the fashion shows, the museums, the stores." Izzy thought back to the stack of magazines by Angie's bed in their old house. She read anything that had anything to do with life in the big cities. Angie wasn't going to stay in Thompson a moment longer than she had to.

"Angie always did have expensive tastes." Rick took her brief silence as an opportunity to voice his opinion.

"She just knew what she liked. Sounded good to me. We talked about going when she was done with college. I wanted to see London.

And Italy. Rome. Maybe Budapest. Don't know why. Think I saw it in some movie a long time ago, or maybe read about it in a book."

"I always thought that her and Brian might . . . might go out sometime. They would have made a cute couple." Rick said, changing the subject.

"They didn't have much in common," Izzy said. "They would have been miserable together."

"I think they would have done all right. Lois and me, we didn't have so much in common when we started dating. But we got along good, and things just worked out. Sometimes time makes the heart grow fonder."

Rick moved again. Now he was directly behind her on his side. His hand settled onto her, slowly caressing her arm and sliding down to her hip. Izzy's skin crawled as he pulled her closer to him.

"I think it's 'absence makes the heart grow fonder.'" She grabbed his hand to push it off her. He resisted and squeezed her tighter. She clenched her fist and wondered what he would do if she drove her elbow back into him. Something told her it wouldn't have helped, and would have only made things worse.

"Time will do it too, Isabelle." He said it low and soft. He nuzzled into her hair. She squirmed away.

"Rick. No." She teetered on the edge of the bed. He seized her leg as she swung it out from under the covers.

"It's too cold out there, darling. Stay." His rough hands pulled her back into the bed.

"Rick, let me go!" Panic surged through her. He had never touched her like this before. "What are you doing?" she cried.

"Darlin', stay. There's no reason to get up. We can just snuggle for a bit. Reward ourselves for all our hard work."

Izzy's last meal came perilously close to disgorging. She pushed at his hands, but his grip only tightened. Her fingernails dug into the back of his hand, and, for the briefest of moments, she thought he would let her go. His hands clutched at her again, and now his leg pinned her to the mattress. He snatched her wrist as she punched his side, and trapped her arm under his elbow.

"I love you so much, darlin'." His beard scratched her neck as he bit her collarbone. She struggled again and landed a punch to his cheek with her free hand. He barely noticed. He slid on top of her, purging the air from her lungs in a violent cough. His face moved. In a flash, his mouth was on hers. His breath, hot and rancid like rotten meat, pushed into her mouth. She tried to turn her head, but he held her still. She choked as he slid his tongue along her lips.

She screamed, but he enveloped her, cutting off all sound. His hands groped, found the gap between her tunic and her pants, and lifted the hem of her shirt. His hand slithered over her exposed skin, sliding first up to her chest, then plunging down, tearing off her thin clothes and undergarments. Still his mouth attacked her, strangling every attempted scream. She gagged and bit down. A metallic taste filled her mouth, and for a second she thought she had driven him off. She gulped two breaths of fresh air. Then he was back on her.

She clawed at the bed frame. This time, nothing came between her and *him*. The faintest of protests escaped her throat.

He did not listen, and he did not stop.

When it was over, he fell onto her and lay motionless, his weight nearly crushing her. Tears burst from her eyes. She pushed on his shoulder. He slid off without a word.

She rolled away and fell onto the floor, the cold air shocking her into a fit of coughing. Her whole body shook. She pulled her clothes tight around her. In the dim light from the window, she could just make out the whites of his eyes. He started to move, stopped, and slowly rolled back over to the other side of the bed.

The pain. *Oh God, the pain.* She crawled to the stove. The burn wouldn't stop. Blood ran down her legs. The agony grew worse, moment by moment, till she could no longer breathe. She vomited onto the stack of wood by the stove. A slimy mixture of blood and vomit drooled from her mouth. She heaved again, until nothing remained in her stomach. The smell of her stomach contents mixed with the smell of *him* forced her to gag again. She collapsed onto the hearth.

Oh, Angie!

What just happened to me?

Why?

Why would he?

Why, Angie?

Why?

Angie, how could you let this happen?

How could you leave me with him?

Outside, the wind whistled through bare branches and shook the walls. Ice and snow pelted against the window. Invisible drafts sliced through the room and leaked around her all-too-thin clothes. What was the temperature? Forty below? Fifty? With the windchill, minus sixty? Going through that door would be escape, one way or another. In ten minutes, twenty at the most, it would all be over.

Angie did not answer her pleas, and Izzy's legs could not lift her to take her out into the storm. The moss she had previously shoved into the gap in the wall fell back out, as if it had not been able to stand up to the wind. A cold gust ripped across the room and onto her exposed skin. She yanked a blanket from the bed and curled up next to the stove. The pain would not stop, and she did not sleep.

CHAPTER 12

Jake

(Summer)

Jake rolled over in his sleeping bag and winced. A sharp rock or a stick, somehow unnoticed when he'd set up the tent the night before, centered on one of his vertebrae and threatened to dislodge it. Jake shifted his position again, but whatever comfort the bag had once provided could no longer be found.

Six days of hard travel had left every muscle tight, every joint sore, and every callus raw. His body didn't want to get up, and neither did his brain. Though he'd been exhausted the night before, sleep had not come easy, nor had it been deep. Every noise outside the tent triggered worry of a bear or wolf attack, or of a raccoon stealing his food. He had camped a thousand times, but never alone. On no other trip in his life had he ever been so completely and utterly alone. That truth kept him awake even when the ground wasn't rocky, and the woods were quiet.

Sleep or no sleep, it was time to get moving. He pulled on his boots and exited the tent.

Days of sunshine had finally surrendered to sullen skies with a misting drizzle. The tops of the trees swayed and bent. Leaves curtsied as water dripped and splashed to the ground below. The drip of rain off his hat brim added to lack of sleep put him in a mood fit to match the foul weather.

Amos had warned him that the trip would be hard, and Jake had heard the words. Hearing and listening, however, are two different things. He had always believed, right up until the moment Amos had died, that the two of them would be able to do this trip—that somehow, with spring, his grandfather would regain his strength, and together they would make it out. Now, less than a week into the three-week journey, he knew exactly what his grandfather had known. Life here was *hard*. For the first time, doubt crept into his mind. With this doubt came more fears that something horrible had happened to his father. If Dad couldn't make it out . . . Dad, with his twenty years' experience in the bush. Strong, fit, *Dad*. Jake searched for another explanation as to why his father had not come back for them. There had to be another explanation. Yet Jake could think of nothing.

Jake stood by the canoe. The rain hitting his shoulders felt as if it would pound him into the forest floor like a hammer would a tent stake. His feet, however, weren't swallowed up by the earth. With a little effort, he moved them. His father, Jake reasoned, wouldn't have stopped until or unless he could no longer move. Jake wouldn't either. And, if his dad was still alive, Jake would find him.

His gaze turned southward. Somewhere ahead, not too far, was a river. That river would get him out of the bush and allow him to get back in the canoe and rest his exhausted legs.

He cleaned up his camp and moved on.

Two hours later, he slid the canoe into the river. The flow headed north. Jake pointed the bow southward and worked his way against the current. The water, not so long ago ice and snow, was freezing cold. Paddling upriver was faster than breaking trail through the bush, but not by much. Twice, Jake pulled in to shore to lift the canoe around rocks that funneled the flow into a chute no wider than the canoe was long. Each time he got out, he lamented the loss of time and the extra effort required to travel the distance.

The banks steepened as the river sawed its way through a ridge.

The speed of the current increased. Jake dug in with his paddle, propelling the canoe from eddy to eddy. The rain from the clouds above mixed with the mist generated by the moving water beneath him. The channel tightened further, till, from the center, Jake could touch both banks at once with his paddle. In some places, the water moved so quickly that the paddle could barely gain any traction. Instead, Jake poled the canoe with a piece of driftwood. The steep sides slid ever higher as he pushed forward.

Get out while you can. Scout the line, Amos's voice warned.

But Jake could see a curve in the river coming, and with the way the ridges seemed to be dropping nearby, he knew that once he was past this bottleneck, the river would open back up. He pushed on.

Ahead, however, in the middle of the curve, a jumble of broken logs held back the flow, blocking his passage completely. The pile breached the surface nearly to Jake's height. Water boiled around the logs, surging between the gaps. Broken branches swung and twisted as the pressure whipped them back and forth. Soon the weight of the water built up behind this dam would overcome the strength of the wood, and the whole mess would shoot down the little canyon like a runaway freight train.

Jake rammed his driftwood pole into the rocky riverbed to steady the canoe. The sides here were too steep to climb. To turn around and head back to a more friendly start to the portage would mean losing an hour's hard-earned gains.

He eyed the pile. It would only take a minute or two to scale it, dragging the canoe with him. On the other side, the slow open water of the backed-up river would be almost pleasant to paddle after so many days fighting the bush.

Jake pushed closer to the pile. The canoe lifted as water seethed from a gap below the surface. He steadied himself by grabbing at one of the logs. The continuous spray had stripped the bark, leaving the wood slick. With one hand on the log, he grabbed his pack with the other and slung it over his shoulder.

The pack secure, he held the forward strut on the canoe with his free hand and transferred his weight to the log. It bent under the extra burden, dipping perilously close to the frothing surface. Relieved of its passenger, the canoe bobbed even more and threatened to break free of Jake's tenuous grip. He clamped his fingers down on the aluminum until it felt like he would crimp the metal. He shifted his feet, searching for solid footing. The log bent farther under the additional weight. Even over the roar of the water and hiss of the spray, Jake heard the wood crack.

Jake nearly jumped back into the canoe right there and then, but just as he started to move, the water lifted the bow out of the water and pushed the canoe toward the pile. Jake pulled with all his might, and the canoe slid onto the pile next to him, until only the stern remained in the current.

The pile, which he could now see was almost like a tiny island, was longer than it was tall by a factor of five. A dozen trees jammed into the thin cut in the rock. Loose branches filled some of the gaps. Weeds and grass stems piled up within the muddle. Tree trunks jutted up at odd angles, forming a three-dimensional maze.

Amos's words of caution fluttered through Jake's brain again. He could still go back down the pile, back along the river, and find a place to start a more normal portage. But the open water beckoned, tantalizingly close. He leaned forward, tested the next logical footstep, and inched ahead.

The canoe squeaked a protest each time he moved it. Twigs and splintered wood scratched at its bottom. Jake lifted it as best he could to avoid the sharpest of sticks, but he didn't dare try to carry the entire mass. He leaned on the canoe while finding his next foothold on the slippery wood.

Halfway across the pile, he came to a tree lodged straight across the gorge. A narrow gap under it appeared easier to pass through than the jumble of branches above. If he used the canoe as a bridge, then pulled it back up from the opposite side, he'd be able to reach the other side of the gap without even getting wet.

He barely paused before sliding the canoe into the hole beneath the tree.

The bow bobbed and jerked as the foaming water whipped it one way, then another. He steadied the craft and pushed it farther into the breach. The fit was tighter than he'd expected. The gunwale barely fit under the obstructing tree, but he managed to steady the boat, and then climbed in.

Halfway across, the pack on his back snagged on the stub of a branch, stopping him in his tracks. Jake's pulse raced. He worked his arm up over his head and gently pried the offending branch upward off his pack. Above his head, the tree trunk shifted, but held. He removed his pack and food canister and started forward again. Three times the canoe bumped up against the trunk, and twice the trunk moved, only to slide slowly back into its original position.

Getting out on the far side was no easier. Jake tossed his pack onto a stable part of the pile to lighten the load. He stood in the bobbing canoe, fought for balance, then leaped across the remaining gap. As he landed, his left foot slipped on a slick log and shot backward into the water. The canoe was propelled backward as well, the current spinning the bow to the left, out of his grasp.

Jake scrambled to his feet, turning to grab the canoe before it slipped completely out of reach. The fingers of his left hand latched on to the bow, but the branch he held on to with his right broke and gave way. Jake pitched forward into the freezing water. The flow tore at his legs. His mouth filled with water. He coughed, gulped more air, and held it deep in his chest as the suction pulled him under the canoe. The canoe began to roll. Jake searched with his right hand for something—anything—to use to pull himself back up above the water. He curled his legs, pressing his knees against the gunwale. More water poured over him and into the canoe, forcing him down, deeper into the pile. His lungs burned. His right hand finally found a handhold. With a kick of his legs, he broke the surface and launched himself into the branches above. The branch bent and torqued toward the water. With his every movement, it sank lower into the water. But as it sank, the tree it was attached to rolled and pulled him clear of the hole in the middle of the pile. Jake rode the tree as it completed its roll. By the time the roll stopped, he was even with his pack, perched on a solid part of the pile, and out of immediate danger. He dropped down next to his pack and put his hands on his knees.

Jake shook from head to toe. Only his tenuous grip on the canoe had saved his life. It had all happened so fast. Had his right hand missed that thin branch, he would never have made it. Had the tree not rolled just the way it did, he would have been trapped underneath it. He was lucky to be alive, and he knew it.

But he also knew his life had just gotten a lot harder. For under that tree, his canoe, now filled with water and pinned down by the flow, was lost. He'd seen canoes submerge before—on one guiding trip, two clients had flipped in a rapid and buried the bow under a waterfall. It had taken six of them—and a bunch of ropes—to drag it free. Even if he could get the tree off the boat—which was a big if considering he had only a little hatchet and his machete—and even if the pile didn't collapse in the meantime, he'd still have to lift a massive amount of water to free the canoe. By himself, he'd never be able to do it.

Jake cupped his face in his hands in a silent plea. After a moment, he tried to push the tree off the boat, just in case the force of the water's flow would somehow lift the canoe. But the tree, having settled into a new equilibrium, barely moved. The canoe sank deeper.

He had no choice. He couldn't stay there. Every minute he stood on the logs was another minute they could all break free and crush him as they tore downriver. He grabbed his pack. The logs under his feet shifted. A loud crack shook the pile. He glanced back at the canoe one last time, buckled the pack up tight, and slid over the next set of logs.

Beyond the pile of logs, the steep sides of the gorge slowly dropped lower. Jake worked himself along a narrow ledge, holding on to the roots of trees which had grown into small fissures in the rock. He pulled himself over the top of the gorge after ten minutes of careful navigation. He collapsed at the top, shivering and shaking. After a moment, he crawled back to the edge and tried to think of another way to free the canoe. With a chainsaw, safety ropes, and a crane, he might be able to get it free. He had none of that—just his inadequate hand tools, and sopping wet clothes he desperately needed to dry.

Jake forced himself to his feet, turned and stumbled inland, looking for a good place to start a fire to warm his chilled body. His father's words again ran through his head. *Shelter. Fire. Water. Food.* But now, he added another critical word to the mantra. *Canoe.*

Finishing his journey would be impossible without one.

CHAPTER 13

Izzy

(Winter)

The storm lasted five days. On the sixth day, the temperature drifted upward to just ten degrees below freezing, which felt almost balmy to Izzy. Rick set out at first light to check his trapline.

"Don't go too far," he said as he zipped up his parka.

"Okay."

"Keep the fire going."

"Yeah," Izzy said bitterly.

"Get some more moss for those gaps."

"I'll see what I can find."

"And restock that woodpile. It's going to get cold again tonight. I'll be back by dark."

With that he disappeared, and she finally had the cabin to herself.

It was a relief to have him out of the cabin—out of the cabin and away from her. After that first time, once Rick had crossed that line, he had shown no mercy. He said he loved her. He told her that this was what people who loved each other did. He said it would get better . . . feel better . . . eventually.

Lies. All lies. The pain was brutal . . . searing her from the inside out. She hurt . . . everywhere, in a never-ending kind of torment she couldn't ignore, but couldn't bear to think about. In the dark, she tried to think about Angie, but pleasant memories could not break the surface of her anguish. She tried to think about her parents, but all she could remember was the horrible way they had died, and how alone she now was. Alone, but *not*, in the worst possible way. He told her how much he needed her. How he was so happy they were together. How he hoped they would always be together.

The words hurt almost as much as the act that followed them.

For all of Izzy's desire to be strong, the act of being strong seemed more than she could bear. Stepping out of the cabin felt like breaking out of jail. But there was no escape from this prison.

Snow had piled up nearly to the roof, wrapping impenetrable walls of white around the cabin to the east and west. The wind still ripped across the lake, like a sentry standing guard. She could not outrun that. She could only survive, or not survive.

It took Izzy an hour to dig a channel through the deep bank to the door of the outhouse to dump the pail they had filled during the storm. Finding firewood required going inland to where, under the shelter of tree branches, the snow was barely knee deep instead of over her head. Digging out already downed trees was impossible. She had no choice but to search for dead branches still hung up above the snow and reachable.

By noon, barely half the woodpile had been rebuilt and Izzy was exhausted. Five days of rest should have allowed her time to rebuild her strength and energy, but the five days had not been restful. Not for her. She tried not to think about it as she worked, but every time she came back to the cabin with another load of wood, her sense of panic rose. Every time she opened the door, she feared he would already be back.

She ate her meager portion for lunch as she ogled the rest of the drying meat on the rack. They were still rationing the deer as if it alone would have to last them through the winter. Rick knew exactly how much remained. His orders were strict, and Izzy still remembered what a truly empty stomach felt like. She made do with her ration.

She wandered farther inland after her lunch, her trail marked with the small hatchet strapped to her wrist. Even with the snowshoe tracks, it was far too easy to become disoriented and end up walking in a circle. In the first two weeks at the cabin, when the snow wasn't quite so deep, they had gathered wood from close by. Now she had to go farther each day. When Rick was around, he'd chop down an entire dead tree. She didn't have the energy or the power to do that.

The ground rose as she trudged north. At first, the shallow grade offered little resistance, but after ten minutes the rise grew steeper until she reached a gravel ridge as high as a six-story building. The trees stopped just short of the slope. She climbed the incline, struggling to maintain a foothold on the ice-covered dirt. The hatchet swung freely from its rawhide strap, banging into her ribs as she ascended. Only a thin layer of snow covered the top, as if the bulk of the ridge had frightened the wind into going up and over and holding its white cargo to dump on their cabin instead.

An impressive view greeted her from the top of the esker. To the north, the ridge sloped steeply downward. Trees fought back against the force of the predominant winds. To the east and west, the ridge ran to the horizon. To the south, toward the cabin, she could just see over the tops of the snow-covered trees below. The lake extended as an expanse of white beyond the limit of visibility. The slightest wisp of gray-blue smoke drifted out of the cabin's metal chimney, reminding her of the need to feed another stick into the fire. Rick wouldn't be happy if it was out when he returned from hunting.

She stood on the ridge as the sky grew. For the first time in months, she could see beyond her immediate surroundings. Last summer, being caught in the open had been something to fear. Here, from the top of this ridge, the size of the earth frightened her. The northern sky dwarfed the tiny, isolated cabin. There was nothing left beyond this desolate view—nothing to go back to. The flu had only been the start of the destruction. People had done the rest.

After the flu, Izzy had followed Angie wherever she went, stumbling through day after day of grief, oblivious to anything but her loss. Her mother. Her father. Her friends.

All dead or gone.

Neither of them had even had the energy to go to the store to get groceries. Rick saved them then. He found them food and gathered supplies. When the remaining survivors began to hoard what they could, the stores had emptied so fast. The flu had killed so many—yet it took only a few weeks for the survivors to eat what was left. Thompson, dependent on trucked-in food and fuel, had been forgotten.

The trucks would come back, the weakened flu survivors all said. The trucks never did.

No one rationed what they had. The food had always come. Everyone ate three meals a day until one day there was barely enough for one. A discovered can of tuna, long hidden in someone's pantry, seemed like a banquet fit for a king. Those had been the good days.

Then the starvation began. The true starvation, where the energy it took to find food exceeded the return from eating it. Every house had been ransacked. The people who could leave, left, and never came back. No one ever came back. Those who stayed, changed. Good people—people who would have given the shirt off their back in the good times—protected what they had until it, too, was gone. Hunger changed them all.

But Rick again had saved them. He took them out of town when there were no other options. Angie had been there, pulling Izzy along, telling her it would be okay. Telling her that they would make it, one way or another.

Izzy glanced back to where the thin curl of smoke betrayed the location of the cabin, and the bed inside.

Angie, why didn't you stop this?

Her sister remained silent.

More memories. Memories of conversations—whispered conversations between Angie and Rick that Izzy had been too stricken to hear to when they happened. The whispers grew louder now. Now, she heard them clearly.

"Don't you ever—"

"Never! You understand me?"

"Never!"

And then she realized Angie *had* done her best to stop it. Izzy knew, in a moment of clarity, what had happened to Angie.

That day.

That day Izzy had killed the deer. Rick and Angie had been gone. Angie had left Izzy alone for the first time in forever. And Angie had been so upset, so different, after she came back. Izzy had always thought it was about the deer. Angie became distant—angry. Not with Izzy. With Rick.

Rick had . . . had done the same to *her.*

Oh, Angie! Poor, Angie!

And yet Angie had stayed. She had stayed; had gone through *that* for weeks after that day and said nothing. *Why would she have done that?* In the instant that followed, Izzy knew why. *Survival.* Angie had done that, with him, to survive. To allow *both* of them to survive. The realization came in gigantic, body-shaking sobs. Her sister had done the unthinkable. And then she knew she would have to do the same, because Angie had done it for her. For Izzy not to survive would be to dishonor Angie's memory, to waste her sacrifice.

Izzy's duty was to survive, and then to escape—or everything Angie had suffered through would be for nothing. Izzy couldn't do that. Not now that she knew it all.

She stumbled over to a cluster of gnarled trees that had shied away from the predominantly northerly gusts. Instead of giving up altogether, the trees had done what they could to survive. Living in the depths of the ravines, away from the wind, would have been easier. But that was not their lot; that was not where their seeds had fallen and taken root. And though their life was hard, their roots grasped at the shallow soil, held tight to it, and the trees survived. Where others with thinner roots would have fallen in the slightest gust, these trees had fought the cruelty of the extended winters and lived.

Izzy put her hand on one of the branches. The branch barely moved. It resisted her pressure. It had adapted. It had grown strong where it could.

From this ridge, she could see the curvature of the earth. No one was out there. No one was looking for her. No one would save her.

Escape would be completely up to her.

She stood on that ridge for a half hour, watching the clouds move, until the chill of the day settled through her clothes. Rick would be back soon, and she had work to do. She would have to do that work, and more. She would have to recover her strength. She would have to learn how to hunt for her own food. She would have to learn how to navigate the wilderness. She would have to find a way to make her own supplies and tools. But worst of all, she would have to bide her time. She would need to survive in that cabin until she could survive out here by herself. In the snow, she would be too easy for him to find. In the summer, however, when the days were long, the weather warmer, and food easier to come by—she could go then. Back to Thompson, and whatever—whoever—was there.

And if there was no one there, she would go south and keep going, until she found . . . a new life . . . away from him.

She worked her way back down the esker, grabbing an armful of branches from a hung-up deadfall as she returned to the cabin.

Rick was waiting by the door when she arrived. A long, silver canoe lay on the snow next to the cabin.

"Where the hell have you been?" he asked.

"Getting firewood." She held up the collection of branches as if he couldn't see them. "Where'd you get that?" She tipped her head toward the canoe. She dumped the sticks unceremoniously on the pile inside the cabin. Clumps of snow dropped onto the floor.

"Did you have to go all the way to Winnipeg for it?" Rick ignored the question about the canoe. Blood covered his hands. A freshly skinned and gutted rabbit lay on the kitchen table. A dead ptarmigan lay next to it, its head at an odd angle to its body, its feathers flayed with spots of red.

"No . . . just had to find wood not covered up by the snow."

"How long were you gone?"

"Not long . . . ," she said with a bit of hesitation. Rick simmered.

"What did I tell you before I left?"

"You told me to get wood and find some moss."

"And what else?"

"And . . ." And she remembered. The stove. She glanced at it.

"You let the fire go out." He grabbed her by the collar of her coat and dragged her over to the stove. The coals were gray and cold. He pushed her face against the cold metal.

"You feel that? You feel how cold that is?" The cast iron sucked the heat from her exposed skin. He pulled her up and glared at her.

"I'm sorry, Rick. I didn't mean to . . . I thought about it while I was out there. Really I did. I just wanted to get as much wood in here as I could, in case it storms again." Izzy's stomach churned.

Fire, out here, was everything. Without it, they wouldn't last a night. Not in this cold.

Rick paused. "We can't let it happen again. You understand?" His anger slowly subsided.

"I know, Rick. I know. It won't happen again."

Rick's grip on her collar relaxed. "There's another half hour of daylight left. Get out there and get some more wood. I'll get this bloody thing relit." He picked up the flint and striker from the mantel, growling and cussing as he did so.

Izzy pulled her coat tight and rushed out the door, back into the cold, deep snow, barely giving a passing thought to the canoe by the door.

Summer couldn't possibly come soon enough.

CHAPTER 14

Jake

(Summer)

Jake rose before dawn, cleaned up his camp, and ate breakfast while the sun climbed to warm the valley. A thick fog settled between the trees, drowning out any noise he made. The incessant buzz of mosquitoes patrolling the lowlands droned in the background. Jake's vision extended just a few meters beyond his camp. His traps had been empty again. He didn't bother to fish.

Away from the river, the air lightened and the fog lifted. The heavy woolen layer that had covered the area the previous day gave way to a pleasant sky dotted with puffy clouds. Drops of dew from the tangled brush soaked his pants and chilled his legs.

His body hurt from the battle with the logs. A bruise on his knee nearly matched the color of the camouflage cap pulled low over his brow. Red scabs—on scratches delivered by the tree that had saved him—covered his hands and face, providing landing strips for the attacks of the morning's gnats.

It was easier walking in the bush without the canoe, but as he caught a glimpse of the river below, he knew that with its speed on flat water, he would already have paddled the length of that river and been on the next lake. He tried not to dwell on it.

He spent more time foraging for edible plants as he worked his way south. A few, like dandelion leaves and lamb's-quarter, could be eaten right off the stem without cooking. Twice he found large clusters of tiny, wild strawberries. Bear scat piled around every berry patch. Plants crushed by sleeping animals sprang up like traps as he passed by. Most bushes had been picked clean. Jake salvaged what he could and kept going. His gun, so long strapped to his pack while he portaged, had been pulled from its case. He held it in his hands, loaded and ready.

His rifle was too powerful for most of the small animals of the area. His grandfather's Colt, still wrapped in a towel and stuffed deep in his pack, was no better. For birds, squirrels, or rabbits, the rifle would likely not just kill them, but would blow them to bits, leaving nothing to eat. Jake had considered other long-barreled guns; they had had three options at the cabin: a .22 rifle, a 12-gauge pump shotgun and the .308 rifle. But he could never have left the .308 behind.

His father had put an air rifle in Jake's hands at the age of six and started him target shooting. When Jake was eight, Leland let him try a single-shot .22-caliber rifle. The noise was louder and the kick more substantial, especially for a skinny boy barely taller than the gun was long. He had balanced the gun by bracing it with his elbows on a downed tree. He learned how to maintain that rifle. He learned how to shoot, how to adjust for wind and gravity, and how to lead a moving target. By the time he was ten, he could hit cans swinging on a rope from forty meters away. This winter at the cabin he'd hit a running snowshoe hare from eighty meters in knee-deep snow—a shot Amos had recounted with pride for weeks.

He was ten when he took his first deer: a small five-point buck. Jake field dressed it himself and helped butcher it. The hunt, the kill, and the butchering had not fazed him. The death didn't revolt him. It had been clean and quick. It wasn't a kill for sport—his dad would never have allowed that. Amos had shown him how to honor the memory of the deer by sprinkling loose tobacco on the ground by the carcass. "The forest," Amos said, "has a memory that will outlive man."

Jake's father gave him the Remington 700 for his twelfth birthday—a gun of superb quality and craftsmanship, and one he took great care to maintain. The kickback from the heavy rounds hurt Jake's shoulder after each shot. Still, he practiced religiously. By fourteen, he was the best shot in the family, so good that his father often wondered aloud if that gun was actually part of him.

As late afternoon approached, Jake changed his style of hiking to reduce his noise. He kept to his planned path as his eyes scanned for a substantial meal. He placed his feet carefully to sidestep breaking twigs. He adjusted his stride to avoid brushing up against branches. He moved across cluttered ground, barely making a sound. He bypassed shots at a couple of small birds. He had to choose his shot: once he fired his gun, the sound and its echo would disperse anything else worth shooting, and hunting would be unproductive for hours.

He crested a small, false peak on a ridge and silently brought the gun to his shoulder. Thirty meters ahead and upwind, a raccoon dug in the remnants of an old tree stump, searching for grubs. Jake leveled the rifle and aimed. He pressed the safety off with a barely audible click and took a pulse-slowing breath. As he exhaled, he squeezed the trigger.

The retort shook the valley. The force of the bullet's impact flung the body end for end, sending a spurt of blood across the ground like a flick of red paint from a dipped brush.

Jake clicked the safety back on and cleared the spent casing from the gun while covering the distance to his kill. The body lay curled in a ball. He prodded it once with the blade of his knife and rolled it onto its back. The field-dressing process was quick. He sliced through the skin along the breast, drained the blood, and removed the entrails. The heart and liver he set on a piece of plastic for safekeeping. He skinned the animal with a practiced hand, trimming the meat off the carcass and wrapping it in the plastic. Raccoon meat would be a welcome change from the deer jerky and fish he had been eating almost continuously on this trip. With no place or time to dry the skin properly, he left it on the ground, neatly rolled up as a sign of respect. *The forest*, he reminded himself, *has a memory that will outlive man.*

He moved on as soon as his gear was repacked. The smell of blood would be strong in the area of the kill, and would draw larger predators. This spot was too exposed to stay in long. A half kilometer later, in the shelter of two boulders, he cooked the meat over a small fire. He didn't stop long. A few minutes after the food was cooked and either rewrapped or eaten, he set back off into the trees. Daylight was not to be wasted.

His compass steered him ever southward. With a full stomach, his pace quickened. The pain in his joints and muscles faded into background noise, like the hum of a fan. The surroundings alternated between dense forest, thick brush, and swampy lowlands. He took his bearings often from any high, exposed place he could find. The area showed no signs of human habitation. There were no abandoned campsites, no trash, and no old trails that weren't made by animals. The skies remained vacant.

He settled in to a rhythmic walking pace much like the paddling pace he had found while canoeing. Walking through the brush was like paddling into a bow-on crosswind that fought progress with every stroke. Roots grabbed at the toes of his boots. Vines grabbed at his shins. Mosquitoes and blackflies hovered around his head and launched attacks onto whatever exposed skin he had left, whether it was previously bitten or not. Jake covered up what he could. He stuffed scraps of cloth from an old shirt under his cap to protect his neck and ears and walked with his mouth closed. Still, he constantly swatted the pests away from his nose and eyes. On the water, the breeze would have blown them back. In the thickets surrounding the lake, the air barely moved and the bugs never ceased their assaults.

It was the distraction of the bugs that allowed him to approach the bear so closely without noticing. The wind, what there was of it deep in the woods, was blowing in the wrong direction for them to smell each other, and Jake missed the telltale snuffs from the bear as it blew the marauding mosquitoes from its own nose while it ambled through the bush.

They were ten meters apart when they finally detected one another. Jake froze, as did the bear. In deep shadow, its black fur had rendered it nearly invisible. A small patch of tan tipped its nose. Jake guessed its weight at a hundred kilos easily, perhaps a hundred and fifty. A slick of dew clung to its fur. Blackflies buzzed around its head. The bear flipped its ears in an instinctual rhythm. It uttered a rumbling growl and sniffed the air. Jake's lungs locked tight. He stole glances to the sides to see if there were cubs about.

"Whoa, big fella." His finger moved slightly toward the safety on the gun. A round sat ready in the chamber, but this was a single-shot gun. If he fired and missed, or if he only wounded the bear and then it attacked, he would have no time to crank the bolt for the next round. The .308 was a deer killer. It could kill a bear with a good shot. He had done just that the previous winter. Back then, he had the safety of a backup shooter in Amos, the distance to allow time to reload, and the time to aim a shot at a bear completely unaware of their presence. At that moment, he wanted the Colt handgun. A bigger caliber. A bigger punch. An automatic reload. But it was zipped deep inside his bag.

The bear dropped its head as Jake adjusted his grip. It fixed its eyes on Jake.

Another snuff. A short surge forward.

Jake yelled at it. "Whoa bear! Whoa bear!"

Another surge. It glared at him. Jake yelled again.

The bear rocked back on its legs, sniffing the air once more. Jake released the safety. The bear jerked at the sound. Jake held his ground and the standoff continued.

Don't do it. Don't charge, bear.

"Whoa bear!"

Jake knew not to run. Prey ran. Competition charged. Respect held ground.

Jake held his ground, but slid his right foot slightly backward to a better shooting position. The bear responded by lifting up onto its hind feet. The bear was bigger than Jake had first thought—easily his height, with paws the size of salad plates. Its curled claws were dirty, but razor sharp. Deadly.

Jake considered the bear spray canister clipped to his shoulder strap. That was an option, though not a great one. The bear was in range, but perhaps too close to deploy the canister quickly enough. And Jake would have to let go of the gun to use it.

He could fire a warning shot, but his father had told him to always shoot to kill in a situation like this. *When you have no second shot, make the first one a damn good one. If you leave a bear wounded, it only comes back angry. And an angry bear does a lot more damage than a dead one.*

The bear dropped down to its front feet, waddled backward, and growled. Jake took a slow step in reverse, adjusting his grip on the stock of the gun just slightly. The bear took another step backward. Jake did likewise. The bear grunted, swung its head away from Jake, and ran up the hill into the brush, crashing through like a bulldozer. Leaves and broken branches flew in all directions. The bear checked behind itself two or three times before it disappeared from the trail.

Jake shivered, then reengaged the safety on the gun and wondered when his heart would resume beating.

CHAPTER 15

Izzy

(Winter)

Izzy held the pine branch at arm's length and inspected the tip. It looked like it might be able to pierce something besides snow. Looks, she knew, could be deceiving. She practiced throwing it at a stump a few times. From ten meters away, she hit the stump once in ten tries. That shot barely nicked her objective. It would be a miracle to hit a moving target, and only the luckiest of strikes would kill something. She left the spear behind a rock along the base of the esker. Depression chased her as she wandered back to the cabin. Without a gun, killing any animals for food would be damn near impossible. She would have to steal what food she needed from Rick's stock. It would be heavy, and it would be all she would ever have. When it ran out, she would be hungry. Even if she made it to Thompson before her supply ran out, the town might still be empty—or worse. And she would go hungry.

She stopped by a tree and picked a handful of pine needles for tea. A squawk from above led her eyes to a complaining crow, angry that she had dared to steal from his domain. As it flapped its wings, a pinecone picked clean of seeds dropped from its grasp. It missed her head by an inch.

"You little bugger," she said as she picked the cone up. She hurled it into the branches. The coal-black bird barely moved as her aim went wide. It squawked again, almost teasing her, daring her, to try again. She picked up another cone and threw it as hard as she could. The cone bounced off a branch just below the crow's feet. It stepped sideways and fluffed its feathers, now slightly perturbed by her presence and gall.

"If I had a gun, you'd be dinner tonight, bird." Izzy bent down and picked up another cone. Even a BB gun would have worked. She kicked herself for not having looked for one when they were in town. Before the flu, every boy in Thompson had at least one. Brian had three or four. When they were on the run, Rick had looked to grab real guns with a high caliber, but those that hadn't been taken by other people were locked in thick-walled safes. She had never considered finding anything for herself.

The crow squawked again, hopped off its branch, dropped a few feet, flapped its wings, and disappeared into the trees. Izzy turned and moved on. Her thoughts drifted back to Brian. He had taught her to shoot the BB gun in the backyard and had taken the blame when she broke a window on the house next door. The guns had been taken away for a month. Brian hadn't really been fazed by it, though. There were plenty of ways, he said, to cause trouble if you really wanted to.

She stopped walking and looked back to the tree where the bird had been. Brian had lost the gun, but he had still had his slingshot. And he was damn good with that. He could take the top off a flower from ten meters away with a piece of pea gravel. During the month the guns were locked up, he left a perfect circle of dents in the wooden fence in the backyard, showing her just how good his aim could be.

She didn't have his slingshot, and she didn't think she had anything elastic enough to work as a slingshot. Rubber didn't last long in this kind of cold. A slingshot, though, wasn't the only way to make rocks travel far and fast. She had once seen Brian fashion a sling from a pair of old shoelaces and a piece of cardboard. She could make something similar: a couple of thin strips of rawhide and another doubled-up piece of hide. She could make that easily. She could practice every time she was out foraging. Slings had been around since the beginning of time. If some Neanderthal could use one, she certainly could.

She gathered another armful of sticks and ran back to the cabin. She had a few hours before Rick returned, and she had a new weapon to make.

It took far longer to learn how to use the sling than it did to make it. For such a simple tool, a thousand things could go wrong to cause the rock to miss its target. Twice, she nearly shot herself in the head by releasing at the wrong instant, and once, the rock careened off a nearby tree only to bounce back and strike her shin, leaving her with a softball-sized purple welt and a trickle of blood. She limped for three days from that one. Rick never asked why.

She practiced for two weeks before she gained the slightest bit of control over the trajectory the rock took when it left the sling. It took another week after that to work out distance.

A month after she had first started, Izzy looped the rawhide strip around her ring finger and clutched it against the palm of her right hand. She pinched the other end of the strap with her thumb and index finger. She removed a twist from the line, then dropped a frosted pebble into the cradle. The sling was ready to fire.

Finding stones under the snow and ice was hard enough, but finding the right size, shape, and weight for her new weapon had been even harder. The best stones were from the esker—ones that had been ground into smooth, rounded pebbles by centuries of glacial pressure. Flat stones tended to curve unpredictably when thrown hard. The perfect stone was round and about the size of a golf ball. In the summer, they would be easy to find. In the winter, they were not.

She leaned back on her right heel while at the same time rotating her arm back as if she were about to throw a baseball. Too much bend in the elbow, and the rock didn't hold a flat trajectory. If her arm was too straight, her accuracy dropped, and the odds that the two strands of rawhide would twist increased dramatically.

Her arm shot forward in the direction she wanted the rock to go. She gave one last snap of the wrist, while simultaneously releasing the trailing line from between her thumb and index finger.

This rock cracked into the wooden target she had placed on the stump, sending broken pieces off in three different directions. She smiled. A collection of mulched wood decorated the snow like chocolate sprinkles on a sponge cake.

She stepped back five steps, picked a different spot on the splintered stump, dropped another rock into the pouch, aimed, and fired. It missed her chosen spot by half a meter. She reloaded and let go again. A hair to the left.

She flexed her fingers and rubbed her hands together. Flecks of snow drifted through the skeletal canopy overhead. Somewhere to her left, a crow cawed. She pulled her last rock from her pocket and dropped it into the pouch, ready to aim. She flexed her shoulder. The joint ached with every move—not a painful ache though: a productive one. On the second day of practice, she'd thought she would never be able to lift her arm again. That ache had faded as she worked, and when she was sure Rick was deep in the woods working his trapline, she returned to practice, hurling twenty or thirty rocks each time.

The crow sounded its cry again, and she turned toward it. It was time to try the sling on something that moved. She crept as quietly as she could on her snowshoes. Her eyes alternated between scanning the branches for the bird and watching her footing. The sling she held loose by her side. It bounced against her leg like a gunslinger's holster.

A movement on the ground ahead stopped her in place. She expected the black wings of a bird, but there was only white. Her eyes scanned the tree. Had the breeze knocked a clump of snow from a branch? She paused. The wind was calm, the tree devoid of everything including leaves. Her eyes drifted back to the ground. A hint of shadow—something slightly darker than the white of the snow—shifted just slightly. The thin outline of a camouflaged hare pulsed against the field of white and faded.

Izzy pulled her arm back. The rock felt light now in the sling, like it would rather soar away into the sky than fly straight and true. She pinched hard onto the lead strand, shifted her feet ever so slightly, rocked back, and launched the stone forward.

The rock smacked into the hare's back, bounced off at an odd angle, then embedded itself into the powder an arm's length away. Izzy rushed forward, struggling to pull her knife from the handmade sheath on her belt. She didn't need it. The hare was already dead. Izzy stood over it, not yet daring to touch it. It was dinner, certainly—but it was far more than that. It was a sign of self-sufficiency. With this sling, she could survive on her own. She could escape from the cabin and make it back to civilization. She would never run out of ammunition. She could make three or four slings and be set for months. Years, even.

She picked up the hare by the scruff of the neck. Tonight, regardless of what Rick brought in, they would eat a full meal. More food was a good thing. She pocketed her sling and headed back to the cabin almost at a run, slowing only to make sure she didn't drop her precious cargo.

By the time Rick returned, she had skinned and gutted the hare. Thin slices of meat were already cooking for the evening meal. The stove was stoked and warm, the water pails full, and the kettle hot. The woodpile inside was enough for three days, even if the temperature dropped. The pile behind the cabin was enough for another week. There would be nothing he could criticize or punish her for today.

Rick entered with only a single bird, another ptarmigan, on his catch line.

He glanced at the stove first, then at the wood pile. "Light day today, Isabelle. Damn wolverine raided my traps again. Son of a bitch took two of them. White fur everywhere. Got a bird though." He held it up.

"That's okay," Izzy said proudly. "I got dinner tonight." She pulled back the cover on the frying pan, showing the prepared meat from the hare, ready to eat.

"Where the hell did that come from?" Rick asked. He looked at the meat-drying racks. It took him only a second to realize she hadn't used any of that.

"I killed it," she said proudly.

"With what?" He stepped closer to the pan.

"This." She pulled the sling out of her pocket proudly. He glared at her and snatched it from her hand. Ice sluiced into her stomach. He held it up by the window.

"You made this?"

"Yes."

"Why?"

"I thought it would be good for both of us to be out hunting. You know. Just in case." She looked at the single, now pitiful-looking bird in his hand, then back at the meat in the pan.

"You don't need to be worrying about that. I'll do the hunting." He balled up the sling in his hand. The shock on his face faded, and for the briefest of seconds, it turned to something she had never seen before. That look disappeared in a flash, replaced with something she *had* seen before: anger. She saw it blossom and bloom, and that spurred a rise in her temperature as well. How could he be angry at her for bringing in food? He never minded when she found nuts or brought in water.

"It's not like we're living a luxurious life out here, Rick. You should be glad I brought something home tonight. If you don't want it, fine. Don't eat it. More for me." She slammed the pan down on the top of the stove. The lid bounced and fell to the floor. She muttered a curse word under her breath and bent to pick it up.

The back of his knuckles smashed into her left cheek as she stood up. Her head snapped back. The lid again flew from her grasp. Her already aching shoulder crashed into the cabin wall, sending jolts of pain flaring through her entire body. Her head missed the edge of the stone mantel by a hair's whisper. Blood filled her mouth as she slid to the floor. She choked on it, spraying a thin red mist across the room.

Rick watched her regain her wits, waiting until he was sure she could see what he was doing. He opened the lid on the barrel-shaped stove and dropped her sling into the fire.

"You don't need that," he said as he turned back to her. "Whatever we need, I'll get. Your job is here, in the house. You don't need to be out there. You have no idea how dangerous it is out there." He looked at the pan filled with the ready-to-cook hare, picked it up, and calmly dumped the contents into the fire. Izzy watched in horror. A line of blood and saliva spilled from her lips. The smell of burning leather wafted through the cabin. Rick closed the lid, glowering at her.

She touched the inside of her cheek with her tongue. Her teeth had dug deep gashes into the flesh. She winced.

"I'm sorry darlin'. Didn't mean to do that." He reached down and caressed her cheek. "You'll be fine. No damage done, right?"

Izzy shook her head ever so slightly, more out of disbelief than agreement, but Rick took it as assent.

"Good. Get yourself cleaned up. And then pluck that bird," he said as he turned away. "It'll do for dinner." He left the cabin with barely a pause, not even bothering to help her back to her feet.

Izzy leaned back against the hearth and swallowed another mouthful of blood-laced spittle.

There had been no warning, nothing but the look on his face . . . and that strange look that had briefly crossed his face before the anger. She closed her eyes and memorized that expression. The shock. The anger. And the look in between.

Her pulse quickened. She knew what that expression was. Fear. *True fear*. The fear of realizing that she could get the one thing she would always need, the one thing he had always provided: food. With that ability, she could go anywhere, do anything, *without him*.

She looked at the stove. The sling was gone, but she could make another. The next one she would hide, and the meat she caught she would keep for herself.

He could have his anger. He could make her life hellish. But she would always remember that look of fear on his face, and someday, when the winter was over, she would make his worst fears come true.

She would leave, and *he* would be completely alone.

CHAPTER 16

Izzy

(Spring)

The stranger's appearance in their camp in the middle of spring changed everything.

Perhaps it was inevitable that someone would find their cabin. The smell of wood smoke permeated the surrounding forest and lingered over the lake. Every hunt-and-salvage mission left footprints in the winter snow and in the spring mud. The sounds of chopping wood could not be camouflaged.

The man was ashore and standing in front of Izzy before she knew he was there.

"Howdy." He wore a deerskin jacket with a rabbit-fur vest. His pants were darker, almost black. *Moose hide,* Izzy thought. The apprentice seamstress in her looked critically at the garment's seams. They were higher quality than even her latest creations—almost as if they had been done by a machine with real thread, not the fishing line she had been using all winter.

The lighter outline of sunglasses stood in stark contrast to the rest of his wind-burned, sun-darkened skin. A long braid of dark hair, stranded with gray, bounced on his shoulders as he turned his head. Izzy stopped what she was doing and took a step backward in the direction of the cabin. She twisted the grip on the rock she had been using to scrape a hide so that the cutting edge faced out—now more of a weapon than a tool. Her pulse thudded in her ears.

"Where's your folks?" the man asked. He glanced at the closed cabin door, then shifted his gaze to the drying racks on the east side of their cabin. The tangy smell of smoked meat filled the air. That he had come so close without Izzy knowing triggered panic within her. Izzy nodded toward the door. She didn't know what to say. Rick was in there taking a nap.

"Inside?"

"Yes."

"What's your name?"

"Isab—Izzy."

"Nice to meet you, Izzy. I'm Bill Six Rivers." He tipped forward in a little bow that seemed almost gallant. Izzy couldn't help but smile. The panic dissolved into a slight flutter in her stomach. He returned the smile, and her grip on the rock relaxed.

"Nice to meet you, Bill." Izzy emulated his bow. "Where did you come from?"

"The lake." He pointed to a red canoe emblazoned with a bright yellow stripe, beached to the east. He took another look at the cabin, then back at Izzy. "How about you? Where are you from?"

"Thompson."

"Been here long?"

"Six months or so, I think. Hard to keep count," Izzy said. Days had blended into weeks, and the weeks into months.

"Wintered over, eh?" He looked at the deerskin she had been scraping, then at the stack of firewood by the door. Half a dozen other skins that they had yet to do anything with covered the pile. "Looks like you did pretty well for yourselves."

Izzy nodded. Rick had been right to choose this place. Beyond the first three days here, they had not gone without at a single meal. There had been small meals, but there had always been something, even without her hunting.

"We've done okay," Izzy said. A brief surge of pride warmed her cheeks. They had made it, and though she hated being cooped up in such a small place with Rick for so long, she did not contest, even in the back of her mind, that he had provided well. Their last month or so in the bush before Angie died had been miserable. These last six had been almost luxurious. She had even put back on some of the weight she lost the previous summer. Her body had begun to grow once again.

"Did you winter over out here too?" Izzy asked.

"I spent some time in the bush. Some time in town," he said with a shrug. His eyes moved off her, slowly scanning the cabin and surrounding woods. The trees were just starting to come into their full spring foliage. In another month, the cabin would be invisible from the lake.

"Which town?" Izzy asked. She almost stood on her tiptoes at the mention of civilization.

"South Indian Lake for a while." He paused. "And Thompson, too. Not too long ago."

The mere mention of her hometown sent Izzy's heart racing. "You were just there?"

"A few weeks ago. Left at the breakup. Stopped by Laroque, then came up this way."

"What's it like now, in Thompson? There were a lot of gangs there when we left. Is it safe now? Are there people there? Food?" Her questions spilled out like a river breaking free of ice after a long winter. If Thompson was safe, she could really go back. She could leave Rick and go *home*! Maybe this man would even take her—

"It's better now, I think." His smile slowly faded. "I heard some pretty bad stories though. There's folks there who went through some pretty horrible . . . stuff."

Izzy nodded. Their eyes locked. The clack of the latch on the cabin door broke their connection. Bill's body stiffened as the door opened, and he glanced from Rick to Izzy with a troubled expression.

Rick strolled toward Izzy. "Hello, Bill."

"Rick." Bill said Rick's name as if he were spitting acid from his mouth.

"Didn't know you'd made it through," Rick said.

"Almost didn't."

Rick's face held an impassive stare. Izzy knew this voice. Rick had many voices, and this one meant she was already in trouble. He covered the distance to Izzy in slow, purposeful steps, then edged into a position to her left, a step ahead of her.

"You know each other?" Izzy asked.

"Bill and I go way back."

Bill's eyes again flicked to Izzy and back to Rick. Izzy felt like jumping out of her moccasins. If they knew each other, there was a chance that Bill would be able to stay for a while. If he stayed for a while, she could convince him to take her back.

"Why don't you go inside, Isabelle, so Bill and I can catch up."

With a purposeful shuffle of his feet, Rick inserted himself into the space between Bill and Izzy, partially obscuring Izzy's view of their visitor. Izzy wasn't doing what Rick wanted, and she knew she'd hear about it later.

"You two are a long way from town."

"Town wasn't so safe last year," Rick said, turning back to Bill.

"It's safer now, I think." Bill seemed to be measuring his words. "Maybe you should think about heading back."

"Harder for trouble to find us here."

"Seems like you have a habit of attracting trouble no matter where you are."

Izzy craned her neck around Rick. The men's eyes were locked in some sort of duel. A vein throbbed on the side of Rick's forehead.

Bill did not back down. "I'm sure Izzy there would like to get back to town. The bush ain't no place for a girl her age to be ... all alone."

"She ain't alone, Bill. She's just fine."

"Really? Izzy, are you fine here? If Rick wants to stay, that's his business, but we can go back if you'd like. There's good people in town now. People I'm sure would be happy to see you."

He smiled. It wasn't one of Rick's fake smiles, Izzy could tell. She nodded, and her feet began to move forward. Bill would take her back. Bill would get her back to safety. Rick couldn't stop him.

Rick put out his hand to block her path. "She's fine, Bill. You'd best be on your way."

"She's fine? Like my Cammie was fine? You don't even know when you're lying, do you? Come on, Izzy. Let's go. I'll take you home." He offered his hand to Izzy.

Rick continued to block her way.

"You know, they should have strung *you* up for what you did," Bill said, his cordial voice now dissolved to anger.

Rick shook his head. "Cammie *was* fine. Everyone knew that. Everyone but you and her. That girl had problems. You may not want to hear it, but even the cops knew that." His voice dropped lower. He pushed Izzy back toward the cabin.

"You think I'd take the word of someone like you over my own daughter's?" Bill stepped forward, narrowing the distance between them.

Izzy leaped away from Rick's outstretched arm. Somewhere in her mind, something clicked. *Cammie*. Brian had dated a Cammie for a while back in high school. Cammie had been around a lot in those days. Then, suddenly, she wasn't. And Brian had been so upset. There had been arguments between Brian and Rick. Big ones. Izzy had heard them all the way from her house. She had asked Angie about them, but Angie said it was something personal. Rick stopped coming over. There had been no ice rink that last winter before the flu. Izzy's father hadn't said why. It all made sense now.

Brian had left for college and then Rick had moved out. The day before Lois died had been the first time Izzy had seen Rick around in months. She hadn't thought much of it at the time—they had all been so sick, and Rick had saved them.

But Angie would have known. Angie had known why Rick was no longer welcome at their house. She had known what Rick had done—what Rick was—

Oh God, she had always known! The hair stood up on Izzy's arms. Angie had *always* known who this monster truly was.

"This ain't about Cammie. And this ain't about you, Bill. The world's changed. And whatever it is now, ain't what it was then."

"Whatever it is, Rick, it ain't this." He pointed his finger at Izzy and began a slow circle of Rick, toward Izzy, while maintaining his distance. "I'm not gonna stand by and let it happen again."

Izzy stepped to the side to get around Rick, but he moved, quick as a cat, to block her.

"Cammie was just confused. She was a sick girl."

Bill clenched his fists. "Don't you go talking about her. Not like that. Whatever was wrong with her was *your* fault. She was perfectly fine until she met up with you. She wouldn't have done what she did if it hadn't been for you."

Bill wagged his finger at Rick's face.

Rick didn't move. "I think you should leave, Bill—before you do something you'll regret."

"Lois knew, didn't she? She knew what you did. That's why she threw you out."

"Lois didn't know nothing. Just like you don't know nothing."

Bill stared at Rick. "I know what I know. And I know you're

up to no good out here." He turned back to Izzy. "Izzy, let's go. I'm getting you out of here."

"Isabelle, get inside!" Rick ordered.

Going back inside was no longer an option, now that she knew it all. She was leaving with Bill, no matter what Rick said.

Bill tried to shoulder his way past Rick to Izzy. Rick pushed him backward. Even as light as he was now, Rick still knew how to use the power in his legs. Bill stumbled to the ground.

"You should go, Bill. Before you get yourself hurt."

Bill jumped back up, his intent clear. He took two steps and lunged at Rick.

Rick was faster. In a flash, the Glock was out of the holster hidden under his coat. On Bill's second step, Rick pulled the trigger. The bullet flew from the chamber, straight into the bowed forehead of the man who would have been Izzy's savior. Rick took a single sideways step like a matador avoiding a charging bull. The impact from the bullet drove Bill to the ground. He was dead before he hit it.

Izzy screamed. The exiting bullet had removed Bill's hat and torn a baseball-sized hole in his skull. A gray and red mass flowed out of the hole. His body jerked once and stopped. She screamed again.

Rick stood over the body, the gun still trained on the man's back. The woods fell silent. Even the wind seemed to have stopped moving the treetops. Rick spat on the ground next to Bill, then turned to Izzy.

"See what you made me do?"

He rubbed his beard with the crook of his elbow, then slowly holstered the gun.

Izzy couldn't speak. For all the bad things Rick had done, she had never actually seen him kill anyone. Those men—the ones who had killed Angie—that had been different. That was out of her sight, and necessary. This time—this man—Bill—had tried to help *her*. And now he was dead.

"Why don't you go inside, Isabelle. You don't need to see this."

He tapped Bill's shoulder with the toe of his boot.

Izzy stared at the body, wishing it would rise up. She blinked twice, hoping that the simple act of refreshing her view would alter it somehow—that this horrible image was a hallucination—a nightmare. She had seen blood before—had butchered dozens of kills—but this blood looked different—was *real*.

"Get inside, darlin'. I'll take care of this."

Rick gave her a gentle push toward the cabin. Izzy turned and began a slow amble back to the door, her mind buzzing with images and words she could barely comprehend.

Loudly though, and now very clearly in her mind, even above the buzz, a months-old image rose to the forefront: an image of a dead deer on a counter in a house very far away, springing to life and whispering four little words.

Run, Izzy. Run now.

CHAPTER 17

Jake

(Summer)

For seven days Jake fought through thick underbrush, swampy ground, and cold streams. The fish, already filled with a never-ending supply of blackflies and mosquitoes, refused to take his bait. Animals tripped his traps, but somehow escaped. His food canister grew lighter by the day. Heavy weather blew in, soaking every stick of firewood. His damp clothes never had a hope of drying. He trudged on. *The North*, he reflected, *could be cruel.*

His boots became a problem as well. They had been good boots when the family had arrived at the cabin the previous summer. Continuous use took a heavy toll. The laces frayed and broke. Rocks gouged the soles. Repeated stumbles wore the leather thin on the outside of the right boot. His feet had grown half a size since they had bought the boots. Day after day of walking scrunched his aching toes into the end of the boot. He tried his running shoes for a while, but the synthetic leather and mesh offered no resistance to the sharp thorns and fetid water. He wrapped soft pieces of moss around the toes threatening to blister and went back to his boots, which caused him to limp slightly. It was that or risk a barefoot hike through kilometers of thorns and sharp sticks. He considered cutting the toe caps off his boots to allow more room, but that was a last resort, and one he couldn't convince himself to try . . . yet. *Measure twice, cut once*, his dad's voice warned.

In the swamp, trees grew at odd angles and blocked his path. Tangles of roots corrupted Jake's footing. Creeper vines covered everything, slathering him with slime each time he touched them. Belt-high stinging nettles, relentless in their attacks, filled in the gaps. The patches of open track he did find were ankle deep with stagnant water. Hip-deep holes tried to drown him. The rain chased him and switched from drizzle to squall, then slackened to a fine mist. Small birds fluttered overhead and laughed at him.

You don't belong here.

The inclement weather did not help. Jake's nose dripped constantly. When he stopped and was able to light a fire, hot tea relieved some of the chill. What he really wanted was to immerse himself in a tub of hot water—to soak away the aches and pains that grew by the day.

Rescue fever enveloped him. He envisioned a helicopter spotting him as he waved his arms, signaling for rescue. He pictured his father leaning out of the chopper, pulling him in, asking him how he had managed to come so far, proud of his boy, who had navigated some of the wildest terrain left in the country, all alone. Jake imagined a return to town, surrounded by reporters and doctors, marveling at his condition.

How did you survive? they would ask.

My dad and my grandpa taught me everything I needed to know, he would reply.

His school would celebrate Jake Clarke Day. The prime minister would call to congratulate him. Jake would smile and be modest and say it was no big deal. His dad would know though, and be so proud. The planning of this celebration kept him moving, constantly scanning the gray skies for his rescuers.

No one came.

At night, he had no flashlight and no moon to see by. The stars hid behind a thick ceiling of clouds, and even if it had been clear, none of that dim light would have reached through the impenetrable canopy. On the seventh night, he walked until darkness enveloped him so tightly that he could no longer see his hand in front of his face. He hacked off a few low branches from a nearby tree, nearly losing his machete in the muck when his numbed hands slid off the mud-encrusted handle on a backswing.

He stacked the branches on the ground and removed the tent fly from his pack. He wrapped himself in the fly, pack and all, and squatted down on the spruce branches. The cuttings kept him somewhat out of the mud. Water dripped from the trees. Branches rubbed against each other as the wind blew overhead. Unseen critters scurried about in the murk. Jake catnapped through the night, his eyes closed, but his mind wide awake and his body miserable.

He moved with the dawn. The clouds thinned and for one brief moment—perhaps thirty seconds—the sun shone directly on a muck-covered boy stuck deep in a marsh in the middle of nowhere. Jake absorbed what he could of the little warmth it offered. The hole in the sky closed. Jake paused, then continued his fight.

On the afternoon of that eighth day in the swamp, the ground began to change. The land rose. The water drained away. The thick brush subsided, and Jake made his first true camp in days. His boots were a mess. Had he been in civilization, he would have thrown them straight into the trash. The swamp wasn't a place for leather. It was better suited to rubber boots and hip waders. He removed the laces and the insoles, opened the boots as far as he could and dried them by his fire.

His food was gone. A few rogue crumbs of jerky rattled around in the canister, but not even enough for a mouthful. He used it to bait his traps, of which he set about a dozen that night, none more than a hundred meters from his fire. His sodden clothes hung on him as if his shoulders were wire coat hangers. His chest hurt with every heartbeat. Death, he knew, lurked in the darkness. He could feel it approaching, stalking him. Without food and canteens refilled with boiled water, it would come, and it would take him.

He resorted to eating the unthinkable that night. He caught a crawfish in the stream, cooked it on a spit, and ate it, carapace and all. He scrounged some small beetles from a rotting log, a slug from a leaf, and two snails from the underside of a rock. Only after washing those down with water did he appreciate why his father had once doubted the viability of surviving on those barely edible options for any length of time.

But his father had never, as far Jake knew, been as desperate. He had never wasted away like this and weighed two-thirds of his weight from just a year before. Jake made do with the bugs, and crossed his fingers that his traps would be full in the morning and that none of what he'd eaten would make him any more ill.

The spirits of his ancestors watched over him that night and kept death at bay. Four of his traps were sprung by dawn. Three held prizes: two squirrels and a rabbit. He scarcely had the energy to celebrate. His fingers, wrinkled from the constant sogginess of the swamp and stiff from the unseasonably cold temperatures, struggled to gut and remove the fur from the critters. He cooked them over his small fire and ate slowly. The food worked its way into his system, but the chill would not leave. His hands shook. He stared at his fire as the wet wood sizzled and burned down to coals. It took all of his willpower, two hours later, to gather his gear and head south up another ridge, down into another shallow valley and back into deeper forests. To sit for even another half hour with his body barely able to maintain its core temperature would mean death, and he knew it. Getting back on his feet would keep the reaper away, if just for a few more hours.

In the forest, a thick carpet of fallen needles cushioned his steps. The size and height of the trees prevented the low ground clutter so prevalent in the valleys. Through the trees to the south, the canopy seemed brighter. He picked up his pace. Within a minute, he stood at the bottom of an immense esker, easily the height of the tallest building in Thompson. Sparse grasses and a few stunted trees were all that had taken root on the pile of sand and gravel. Jake scrambled up the side, using those few trees and blades of grass as handholds to pull himself along. The sand gave way as he attempted to summit the aeons-old pile of glacial debris. He crawled to the top on all fours, pulled himself to his feet using a gnarled jack pine for support, and took in the scene before him.

A kilometer ahead, perhaps two at the most, the forest ended at the shore of a massive lake. A breeze from the north whipped away the bugs that had followed him up the hill, stirring whitecapped waves on the lake. In the farthest distance of the horizon, a gray line indicated either the southern shore or a low cloud bank moving south with the wind.

Jake pulled out his map, nearly losing it to the gusts. There were only two lakes this large in this part of Manitoba. And to reach one of those would have taken a massive miscalculation on his part. That left one option: Northern Indian Lake. And if this was Northern Indian Lake, then across the lake and within another week's march was Laroque—if he could get across. To the west the mighty Churchill fed this lake with water, and to the east the Churchill resumed, pulling the water back out. The lake, as large as it was, was really just a reservoir for one of the biggest rivers in the province. With a canoe, the town was three days' paddle away, and nearly straight south. Walking around this lake and finding a way over the fierce Churchill and all its tributaries could take the rest of the summer.

A glimmer of a smile crossed Jake's weary face anyway. Getting out of the swamp alive had been a major accomplishment. Getting across the lake without a canoe, and without drowning, would be an even bigger one. That, though, was a concern for later. First, he needed to get down to the lakeshore. *One goal at a time,* Amos's voice reminded him. *Use high ground to get your bearings. Know where you're going before you set out. Makes it more likely you'll actually get there.*

Jake double-checked his map, took a solid compass reading, and scanned the shore for points of reference. Only once he had done everything Amos would have advised, did he stow the map and begin the long slide down the gravel to the forest below. His pace was quick and his spirits high.

He'd find a way across the lake, he told himself, even if he had to build a raft.

CHAPTER 18

Izzy

(Summer)

This time, she would heed the warning. She would run. But first she needed new slings and extra moccasins. She had to pack supplies for the trip: extra food, extra clothing, and whatever tools she'd need to survive—out there—alone—for days, if not weeks. She gathered these things while Rick was gone, wrapped them in a piece of heavy plastic she hoped Rick wouldn't miss, and hid them in a big, hollowed-out maple tree to the east of the cabin.

There were some things she wouldn't be able to hide prior to running. Rick's flint and striker. She needed that. She needed a water bottle and her knife. She couldn't go anywhere without her sleeping bag. A pot for boiling water was essential. Rick would notice the instant any of these things weren't in their regular places, and she could not forget what had happened to Bill.

Even dead, Bill was the key to Izzy's escape. Rick had kept Bill's canoe. It was half the size of the aluminum behemoth stored behind the cabin. That small canoe would allow her to cross the lake.

Getting across the lake wouldn't be easy, but it wasn't the only difficult part of her plan. When Rick wasn't using the canoe—which was rarely—he kept it out of sight behind the cabin, covered by an old tarp. Izzy had tried to move it twice. While Rick was able to shoulder it without breaking a sweat, Izzy was only able to slide it across the ground. Dragging a canoe across the forest floor made a lot of noise, and if Rick was anywhere nearby, he would come running.

And that was the other problem. When he wasn't using the canoe for fishing or salvage trips, he rarely strayed far from her little prison. In fact, he stayed closer than ever. He spent the rainy days putting together new gizmos and gadgets that made the cabin feel all the more permanent. He built a more substantial smokehouse. He found a hand pump at a nearby deserted cabin, and combined it with a length of garden hose and a deep pot. Just like that, they had running water and a kitchen sink—a sink she would be stuck at for the rest of her life, if Rick had his way.

In her mind, she mapped her path from one part of the cabin to another, gathering her supplies and adding the ones stored in the hollow tree. She'd drag the canoe to the shore and hop in. Her skills at handling a canoe weren't great, but she was a quick learner. As long as she was out of sight by the time Rick returned, she'd be fine. In theory.

Still, there were daunting challenges. Rick never left the cabin without the compass, and it was the only one they had. She stole glances at the maps when he was gone. She didn't know for certain exactly where they were. Rick had never told her the name of the lake. Some features stood out to her and matched one that seemed to fit: a large, long lake that ran east to west, with a spit of land that looked like a nose to the east of the cabin. Across the lake and slightly to the west, a river entered from the southwest. That river would take her to civilization. She didn't have to get all the way back to Thompson—not on her own. She traced a route to Laroque following the river. If, once across the lake, she always walked up the rivers and clockwise around the next lake, she knew she would end up in Laroque. Of course, it wouldn't be that simple. There were dozens of rivers entering each lake. She'd have to pick the right one.

She'd have to work her way through the dense summer forest, too, but once across the lake it would just be a matter of will, and she had plenty of that.

Without a true calendar, Izzy relied on guesswork to calculate the start of summer. The longest day of the year should have been the perfect time to run, but a weeklong string of cold showers dropped into the region, leaving the rivers high and Izzy's spirits as drenched as the surrounding landscape. With the wet weather came the blackflies, thick as tire smoke and impossible to endure without full skin protection.

Rick grumbled through every meal, and, if stuck inside due to the weather, napped often, ate little, and talked even less. Izzy nervously awaited a good stretch of weather, if only to push him out of the cabin for a moment's peace.

She counted the days through late June. Rick hovered close, never leaving for more than a couple of hours.

"The fish are biting today!" he said each morning. He spent every day in the canoe within sight of the cabin. At the end of each day, they crammed the smoker full with more drying fish. By the end of June, every shelf in the cabin overflowed with food, to the point that catching more than they could eat in a day was almost a waste.

"Damn wolverine's back." Rick came in one morning near the end of the month. "Sneaky bastard ate right through the smokehouse wall last night. Knocked all the racks down. Made one hell of a mess." He reached above the door and grabbed the rifle.

"You going looking for it?" Izzy's hopes surged. The weather was good, the day young. Her legs and arms were fresh and ready to paddle. If Rick was gone for even a few hours, that would give her enough of a head start.

"I'm going to go kill it, is what I'm going to do," he said.

"You sound pretty sure this time," she said with a bit of a smirk.

"Saw the bastard running off with a whole stringer of fish. Followed it to that big ol' hollowed-out maple off to the east. If I can get back there fast enough, I'll take that sucker out, even if I have to chop that damn tree down." He picked up the ax from the corner. Izzy cussed to herself. She needed him to head west, not east. Her supplies were to the east. And then it dawned on her. There were lots of maple trees around the cabin, but not many Rick would describe as big and old and hollow. She swore again, this time aloud.

"Don't worry, darling. I'll get it. We'll be having wolverine stew tonight."

"I'll come with you," she offered, taking a few steps in the direction of the door.

"Naw. Stay here. Those things can get a might ornery when they're cornered. Wouldn't want you to get that pretty face hurt." He pulled the door shut behind him as he ran out.

Izzy looked at her backpack, sitting innocently in the corner. She could fill that with supplies in minutes, and add a few extra pieces of leather and rawhide to make whatever she needed. Rick's pack was also in the corner. The maps were there. And clipped to the shoulder harness was the compass. She paused for the briefest of moments. She would have only a few minutes head start—so little time to load the canoe and drag it to the water. If Rick caught her, he would likely kill her. On the other hand, if he found that pouch and all her supplies in that tree, he'd probably do worse.

She stepped toward the corner where the backpacks lay. The first step was the hardest. Then her feet moved faster. She grabbed her pack and stole the compass from Rick's. The maps were carefully folded and sealed inside a plastic bag. A stack of meat was next. She crammed her sleeping bag into the center of the pack. There would be time for rolling it properly later.

A noise from outside stopped her in her tracks. For a moment, she thought Rick had already returned, but after a second she realized it was only a flock of geese passing overhead. She shook her head and forced herself to focus on her task.

The sound of a shot, then a second, cracked through the woods. This time, she didn't stop moving. She grabbed a roll of fishing line and a package of hooks, a spare dishcloth, and the lightest of their pans. Her poor packing meant that before she had even half of what she needed, the pack was already overflowing. She added the hatchet to the side of pack. Her panicked fingers fumbled with the straps. The hatchet fell to the floor, missing her toes by a fraction of an inch. She reviewed what she had stuffed into the nylon pack. Food. *Check.* Shelter. The plastic was in the tree. She grabbed the rolled up tent fly from the shelf. It would have to do. *Check.* Water? She grabbed a spare one-liter plastic bottle. *Check.* Fire? She grabbed the flint and striker. *Check.* Clothes? She had only the thin deerskin tunic on her back. Most of her city clothes had long since worn through. The parka, even at night, would be too warm and too much to carry. Knife. She grabbed the worn knife from the kitchen table.

An alarm went off in her mind. Rick would soon be back. She snapped the clasp on the pack closed, flung it over her shoulder, and raced for the door. Her mind buzzed with the plan. She would miss the moccasins and the slings the most. Those would be the first things she would make when she had time. She stopped as she reached the door. She hadn't packed any extra skins or leather to make a sling with, let alone enough to make moccasins with. Her stock of materials inside was desperately low. Most of it was out back, drying on the woodpile near the canoe.

She ducked out of the door and headed around the back. She flipped over the canoe, tossed her pack into it, and grabbed a full deerskin from the pile. A single skin could make five or six pairs of moccasins—far more than she would need, but she'd worry about that later. She grabbed a paddle from next to the cabin and began to drag the canoe across the ground. The noise it made seemed like it would wake up the entire forest. She rounded the corner of the cabin, eyeing the lake to the south. She knew the exact path that she could quickly drag the canoe through. She'd envisioned this path a hundred times and had even cleared the few remaining sticks out of the way.

She had barely rounded the southwestern corner of the cabin when Rick's massive hand grabbed her shoulder from behind and yanked her backward.

"What the hell do you think you're doing?" he yelled as he wrenched her to the ground. Her legs flew out from under her. The impact with the forest floor rendered her unable to speak. The sun was directly behind him. His dark silhouette towered over her.

Izzy raised her hands to protect herself. The paddle was still clenched in her hand. Rick kicked out at it, nearly breaking her fingers. The paddle flew off into the leaves. Izzy screamed in pain and rolled away. Rick grabbed her by her hair and lifted her to her feet. He dropped a shredded piece of plastic by her feet—the plastic she had used to wrap the supplies she had hidden in the tree. Her spare slings fell to the side. He pulled the backpack from the canoe, then riffled through it with one hand while holding her at arm's length with the other.

"You little bitch." He snatched the compass out of the pack. "I keep you alive for a whole bloody year, and this is how you repay me? You take my stuff?" He jerked her to the side so violently that she thought her neck was going to break.

"You want to run?" He tossed the pack behind him, grabbed the bottom hem of her tunic, and pulled it up and over her head, switching hands to keep ahold of her hair. The cool morning air flowed around every inch of her naked body, and she shivered. Tears scorched her cheeks.

"You want to run?" he yelled again. "Run now!"

"I'm sorry, Rick," she pleaded between sobs. She wrapped her hands around her body.

"Go—swim! Run!" He pointed south and swung the tunic over his shoulder. "You want to leave, now is your chance. See how far you make it before you freeze your ass off—how far you get before wolves pick up your scent. I say you don't last the night." He let go of her hair. Izzy sank to her knees.

"No, Rick, I want to stay." She crawled back toward him. He backed up a step and pushed her to the ground.

"Rick, please, let me stay. I won't do it again." Leaves and dirt stuck to her arms and knees. The cool air sucked away more of her independence with each passing minute. Rick's hovering presence ripped away her will even more quickly. Her desperate sobs turned into a wail as he flipped her over onto her back with his foot, then pinned her down with his boot.

"You do it again, and I'll put a bullet through that pretty little head of yours." He threw the tunic at her and picked up her pack. She cowered on the ground, weeping and shivering as the sound of his footsteps receded. The cabin door slammed. Once again, she was alone.

She slowly pulled the tunic over her head, stood, and limped past the canoe to the edge of the lake. A cold wind ruffled the water and shook her to her core.

There was no sign of a dead wolverine or fresh blood where they normally cleaned their kills. The wolverine had, it seemed, escaped once again.

CHAPTER 19

◄○►

Jake

(Summer)

Jake covered the remaining distance to the lake at a breakneck pace. The forest floor seemed almost manicured—like a city park instead of the bush he'd been fighting for so long. His spirits soared. He imagined putting his hands and feet into the lake's cool, clean water. He pictured catching a fish or two for dinner. He'd left the swamp behind, and now everything would be so much better. The corner had been turned. It was just a matter of time before he was safe.

A massive flock of geese passed overhead as he jogged, trumpeting his arrival, honking and calling out landing instructions to each other. Jake's hopes surged. One of those geese would feed him for days. The lake would provide everything he so badly needed, and a respite from the slog through the bush.

The blast of a single gunshot broke him from his reverie. The echo bounced among the trees before dissipating through the forest. Jake ducked, hunching his shoulders slightly before his secondary reactions took over. He stumbled and came to a stop. A second shot pierced the quiet of the woods.

Jake's head swam with the consequences of the shots. Shots could only mean one thing: people. He turned, searching for his bearings. All thoughts of his aches and pains withdrew from his mind. Somewhere, within earshot, rescue awaited. Jake only had to find it before that chance disappeared. His ears told him the sound had originated from the southeast. He spun that way and began jogging.

"Hello?" he croaked, barely loud enough to be heard over the pounding of his heart. He relaxed, took a breath, and repeated the call, more loudly and forcefully. "Hello! Is anyone out there?" No response. He ceased jogging and listened again. Quiet greeted him. Another call was met with silence.

Jake wound his way between the closely packed trees. The ground had been cleared of deadfall, a sure sign of human presence. It had been the same around his winter cabin. He and Amos had picked up every stick within a kilometer the previous winter to keep the stove going.

Jake's heart raced. He scanned the woods. He sniffed the air. A faint tinge of wood smoke hung over the area. Living by campfires for so long made it difficult to sense, but it drifted by like a sheer curtain. The hairs on the back of his neck rose.

A noise ahead—a familiar scraping noise. Jake's tightened throat wouldn't allow his words to escape past his lips. He raced forward ever faster. A dark, rectangular shadow emerged from the trees. Jake closed on it. An outhouse. Never before had he been so excited to see a latrine. He nearly jumped for joy.

What he saw next halted him in his tracks and nearly stopped his heart.

Ahead, next to a cabin, a girl dragged a red canoe. She was a blond, waiflike creature, perhaps twelve or thirteen years old. Her face was dirty, her hair tangled and matted. She was scrawny, with a body like a feral cat, and wore a crudely made deerskin tunic and moccasins. Jake instantly recognized the canoe she was attempting to move. Jake had sat in that canoe, with its distinctive yellow stripe, a dozen times. If that canoe was here, then Bill Six Rivers was not far away. Jake's heart leaped.

The girl didn't look familiar, though. Bill's daughter, Cammie, had been much older when she died. And Bill, as far as Jake knew, had no other children—and definitely no blondes.

The girl pulled the canoe with all her might. She checked behind her as she pulled it, as if she were being chased. A moment later, Jake knew why. A large, older man caught up to her as she passed the corner of the cabin. He grabbed her with one hand and tossed her to the ground like a rag doll. The man began yelling. Jake couldn't decipher the words, but he knew that whatever they were, they weren't nice. The man grabbed her tunic and ripped it off her body. The girl screamed.

The air left Jake's lungs with a whoosh. His feet took root in the ground. The image of a bear tearing apart a fawn flashed in his mind. Whoever this man was, he was closer to animal than human.

The girl lay sobbing on the ground. She wrapped her arms around her head and pulled her legs close to her chest. The man continued to taunt and berate her. The girl screamed as he stepped on her. Jake's feet broke from their shackles and began to move. But the next sentence out of the man's mouth stopped Jake once again.

"You do it again and I'll put a bullet through that pretty little head of yours." The man tossed the tunic at the girl and stormed off.

The girl struggled to replace her tunic, paused as though gathering her wits, then stood and walked toward the water. The canoe was left where it was.

Jake turned, slid behind the outhouse, and, making sure he kept the privy between him and the cabin, worked his way back into the woods.

PART II

CHAPTER 20

Jake

Jake scrambled back through the woods toward the esker, and away from whatever it was he had just witnessed. He'd get another look at the lake from the top of the ridge and decide whether to go east or west. Neither option felt like a good one. If he could just find another cabin, one with different people, or no people, then he might find another canoe or a rowboat, or materials to build a raft, and get across. He could leave the memory of that wretchedness far behind. Whichever way he went, it wouldn't be anywhere close to that cabin.

He was ten days from Laroque if he had to circumnavigate the lake. Fewer if he pushed hard. Maybe four days if he found a way across the lake. Whoever that man was, and whatever he was doing out here, would be none of Jake's concern once he arrived in Laroque. He jogged a little faster at the thought, taking but few glances south.

Light through the trees outlined the gravel ridge. Jake knew from his descent that the surface on this side was sandier than the one to the north. The winds had blown the lightest of the granules to the southern side. Slowly, over a period of another million years or so, the entire ridge would blow away.

Jake pulled himself up to the top, huffing and puffing the entire way. The climb was brief and intense. But no amount of physical struggle could destroy the image of what he had seen.

The sights and the sounds of that encounter crept back every time he took a breath.

He tried to focus his thoughts as he stood on top of the esker. He scanned for routes to the east and west. Little bays dotted the lakeshore. Dozens of rivers and hundreds of creeks flowed in from every direction. *Water, water, everywhere.* His heart slowed, but his thoughts flew back to the girl. Jake rolled back through the scenes of the encounter: the joy of discovering the cabin; the fear on the girl's face as she dragged that canoe—Bill's canoe—across the ground; the sudden appearance of the man; the violence with which he had grabbed her and tossed her down; how he had stripped her bare without even the slightest concern for decency.

And then Jake imagined living with that man. He imagined what it must be like for that girl—so thin, so desperate—to live under the same roof with that man. Every day. With no hope for escape or freedom. Jake's mouth went dry.

From here, it was ten days' travel home.

One klick to the south was trouble of a sort he had never before seen. This wasn't a bear deciding if he was dinner or danger. This wasn't a swamp trying to keep him lost deep in its bogs. This wasn't a school-yard fight where the teachers would step in and separate the children before they hurt each other.

On the shore of that lake was a dangerous, unpredictable man who had a gun and who had already proven the will to beat a little girl. A man who had *somehow* gotten his hands on Bill Six Rivers's prized canoe. Bill had built that boat with his own bare hands as therapy after his daughter's suicide. He had told Leland that he was to be buried in it when that day came. He would never have sold it or given it away.

Ten more days.

In ten days he would be home and he could send the authorities back to check on the girl.

Jake flashed back again to the look of terror on that girl's face. Was she the man's daughter?

Did it matter?

She wouldn't last ten more days. Not with that man.

Jake stood on the esker and watched a thin line of gray smoke drift from the woods ahead of him, marking the location of the cabin like an emergency beacon. His father had asked him, all those months ago, to do him proud—to do what needed to be done.

Two things forced Jake to run back down the esker in the direction of the cabin: the look his father would have given him if he hadn't, and the expression on the girl's face when that man had appeared at the corner of the cabin. She had known—before she even tried to take the canoe—what was going to happen if the man caught her.

Jake paused at the bottom of the slope.

He removed his rifle strap from his shoulder and slid the bolt backward on the gun to chamber a round. The bullet rose from the magazine. Time and elements had slightly tarnished the brass cartridge. He looked at that bullet, with its hollow-point tip designed to wreak havoc on the internal organs of whatever he hit. He couldn't close the bolt. His hand wouldn't move. Death lived in that piece of metal and fire. Ugly. Human. Death. Deer and bears were animals—food. To be respected, no doubt—but food just the same. Jake had killed dozens of them in his short life; gutted and butchered them, too. Deer blood was no more disgusting to him than oil to a mechanic. But human blood—*that blood would stain.* It would leave a deep, dark patch on his soul.

He pulled the bullet from the chamber, pushed it back into the magazine, then returned the gun to its case at the side of his pack.

He headed south.

CHAPTER 21

◄○►

Izzy

Izzy stood on the shoreline, watching the wind push the water southward. Waves formed once out of the lee of the shore. On the horizon, whitecaps dotted the lake's surface. She shuddered. What had she been thinking? Even if she had been able to get the canoe out into the lake, she would never have been able to get across it, not without capsizing and losing everything, including her life. She bent forward, touching the water with a fingertip. Six weeks ago, this water had been frozen solid. It didn't feel much warmer now.

She looked back at the cabin. The canoe remained where she had left it. Rick had gone inside, taking her pack and all of her things. The canoe was left as some kind of dare. Take it. Try getting away. *A bullet through your head.*

And she knew he meant it. That moment of fear she had seen all those months ago—his fear of being out here all alone—had not appeared on his face this time. His face had shown only rage. Tonight would be brutal. He would teach her a lesson tonight. There was no way around that.

Except there was. If there was no escaping this place alive, there was another option. Her parents were gone. Her sister was gone. Everything good in her life was gone. The hole those things had left behind had been filled with grief and sadness and terror and . . . and Rick. Rick said he loved her. What did he know about love? This wasn't love. She knew love, she had felt it. At home. In her house, with her father and her mother and Angie. The memory of that feeling had faded as Rick filled the hole in her heart with darkness. A web of anger and hatred wrapped her heart now, crushing her soul under the pressure. Living with that all-consuming burden was too much to bear.

She took a step forward.

Frigid water curled around her ankles. She'd bathed in this water daily since the ice had broken up, trying in vain to scrub every last bit of Rick from every part of her. It had been cold then. Today it seemed more than cold. Numbness invaded her feet until tiny shards of ice pulsed through her veins on a trip back to that hole in her heart. She took another step. The hole began to fill. The weight began to lift. A wave pulled at her knees, inviting her in, deeper.

The hem of her tunic touched the water. The next wave latched on to the deerskin and tugged at it. The feeling flowed away from her legs. The hole floated like a balloon, buoyant and calm. Her heart stuttered.

Izzy slid forward into the water. It welcomed her.

CHAPTER 22

Jake

Jake retraced his steps back to the cabin. He weaved his way between the trees and through the brush without making a sound. He didn't know exactly what he would do when he got there. Not yet.

Scout the line, his grandfather advised.

This time, Jake listened to the warning. He scanned the terrain as he drifted over uneven ground like a feather blown by the wind, stalking. He counted distance in steps. He checked the compass frequently, but his eyes remained alert. If the man saw him before he saw the man, Jake knew there would be trouble. He felt it in his bones. The man had threatened to kill the girl. What would he do to a stranger sneaking through the bush around his cabin? Jake's hand touched the bear spray canister on his harness. It wasn't as strong as mace, but in an emergency it would have to do.

Jake slowed further when he spotted the outhouse. His heart pounded in his chest—a sound he was sure carried through the woods like the engine of Jim Bridger's old Piper Cub airplane. The girl was nowhere to be seen. Bill's canoe lay where it had fallen when the man attacked her. That canoe would be the tool he needed to get them both out of there. With a canoe and a few minutes' head start, no one could catch him on the open water—not without a motor on their boat.

Along the back of the cabin, a lean-to protected a large stack of firewood. A longer canoe, silver and massive, sat on two rough sawhorses near the wood. A rack of furs, stretched to dry, hung between two trees. If he had had any doubts before, Jake now knew what kind of man he faced. He was a woodsman, a trapper, a thief, and an abuser, if not worse. Judging by the size of the fur pile, his skill at killing animals was indisputable. At that moment, Jake felt like a chipmunk trying to steal a nut from one of the man's snares.

Jake worked his way around the east side of the cabin. That side had more piles of wood as well as a few small propane tanks, a small smokehouse, and stacks of sealed plastic storage crates. Jake remembered how much work it had been for Amos and him just to keep the fire going, let alone to prepare for the winter. The man and the girl had obviously been here for a while, and planned well.

The sight of the smokehouse reminded him that food was still something he hadn't had enough of today. The morning's meal, eaten after seven days without solid food, now seemed like a very long time ago. His stomach rumbled. He took a sip of water from his canteen to settle it.

His mind spun with options. He could retreat again, find something to eat, and then wait for another day when he had more time to make a plan. That, his nervous insides told him, was the best idea. He could figure out when the man was hunting or running his traplines, see if he could catch the girl alone. If Jake could talk to her, he could find out the real story before he acted.

He also knew that the longer he stayed in the area, the greater the chance he would be discovered. And it wasn't just him that could be discovered. Rick could find his gear. His tent. His traps. His gun. If he lost those, he would again be stuck in the wilderness with a long way to walk, with no food and no way of getting more.

Bill's canoe was so close to the water's edge. He could pick it up and be on the shore in seconds. In the canoe, Jake could reach

Laroque in a couple of days, then come back and save the girl another time. Without it, he had none of those options. That canoe—Bill's canoe—was the key to everything. And Bill would want him to have it. About that, Jake had no doubt. Jake edged closer to it, his eyes darting left and right, looking for any sign of the man.

It was then that he saw the girl, standing on the shore, staring out at the water. Jake sighed with relief to see that she was alive and well. He would swing slightly farther east, away from the cabin, then come back along the shore, and, if she was alone, he'd talk with her, or at least let her know that he was here. If she had no interest in leaving, he'd back away and decide later if he was willing to risk stealing the canoe, perhaps that night.

Jake slipped around a large tree. For a moment, he lost sight of the girl, only to realize that she had moved at the same time he had. She now stood knee deep in the lake. Jake shivered at the thought of standing in that cold water for any length of time. He'd become accustomed to frigid baths, but part of the routine was to get in and get out quickly, and to have a roaring fire nearby. The water temperature here, even in the warmest part of the summer, never reached the point where it was safe to actually swim. But she showed no sense of urgency in her bathing. Instead, she slipped deeper into the water.

It took Jake another moment to realize what he was witnessing. He sprang forward, toward the water, but slowed as he approached the canoe. If he dove in after her, he'd have to pull both of them back up onto the shore. Then they would both be wet and cold and completely at the mercy of the man, wherever he was.

But if he could grab the canoe, get it into the water, and pull her into that, he could then paddle straight across the lake and save them both.

He snatched a paddle from the ground near the canoe and tossed it into the boat. He seized the center stay of the canoe with one hand, tipped it onto its side, and grabbed the gunwale with the other. With a gigantic pull, he hefted the canoe onto his shoulder in an awkward side-carry. He couldn't have gone far with it like that, but he didn't have to. The water was just meters away.

The girl heard his approach, and turned. A look of pure fear upon her face gave way to utter shock. She stumbled and pitched headfirst into the water. Jake raced forward. He hit the shore at a run, took two steps into the water, and tossed the canoe in ahead of him as the girl's hair disappeared beneath the waves.

CHAPTER 23

Jake

Jake vaulted into the canoe, grabbed the paddle, and threw two strokes into the water. He dropped the paddle as the bow reached the girl. The mop of hair bobbed back to the surface. Her face turned to the canoe. She sputtered and coughed.

"Take my hand," Jake said.

She hesitated.

"Take it!" he ordered again. He grabbed at her wrist, which floated just below the surface. Her hand moved away from him. Jake couldn't tell if she was treading water or trying to get away.

"Take it, please!" Jake begged. Still the girl wouldn't grab ahold. But she didn't move away either. Perhaps, Jake thought, she was already too cold to do anything. Or, she didn't trust him.

He paddled the canoe closer to her with his hand. If she didn't cooperate soon, the incoming waves would turn the bow, and he'd have to paddle to remain upright. "You have to trust me. I'll get you out of here."

His eyes met hers, and in a single glance he saw more pain than he could ever have thought possible for a person to hold within.

She moved her hand nearer to his. He grabbed it as soon as it came close enough, and with a jerk, he lifted her up. She kicked twice, helping him just enough to get her partway into the canoe. He reached over her, looking for a belt or pants or anything to latch on to, but except for the thin tunic, she had no other clothes. Jake adjusted his grip on her arm, looped his hand under her armpits, twisted her around, and wrenched her into the canoe. The two fell to the bottom, a tangle of arms and legs.

She was cold. Ice cold. Her skin was the color of a storm cloud— blotchy and gray. Jake glanced back at the cabin. That way lay fire and warmth, and whatever spare clothes she had. Jake extricated himself from under her and grabbed the paddle.

"Are you okay?"

If not for the shivers rippling through her body, she would have barely moved. Her core had probably already reached temperatures where hypothermia killed in minutes. Jake glanced back at the shore.

"We need to go back. You need dry clothes."

"No." She groaned weakly. "No."

"You're going to die out here if we don't."

"I don't care." She coughed water from her lungs.

Jake again glanced at the shore, then at her. She pulled herself up to the edge of the gunwale.

"Please don't go back."

Her eyes dropped to the water. If he turned around, he had no doubt she would throw herself over the side. He put a steering stroke into the water and looked southward. From this low vantage point, he could not see the opposite shore, nor could he see the whitecaps in the middle. He knew both to be out there. He could steer east or west a kilometer or two, come back ashore, light a fire, and get her warm. He drove a stroke deep as a wave crashed into the bow.

The shout from the shore disrupted his thoughts and shook him to his core.

"What the hell?" the man hollered.

Jake turned. The man rushed from the cabin. Jake caught only glimpses of him through the trees. But he saw enough to know that he had to get them out of there, fast. He rammed a stroke into the next wave. Thirty meters now separated the stern from the beach.

"Get back here! Now!" The man released a stream of cusswords.

Jake dropped half a dozen hard strokes into the water. The canoe accelerated with each one. The first hints of the northerly wind pushed him from behind, adding to his speed. He glanced back. The man reached the shoreline. He held something in his hand. Jake didn't have to hear its sound to know what it was. He ducked as the canoe dropped between two waves. The bullet flew harmlessly over his head. The sound shook the lake a moment later. Nearby geese panicked and fled from the surface in a massive, loud burst. A second shot followed. Jake didn't know where it went, but it felt closer. He didn't bother looking back. He timed the next wave, put two quick strokes into the water, and ducked again.

Jake paddled hard again as the wave passed by, his back hunched. He glanced over his shoulder. The distance to shore had grown to almost two hundred meters. The man held a pistol in his hand. Only the luckiest shot with a pistol would now come anywhere close to the canoe. Jake straightened his back and levered the canoe forward with all his might, straight out into the center of the lake.

No more shots came from shore. The man apparently knew as well as Jake did that they were out of range. Jake took no more glances back. Ahead of him, the first of the whitecaps waited, ready to challenge his skills.

In the bow, the girl was not moving. Jake hoped he would have an hour to get across the lake before she succumbed to hypothermia. If she died before they got across, he would never forgive himself.

He grabbed his pack and pulled the sleeping bag and tent fly from it.

"Here, wrap yourself in this." He handed it to her, but she barely reponded. "You need to get warm." He tapped her leg. She had stopped shivering. That, Jake knew, was not a good sign. He gauged the next wave, set the paddle down, and did his best to wrap her up before the following wave nearly capsized the boat. She would be warmer curled up by a fire, but this would have to do.

Jake stared ahead. The wind buffeted the lake's surface. The currents on this lake, even when the wind wasn't blowing, could be problematic. With the wind, it would take every ounce of his strength and energy to navigate safely. And he didn't have much in reserve. The day had been arduous, and his last meal too long ago.

But he would paddle, and paddle like he had never paddled before. Going back was no longer an option.

CHAPTER 24

◄O►

Izzy

Izzy pulled the dirty blue sleeping bag around herself as tightly as she could. Water splashed from the boy's paddle and from the lake as they bounced through a series of waves. Her teeth chattered. She rubbed her hands on her arms to try to warm up. Her stomach roiled, then burst forward from her mouth, spraying a mix of lake water and remnants of breakfast onto the fabric.

A wave cascaded over the bow. The boy apologized and tried to cover her up a bit better. Streams of water curled through folds in the bag, like a serpent trying to steal what little warmth she had remaining. The feeling in her fingers slowly disappeared, only to be replaced a few minutes later with a burning sensation like a thousand needles being shoved into her fingertips, over and over again.

She needed more clothes. She needed her things. Her sling. She needed her sling. So she could hunt. If she could hunt, she could make more slippers. And be warm again.

Still, Rick was back there. She could never go back to him . . . to *that*. She coughed. Another lungful of water dribbled out of her mouth. She could never go back to that . . . alive.

Dead. She should have been dead. It had been so easy to stay under once the water had pulled her in. The hole in her heart had dragged her down with so little effort. Yet here she was, in the canoe, crossing the lake with this boy. He had saved her. Where was he taking her?

The muscles in her chest began to quiver. The teeth chattering stopped. The pain in her fingers abated. Her heart pounded in her ears.

Dead. She would soon be dead.

"Angie," she mumbled. "Angie. I'm cold."

The noise of the surrounding lake faded to absolute quiet.

Cold.

Her thoughts echoed in a vast chasm. The pain subsided.

So cold.

CHAPTER 25

Jake

Arctic air roared past Jake's face. The spray stung his exposed hands. He kept his head on a swivel, gauging each wave in an unending series, positioning the canoe, and praying that this one wouldn't be the one to capsize them. He pushed south, fighting the roiling surface for the better part of an hour and a half. He couldn't stop. In the center of the lake, the land disappeared in every direction. He checked his compass every five minutes, until a glimpse of a treetop to the southwest told him to steer that way.

Massive waves, lifted by the rising lake bed, crashed against the rocks of the southern shore. Jake fought the surging waters until he found a gap in the rocks. His hands ached from his heavy grip on the paddle. His arms shook from the exertion.

He checked the girl. She had barely moved the entire trip, aside from throwing up soon after they set out on the lake. If they went over in the surf, she'd be helpless against the undertow.

Jake steadied the canoe and waited for a wave to pass. He needed to time it so that the next wave would pick them up and drop them onto the gravel shore. A second wrong in the timing, and the wave would fill the canoe with water instead, and roll them under. He pulled hard as the wave passed by. On the fourth stroke, the next wave caught them from behind. Jake braced the paddle against the stern and used it as a rudder, surfing the wave into the beach. The bow touched down a second before the stern. The canoe canted sideways. Jake leaped over the unconscious girl. His weary legs buckled as they hit the land. He caught himself and wrenched the canoe onto the shore. The remnants of the wave that had beached them soaked him from the hips down. He pulled until the stern cleared the outermost reach of the water. The wave retreated to the deeps.

The lake would not take them today.

His chest shuddered with exhaustion, but there was no time to waste.

Shelter. Fire. Water. Food. His father's mantra rang clear through his head. He left the girl in the canoe, grabbed the tent, and hastily set it up in a gap between the trees just a few meters in from the shore. His fingers fumbled with the poles and nearly broke one. He slowed his pace. The tent was his—*their*—lifeline. He couldn't lose it.

The girl didn't move as he carried her into the tent. Her skin was cool to the touch—she was still alive, but barely. Water dripped from his only sleeping bag. He wrung it out as best he could, but covering her in that would be like wrapping her in a wet towel. Instead, he dug his old clothes out of his pack and tucked them in around her. They were rank and soiled, but the best he could do.

His stiff hands worked to light a fire. Maintaining a grip on the flint and striker required a level of focus he no longer had. Somehow the fire lit on the fourth spark. A hastily stacked wall of rocks blocked the wind and reflected some of the heat into the tent. He gathered more wood while waiting for water to boil.

Only when he had enough wood for the next two hours did he let his body relax. He forced his eyes away from the slowly heating pot and gazed back the way they had come. Somewhere close, he knew, was the entrance to the river that would take him to Laroque—and her too if she lasted the night. To get her through the night, he'd have to warm her back up and get her some food. It had been over twelve hours since he ate the last of the food his traps had produced the night before: twelve solid hours of walking, running, and paddling. His body needed an all-you-can-eat buffet and a three-day sleep, not another all-nighter followed by an upriver run. That, however, was not in the cards. He grabbed a couple of cattail shoots and munched on them instead.

The girl was still asleep when Jake crawled back into the tent. He pushed one of his canteens, filled with hot water, into the shirt wrapped around her side and began rubbing her arms, trying, with little success, to get some heat back into her nearly frozen body. When that didn't produce immediate results, he left, returning a minute later with two rocks that had been warming by the fire, and tucked them in next to her back.

A few minutes after that, he entered the tent with a steaming cup of tea. It took a few tries to wake her.

"Hey, come on. We need to get you warmed up."

She moved, but only slightly.

"No." Her objection was barely audible.

"I need you to wake up now. Please. Have some tea." He rubbed her forehead, pushing her matted blond hair back from her face. He held the cup to her mouth. She opened her eyes as the liquid touched her lips. She took one sip, and then another.

He held the cup for her while she drank. Her hands shook as they moved. An hour before, he had not thought she would make it. Now at least he held out a glimmer of hope. Jake swapped the rocks next to her with two fresh from the fire, slipped inside one of his old socks. The girl wrapped herself around them, still shivering.

Jake refilled the cup and forced the additional fluid into her as well. Only when she had downed her second cup and begun to show color in her cheeks did he treat himself to some of the hot liquid. He wanted food, but to get that, he would have to leave her alone, and he wasn't going to do that until he knew she was going to make it.

"My name's Jake. What's yours?" he asked. He rubbed her legs with his dishcloth, hoping the little bit of friction would generate more heat. She pulled her legs back into the fetal position. She did not reply.

"I'm not going to hurt you. I'm just trying to warm you up. We need to get your core temperature up so I can go and get us some food. We need to work together at this or it won't happen." Her eyes opened briefly and she studied him.

"Izzy. My name's Izzy," she said after a pause.

Her eyes dipped closed. She curled tighter into a ball. Jake gave up on rubbing her legs. He peeled off his jacket and covered her with it. "I'll be back in a bit, okay, Izzy?"

She didn't budge as he exited the tent.

Shelter. The tent would be crowded with the two of them, but it would do until they got to Laroque. *Check.*

Fire. He put another log on it to keep it burning. *Check.* He draped the sleeping bag over a nearby tree to dry. With a little good luck, and no rain, it might not be dripping wet in a couple of days. Jake scanned the sky. Thick low-hanging clouds approached, carried by the gusting wind. Jake shook his head, then continued with his checklist.

Water. Jake refilled the pot and hung it back over the fire. He finished off what was left in his cup. He'd need to drink a lot more to replenish what he had lost in sweat during the crossing, but with the pot on the fire, that task, at least, was taken care of. *Check.*

Food. Tapping on his canister created a hollow thud. *Empty.* Now he'd need even more food to keep two of them alive. He wasn't sure how long she had been out in the woods, or how much she had eaten lately. She'd need more than she'd had.

The same, he reckoned, could be said for him as well.

He grabbed his fishing pole from his pack and began casting his lure off the rocks to the east of the camp. He'd fished this lake with his father and grandfather and a small client group many summers before. Somewhere around here, at another small campsite, was a log pitted with practice shots from Jake's air rifle. At seven years old, Jake had been little more than a camp mascot to the clients. He fetched the firewood, cleaned their fish, and picked up their trash. They had treated him well, but they hadn't expected anything out of him.

Now, the expectations were unbelievably high. The responsibility of keeping this girl alive and getting them both back to civilization almost overwhelmed him. Everything would have to go right. He had to get her warmed up. Feed her. Keep her from . . . from trying to kill herself again, until he could get her to someone who could really help her.

And what of that man? That man who had *shot* at him— had tried to kill him for helping this girl. Would he follow them? Would he track them down? In these woods, on these lakes, tracking someone was not easy. That man, however, had skills. The stack of furs behind the cabin had been proof of that. He was a hunter. If he wanted this girl back, he would be coming. And if he came... Jake glanced back to his camp. Toward the pack leaning up against the canoe near the fire. To the gun in the case strapped to the side of the pack.

He shook his head to clear the thought from his mind. Then he cast the lure back into the water as the long summer day drew to a close. First things first: get the girl through the night. Worry about tomorrow, tomorrow.

Still, as the sky darkened, Jake kept a wary eye out to the north, where low clouds continued to gather. A storm was coming.

CHAPTER 26

Jake

Jake caught a whitefish, cleaned it, and cooked it as the last light from the midnight sun disappeared to the west. Farther north, the sun would rise and set only once a year. Here, it would return in less than three hours. This night, Jake understood why his ancestors had celebrated the summer solstice. The sun warmed those who were cold and provided illumination for travelers. Jake needed it for both reasons.

He cleaned up the camp and added more wood to the fire as the fish sizzled in the pan. He ducked back into the tent when he heard the girl stir. This time she raised her head off the ground as he zipped the tent closed. He held out a plate with a large fillet of fried fish.

"Hungry?" he asked.

She nodded. He handed her the plate. She cleaned off half the plate in a single bite. Jake watched with fascination. She then licked the oil off her fingers, instead of wiping it on her clothes or on the tent. Jake appreciated that. Normally, he wouldn't have brought food anywhere near the tent. Bears would smell it for months. Today was the exception to all the rules.

"What's your name again?" she asked as she finished her meal. She reached for the mug Jake still held. Her fingers wrapped around the warm metal, but Jake didn't let go for fear she would lose her grip and spill the scalding liquid on herself.

"Jake. Jake Clarke," he responded.

She paused for a moment, her brow furrowed. "Izzy Chamberlain."

Jake nodded. "Where are you from, Izzy?" he asked.

"Thompson."

Jake's eyes widened. There weren't many towns in the area, but still, hearing that name clenched his throat.

"Me, too." Jake smiled.

"We're going back there?" she asked.

"Yep. Laroque is two, maybe three days' paddle from here. We'll catch a plane out from there and be home in a jiffy." He checked her forehead with his hand. "Do you think you can make it?"

She cocked her head slightly at the mention of the plane. "I'll make it." The confidence in her voice assuaged Jake's fears that she didn't know what was going on.

"How old are you, Izzy?"

"Fourteen," she said. Jake didn't know whether or not to believe her. She didn't look a day over twelve.

"How long have you been out here . . . with . . . that guy?"

"Rick? Since last winter." She shuddered as she thought about it for a minute. "October, I think." She talked slowly, each word taking energy and thought. "Maybe early November. It took us a while to get there." She frowned and bit the inside of her lip. "How about you?"

"Eleven months, I think. Maybe twelve now." Jake checked his numbers.

"Did you get sick, too?"

"Sick?" His mind spun back to his mother's injury and subsequent illness and his grandfather's gradual deterioration. His mother had gotten injured. His grandfather had cancer. Izzy wouldn't have known about either.

"My mom and dad got it, and didn't make it. My sister, Angie, and Rick and I got it, but not as bad."

Jake's eyes popped at the matter-of-fact way Izzy had told him that her parents were dead. The grit in her voice could not have been fabricated. It rubbed against Jake's spine and made him sit up straighter.

"Got what?"

"You know, the *flu*. Didn't you get it? I thought everyone got it."

"The flu? Your parents died from the flu? What? When?" Jake's breath whooshed from his chest.

"Last year." She paused. "I thought you said you lived in Thompson?"

"I did."

"Where?"

"On Prospect. Near the power lines."

"What school did you go to?"

"Parker. What flu?"

"What was your last name, again?"

"Clarke."

"I went to Frontier. I remember a Mrs. Clarke who helped out Mrs. Vaughn when I was in grade three. Do you know her?"

"My mother." Jake swallowed, but his mouth was dry. The teacup was empty. "She died last summer."

"I'm sorry."

"What flu?" He needed an answer to this question. The longer it took her to answer, the more important he knew the answer to be.

"*The* flu. Everyone had it. You didn't get it? But your mom—"

"No, I never heard anything about it. My parents and my grandfather and I were up at our cabin last June, north of Sand Lakes. We were supposed to get picked up, but no one ever came for us. Mom cut herself. Bad. It got infected. No one answered on the radio when we called for help."

"They stopped all the planes once they realized how bad this one was, to keep it from spreading. Didn't help. Where are your dad and grandfather now?"

"What? Start from the beginning," Jake said, ignoring her question. Izzy looked at him, slightly distressed by his tone. He noted her expression and added, "Please."

"I don't know much about how it started. It was a year ago. I was thirteen. I should have paid more attention . . . to a lot of things—" She stopped and studied her plate. "Mom worked at the hospital, in pediatrics. People started getting sick in late June in Thompson, but it was already in Winnipeg before that and a lot of other cities, too. Mom got it first, then Dad and Angie got it, then me. Dad had a fever on Friday and he died on Tuesday. Mom died the next day. Angie and I recovered and moved in with Rick and his ex-wife, Lois. He was our neighbor . . . before. He'd had the flu, too, but he recovered. Lois didn't. Their son, Brian, was out of town, but we never heard from him after the power went out. You really didn't know?"

"No." Jake sat for a moment. His brain tried to process what she had just told him. It seemed so unreal. More questions than answers swirled in his mind.

"So why did you and Rick leave Thompson? Where's your sister?"

Izzy shook her head slowly, then shrugged. "It wasn't safe. Not after the food ran out. Rick took us south into the bush to protect us. Then the weather got cold, and we tried to get back to Thompson for the winter. That's when the gangs got Angie. Rick and I left and went back into the bush. It was pretty rough last winter, but we made it."

"The food ran out? How could the food run out? And gangs?" In the darkened tent, facial expressions barely registered. Only the flickering campfire cast any glow, and that was changed to a dull blue shade to match the nylon walls.

"The grocery stores were empty after a few weeks. Rick said we were all too dependent on the big cities. It was like they just forgot about us. The trucks stopped coming. Most folks only had enough food for a couple of days in the house. Even with all the dead . . . it just didn't last. People went south to get more, but they never came back. By mid-August there were all these people looking for food. They stole. They fought. They killed. People tried—tried to keep it together, but we couldn't. We did the best we could . . . for as long as we could."

"What about the police? The army?"

"Gone. The police that didn't die from the flu—and didn't starve—ran into the bush like the rest of us. The army . . . never saw them. Word was that they tried to help out the bigger cities. They must have just forgot about us."

Jake sat in silence as his brain organized the information into a picture that made sense.

"Jake?"

"Yes?"

"Can I have some more tea? I'm still thirsty."

"Sure." He grabbed the now-cool mug and the empty plate. Cool air spilled into the tent as he stumbled through the gap. Coals burned low in the fire, hissing and steaming as a spattering of rain fell on them. Jake refilled the pot with water, sliced off another hunk of the fish, and threw more wood on the fire. The forest was so peaceful, so quiet. His mind spun with noise and distraction. *The flu?* He'd had what his mom had called the flu a few times, but he had never heard of it killing anyone. There had been gangs at his high school—small, informal groups of kids who liked to pretend they were tougher than they were, but they never went farther than spraying graffiti on the walls of abandoned buildings, starting a few fistfights, or joyriding in a stolen car. The real gangs—the ones running guns and drugs on the news and the TV shows from the US—those just didn't exist in Thompson. Thompson was a good town. With good people. The way she had described it, the good people were all gone, replaced by whacked-out nut jobs.

Could what she had described actually have happened? Could everyone else he knew—his friends from school, his neighbors—all really be dead? Or had her hypothermia caused some kind of weird hallucination? Was this all some elaborate story cooked up by a damaged little girl who, only a few hours ago, had tried to kill herself? If it was a story, then how did they end up with Bill's canoe? It made no sense.

Jake filled the cup, pulled another piece off the fried fish, and brought it back into the tent. Izzy dozed, but woke long enough to drink the tea and eat a little more before falling back to sleep. Jake again swapped out the rocks keeping her warm and left her alone while he cooked more tea and fish for himself. He curled up under the overturned canoe by the fire for a miserable night. Not that he would have slept more had he been warm. There were too may thoughts in his head, still too many questions he couldn't answer.

The answers he *could* find didn't help him sleep.

CHAPTER 27

Izzy

Izzy clawed at the bedcovers, attempting to pull them closer. Cold air leaked around the edges in a dozen places where there shouldn't have been edges. She coughed and shivered. The air drawn into her lungs tasted of mildew and lake water—nothing like the potpourri she kept next to her bed in her room. She shifted again. Something hard rubbed against her side. Nylon crinkled beneath her, breaking the final strands of the illusion that she was safe, at home, in her old bed.

She opened her eyes and sat up. Her lower back throbbed in protest. Above her, the thin roof of a tent bloused as her hair brushed against it. She glanced left, then right. A rock wrapped in an old filthy sock lay against her back. She was alone. Alone, and where? The face of a boy came to her mind, along with a name. *Jake.* Where was he?

She straightened her tunic and exited the tent. Jake lay on the ground, between a large log and a fire that burned low. The overturned canoe offered him little protection from the elements. His eyes were closed, his arms wrapped tightly around his chest. A backpack doubled as his pillow. Izzy did not disturb him.

She crept into the forest a few meters and squatted behind a tree. Her urine burned as she peed. She winced. She recalled the ride across the lake and the vomiting that had accompanied it. The dry heaves had continued unabated, even when nothing remained in her stomach, as if her body was cleansing itself of everything related to

Rick all at once. Her stomach rolled again from the very thought of it. Disjointed images of the previous day flashed in a blur. There were more memories than could possibly have fit into a single day: the wolverine; her ill-fated attempt at escape; Rick's attack; her attempt to . . . put an end to it . . . *Angie would have understood, right*? The boy's sudden appearance. She glanced up, toward the lake. They had crossed the lake, hadn't they? Rick was on the far side now, wasn't he? He had the other canoe, though, and he knew this area. He'd be coming, and coming soon. He wouldn't let her go. Not that easily.

She finished her business, wiped with a few leaves pulled from a nearby maple tree, grabbed an armload of sticks for the fire, and returned to the camp. Jake remained asleep.

She set the sticks on the coals. The wet wood smoldered and smoked before finally catching. She held her hands close to the fire, till the heat from the flames went from comforting to searing. She moved backward a step and studied the boy.

Bits of his story fluttered through her mind. He said he had been lost in the woods since before the flu. He hadn't *seemed* to know anything about what had happened. How could he not know? Was that really possible? Or was he up to something? He had touched her the previous night. His hands had been on her legs. He said he was just trying to warm her up.

Just like Rick.

But she had been so cold—so very cold. After she had warmed up, he had slept outside, with no protection from the elements, while giving her the tent, despite there being more than enough room for both of them. Rick would never have done that.

She turned her attention to his face, partially obscured by a tangle of thick, dark hair. Her rescuer. He had pulled her from the water . . . She could still feel the lake's frigid fingers wrapping around her ankles, fighting him for her life. She could still remember the taste of the water as it pushed down her throat, into her lungs. The boy had saved her and gotten her away from Rick. For that, she was grateful. She wanted to trust him.

The sun began to rise to her right, not to her left as it had been for all these months. They *had* crossed the lake. The boy had said Laroque wasn't far from here. She glanced into the woods. She could head south and find her own way. Without supplies—no food, no slings, barely any clothes, no compass, no way to start a fire—the idea seemed ludicrous. But Rick was coming, and the boy had the things she needed. She could grab what she required and be long gone before he awoke. Now that she was across the lake, she could survive on her own out here, given the right tools. She had planned and trained for a moment just like this. She began to move.

She stood and backtracked to the tent. Her "blankets" had been the boy's extra clothes. He wouldn't miss them. She grabbed the jacket and a pair of his pants. Both were far too big for her. The jacket sleeves extended past her fingertips. She could have fit two of herself into the waistband of the pants. She rolled up the pant legs till they only just brushed the ground when she stood. She'd find some way to make a belt later. For now, she'd simply hold on to a belt loop to keep them up. He had left a pair of old running shoes inside the tent as well. They fit like clown shoes on her tiny feet. She wrapped the laces around her ankles ballet-slipper style to keep the shoes on.

She crawled out of the tent. The boy snored under the canoe. His food canister sat a short distance from the bow of the canoe. She crept toward it. He wouldn't notice if she took a few small bits, she reckoned. Just enough for a couple of days—enough to get her through to Laroque. She grabbed the canister. Empty. Her heart sank. She set it back down.

Fine. She'd have to find food on her own. Fish. Or plants. Rick had at least shown her some of what was edible, so she could add them to their diet without poisoning them both. Now that the snow was gone, surviving in the forest was so much easier than it had been in the winter. She could do this.

She stole a look back at the woods. Without a compass and a map, she'd have no idea where she needed to go. In fact, she had no idea where she was now. What if Laroque was to the west, not the south? What if she wasn't just two days from it? If she missed it altogether, how far was it to Thompson? Another week? There were roads, weren't there?

If she could just find a road and follow it, it'd take her home, right?

If she could hold a straight line south she'd make it, one way or another.

Clasped to a plastic ring on the boy's backpack was a compass. If she had that, at least she'd have a chance.

She edged closer to the boy, barely making a sound as she tiptoed across the ground. A simple carabiner held the compass in place. She extended her arm. The metal clasp released easily from the webbing. She slid backward. The boy did not move.

Now, with the compass in hand, doubts began to creep into her mind. Without a fire and shelter, every night would be brutal. In her original escape plan, she had the plastic tarp, and the flint and striker. She had tried, at the cabin, to start a fire by rubbing two pieces of wood together, but had never even gotten the tip of the spindle warm before her muscles gave out. Rick had once started a fire with a bow and drill setup, but he had only done that to prove to himself—and to her—that he could. He had never revealed the secrets of that tool to her.

She glanced back at the boy's pack. In that pack was everything she would need to survive. If she could just wait until he wasn't looking, she could take it and run. She would just bide her time until that opportunity presented itself. Then she could go wherever she wanted and not be at the mercy of Rick, or this boy.

She glanced at the compass in her hand. If he caught her with it, he would know what she was planning. She had to return it to the pack before he awoke.

She slithered back toward the boy. Her heart fluttered in her chest. Every step seemed louder than it had before. She knelt beside him and reached for the pack.

CHAPTER 28

Jake

Jake's first thought was that the worst had happened—a black bear had picked up the remnant odors of the cooked fish and discovered the camp. His instincts kicked into full gear. He thrust his hands up over his face and rolled away from the perceived threat, expecting at any moment that the sharp claws of the black would rip him to shreds.

A shriek of panic caught his attention. He glanced up at the tent, worried that the bear had gone after the girl.

Instead of a bear, Jake saw only the girl. She fell backward, away from him. Jake scrambled to his feet.

"You scared the bejesus out of me," he said as he collected himself. He stepped forward to offer her a hand up. She sat back on the ground and did not accept his offer.

"Sorry," she said as she shied away from him. Jake studied her. She had dressed at some point in a pair of his pants and his only jacket. One hand hooked fingers through a belt loop. The other held something black. She tracked his eyes and moved her hand out of sight.

"It's okay. Really. I'm not going to hurt you." Jake eased a step backward. To his right, the fire burned higher on fresh wood. He tipped his head toward the fire pit, then bent to warm his hands.

"Thanks for getting the wood. I'll go see if I can't get us a fish for breakfast. There's hot water in the pot there if you're thirsty, or even if you're not. You need to rehydrate if we're going to get you out of here in one piece."

"Sure," she said.

Jake shook his head and smiled. The girl wasn't very talkative— at least not first thing in the morning. Amos had been the same way. *Mornings*, he had said, *are for workin', not yappin'*. But she was alive and mobile, and that was something he had only hoped for the previous evening.

Jake reached down and grabbed his pack. He had stowed the fishing rod back in its case after dinner the previous night. Everything had its place in an orderly camp. Disarray meant leaving things behind when you had to move quickly.

When he picked up his pack, he immediately knew something was missing. *The compass.* Somehow it must have come loose. He scanned the ground beside his bed. Not there. He checked the carabiner on the webbing, half-expecting it to be broken or sprung. Aside from a little tarnish, the clasp remained in perfect working condition. He spun around, hoping to spot the compass among the leaf clutter. He had checked it while waiting for the previous night's dinner to finish cooking, to get a good fix on his location before dark. He remembered clipping it back to the webbing. He always put it back. *Always.* It had been there just a few short hours ago.

Only one thing had changed since then—and she had been right beside him when he awoke. He turned to Izzy.

"Where is it?" he asked.

"Where is what?"

"The compass."

"What compass?"

Jake had seen something in her hand, and now he knew exactly what that had been.

"Hand it over."

"I don't know what you're talking about."

Jake stood and put his hands on his hips. The girl cowered, sliding farther away from the fire, little by little, ready to rabbit. Jake chewed the inside of his cheek. Taking his clothes was one thing. She needed those, and unless he was wearing them, he was carrying them. He should have put them on her the previous night.

Taking a person's compass out here, however, was like sentencing them to death. On the lake the previous day, when land disappeared in every direction and the sun hid behind storm clouds, only the little needle on the compass had prevented them from being lost among the waves for hours. For all these weeks in the middle of the woods, it had been his most important tool. Now this girl he had rescued seemed ready to cut that lifeline. As much as he wanted to help her, he couldn't allow her to endanger them any further. His temper rose.

"Do you know how to use it?" he asked. "I mean, do you really know how to use it? With a map? Without one? Because I do. I've come through a hundred kilometers of bush with that, and I plan to follow it all the way home if I need to. If you know how to use it, and can lead us both home faster than I can, then by all means, keep it. I'll follow you all the way. But if you don't know—if you only think you know—then you should give it back to me. I'll guarantee that we'll be in Laroque in three days, and once we're there, I'll buy you one of your own." She didn't move.

"You're going to have to trust me, Izzy. Whatever happened back there—whatever he did to you—isn't going to happen with me. I'm going to take us home. You have to believe me. But I can't do it without that compass."

Izzy still didn't move. Jake wanted to rush forward and grab it out of her hand. But if he did that, she would never trust him, or worse, the compass could break in the scuffle. Whatever this girl had gone through—whether what she had told him last night was the truth or not—had broken her. He couldn't piece her back together by *telling* her to trust him.

Jake turned away from her and pulled the fishing rod out of his pack.

"I'm going to get us some breakfast. You decide what you want to do. I'll be over there." He pointed to a large rock that jutted into the water like the prow of a ship. She held her position.

Jake forced himself not to look back as he moved away from the camp. He took long, purposeful steps. If she was gone when he finally did turn around, he would have to decide whether to chase her down or let her go. Without the compass, he reckoned he could *probably* make Laroque—but probably wasn't nearly as good as knowing for sure.

He leaped onto the rock, edging closer to the water. Still, he did not look back—not until he had cast the lure as far out into the lake as he could manage. Only then did he turn to learn of her decision.

Izzy stood there, beside the canoe. She bent down to where he had set his pack, then popped right back up. One hand remained on her hip, holding her pants up. With the other, she gave him a little open-handed wave, showing him her empty palm.

She bent back down, picked up the kettle, and poured herself a cup of hot water.

Jake turned his attention back to the water, exhaling slowly. He'd have to keep an eye on her, but at least she hadn't run. Not yet anyway.

CHAPTER 29

◄o►

Jake

After a breakfast of a couple of perch, Jake broke camp, stowed the tent, and placed everything but the sleeping bag in the canoe. Izzy helped, putting the dishes she had cleaned where he instructed. Jake doused the fire, then checked to make sure they had left nothing behind. Izzy was rooting through the contents of the canoe when he returned.

"Where's the other paddle?" she asked.

Jake shrugged. "It must have fallen out back at the cabin. Didn't see it," he answered.

"I can paddle," she said with a bit of a snip. She folded her arms in front of her as if she wouldn't move unless she, too, had a paddle.

Jake shook his head. *Patience,* he told himself. "I'm sure you can. We'll keep an eye out for one if we come across any more cabins. That sound okay?"

Izzy gave a slow nod. Jake pointed to the canoe.

"Grab on. Let's go."

Izzy helped slide the canoe back to the water's edge, then hopped in as Jake pushed the bow into the water. She wrapped her body from toes to neck with the sleeping bag. Jake grimaced. It would never get dry at this rate.

"Be careful with that sleeping bag. It's the only one we've got," he said. Water sloshed over the bow as soon as he said it. Wet dots appeared on the nylon shell.

"Do you have a blanket or something I can use instead?" she asked. She lifted the bag clear of the bottom of the canoe.

"No. Just the bag." Jake ran his fingers through his hair, pushing it back from his face. He leaned forward, wrapped the bag back around her, then pulled the tent fly from his pack and wrapped her in that as well. "We'll just have to make do."

He smiled at her as some sort of apology for snapping. He'd try to dry the bag again before nightfall.

Jake checked the sky. The heavy cloud layer had thinned overnight. The rain and the wind, at least, had moved on. Perhaps, he thought, they'd actually see a day worthy of summer today. The clouds and rain had been around for so long that he had almost forgotten it *was* summer.

"Waves are better today," he said.

"Yeah."

Izzy shifted lower in the canoe, resting her head on a strut. Jake shook his head. This canoe was far too small for even someone her size to stretch out in. Bill had built it for one person, two at the most; two paddlers, sitting upright, not one stretched out like cargo.

Jake steered them westward, guessing that the river to Laroque lay within a few miles in that direction. Without an accurate map and a position fix, trial and error became his next best option. The lake was dozens of kilometers long, east to west. If they hit the entrance of the Churchill, he'd know he'd guessed wrong, and have to turn back around. His gut told him he wasn't that far off his goal. He just didn't know for sure which direction they needed to go. If they didn't hit the river by lunch, he'd turn them around and try to the east.

Jake waited for his rhythm with the paddle to set before he dared return to his questions from the night before. There were so many, and now that they were back on the water, he couldn't distract his thoughts. He needed more answers.

"Izzy?"

She twisted in the sleeping bag to face him. "Yeah?"

"Why were you running away from Rick? Was he—" Jake couldn't finish the question.

She paused for a moment before she answered.

"Does it matter?"

"Does it matter?" Jake echoed. Of course it mattered. He had been shot at. He had nearly died crossing the lake in weather not fit for a boat twice the size of their small canoe. He now had a girl in his boat, one he barely knew—one who had, just an hour before, tried to steal his compass. He needed to know exactly what sort of a mess he had gotten himself into.

"If he was hurting me or not hurting me? Does that make a difference now? Would you turn around and drop me back there if I said he wasn't hurting me?"

"No."

"Then I don't really want to talk about it. Not right now."

She looked at him briefly before diverting her eyes to the nearby shoreline. She said no more. Jake clenched the shaft of the paddle and forced himself to think before speaking.

"Fine." He pulled the paddle through the water and scanned the lake ahead. "You're welcome, by the way."

His mind wandered back to parts of her story: the gangs in Thompson, the flu and all the people killed, the details of the past year she had glossed over. She said her parents had died. She said that Rick's wife had died. Just how many others had died? A hundred? Five hundred? A thousand? More? How many would it take for the kind of chaos she described to kick in? It was nearly eight months since she'd left town for the last time. Would those gangs still be there? If it were all true, it would explain so much.

Izzy fidgeted in the bow, then sat up to face him.

"He lied to me, Jake."

Jake stopped paddling.

"He told me I'd be safe with him, Jake. I was never going to be safe with him."

Jake couldn't hold her gaze. He watched a drop of water slide down his paddle and splash back into the lake. That one statement told an awful truth. For a year she had lived with a man she feared—a man she was dependent upon for survival. A man who had no qualms about taking advantage of his power. Living like that, Jake thought, would be impossible for him to do. He had watched his mother and his grandfather die, living with fear that he would be left alone without his family. Even with all that, he had never really doubted he would make it out—that his situation would end with rescue. He had always believed in himself and his ability to survive. His survival was all within his power.

She believed nothing remained to go back to. She had lived with a horror he couldn't imagine—being trapped with Rick, a man Jake had only seen from a distance but already knew was evil. A man willing to kill to keep what he believed was his.

Jake scanned the water for any signs of humanity. Small waves lapped at the hull.

"I'm sorry. I didn't mean to pressure you. It's just—there's just so much I don't know about what happened. I didn't see what you saw. I didn't have to do what you did. I just want to get home. Back to Thompson. And now—now you tell me it's not—it's not safe there either. And yet you want to go back."

"You wouldn't have recognized the city when we left. It was like some third-world country. No power. No lights. No heat. No gas. Maybe it's better now. Better than this anyway."

Jake imagined the city, once fifteen thousand people strong, devoid of life.

"That was last October?"

"Yeah, late October."

"Did you happen to see my dad? He's a little taller than me, with a green canoe, and would have been heading south through here, looking for help. Bush hat. A blue two-man tent."

"There were lots of people in the bush back then, Jake. I don't remember anyone like that. Besides, we were hiding most of the time. Every time we saw someone coming, we hid or we ran."

"Not everyone could have been bad."

"No, not everyone, but you couldn't tell the good from the bad by looking at them. Hiding was safer. You never knew who you could trust. I was pretty scared most of the time. Rick figured out what to do. So we survived."

"So I was your first chance to leave, to get away from him?"

"No—not the first chance." Her eyes drifted to the bottom of the boat. "The guy Rick took this canoe from—"

"Bill Six Rivers?" Jake stopped paddling. "You met him?"

"You knew him?"

"Since I was a kid." Jake paused. "*Knew* him? Wait. He's—"

"He was a good man. He tried to help me. Rick killed him." Izzy paused. "I'm sorry, Jake."

Jake's chest locked tight. He forced the air from his lungs with a profanity and slammed the paddle against the water. The sound of the impact ricocheted off the trees onshore before dissolving across the waves.

"He and Rick knew each other. From before the flu. Bill said Rick was responsible for what happened to his daughter."

"Cammie? She . . . died. A couple of years ago. Long before the flu."

"Bill blamed Rick for it. He was going to take me home to make sure the same thing didn't happen to me. They argued. Rick shot him."

"*Bastard.*"

Cammie's suicide had shocked them all. Jake had been a freshman. Cammie had been a junior. Jake had been over to her house a dozen times. He had been to her funeral. The whispers had divided the school. Her boyfriend had been white. The word *rape* had spread like wildfire. Nothing raised tension in school faster than racial issues. The boyfriend had been blamed, but never charged. Now Jake knew why. It hadn't been the boyfriend. It had been the boyfriend's father.

Jake looked at the rifle strapped to his pack. It hadn't been out of its case since he decided to try and rescue Izzy without causing a confrontation. Now he second-guessed that decision.

He should have just lined up the first good shot he had and taken it.

He gritted his teeth.

It wouldn't have been that easy.

Nothing about this trip was easy.

They exchanged a look that told Jake she knew exactly where he was emotionally. They had no need to go into it deeper, to dump each other's troubles onto sympathetic but already burdened shoulders. She was young, and Jake had spent the night worrying he would have to take care of her the whole way back, that she would be some lifeless, useless passenger. She wasn't. She was alert and competent and mature beyond her years. There was a reason for that, Jake thought. She had survived for months in the most brutal of circumstances. *An average person doesn't last a week out here,* his father's voice whispered to him. An average person doesn't make it through everything else she had described, either, Jake thought.

He looked at her again. Only a bit of her face poked out from the sleeping bag. She no longer looked like a little girl to him. She looked older and stronger. She smiled nervously back at him.

"Three days?" she asked as she turned her attention to the shore.

"Less than that if we get you a paddle."

"That'd be good." She hunkered down below the gunwale to stay out of the breeze.

Jake checked behind him for any sign that Rick was back there, following them. The lake remained empty.

He paddled on.

CHAPTER 30

Izzy

For six hours, Izzy lay in the bottom of the canoe while Jake paddled westward. A slight breeze from the northwest threw choppy water into their path. Jake chattered on about the current coming in from the west, and how it made this lake so dangerous and so unpredictable. Izzy barely listened. She watched the horizon behind them, half-expecting Rick to materialize from the haze at any moment. The shore moved by at a glacial pace. Once, Jake pointed out wildlife on the shore—a black bear that bolted back into the cover of the forest as soon as it saw them. After so many months in the bush, wildlife—unless it was dinner—didn't interest her. Getting farther away from Rick—and getting home, wherever that was now—were the only things that mattered.

Around lunchtime, Izzy's stomach began to rumble. She reached for Jake's pack and began to undo the straps holding the fishing-rod case to the side.

"What are you doing?" he asked.

"What does it look like? I'm going to fish. Catch us some lunch."

"You know how?"

"Of course I know how." She shook her head. "My father taught me. Years ago."

A half-truth. Her dad had tried to teach her. She had been too squeamish at the time. Rick had done his best to not teach her anything about fishing, but she had picked up a few things. *How hard can it be?* she asked herself.

She pulled the rod from the case and assembled it, careful not to tangle the line. She paused only briefly to guess how the reel worked—it was a spinning rod, not the spincast reel she had used with her dad, but the operation wasn't too different. Still, it took four tries to get the lure into deeper water away from the canoe. She adjusted her position, keeping the tip of the rod well out from the boat, so as not to interfere with Jake's paddling.

Three minutes later, a fish grabbed the lure. Izzy set the hook with a snap, just like she had seen Rick do a hundred times, and began to apply pressure to reel the fish in. A quick turn by Jake left too much slack in the line. In an instant, the fish broke free. Izzy scowled. She reeled in the extra line. Jake grabbed the line as it slid along the hull and inspected the lure.

"Hooks are dull. Need to be sharpened. Should have done it a week ago." Jake shrugged off her misfortune. He dropped the lure back into the water so she could reel in the rest of the slack. "Keep the pressure on the line when reeling it in and it should still work."

Izzy did not reply. Dull hooks or not, if he had kept the boat steady, she would have already had lunch in the boat.

She hauled the lure back in and checked the points on the dual treble hooks herself with the tip of her finger. She drew blood. They seemed sharp enough. She cast the line back into the depths.

Half an hour passed before her next bite. She set the hook and this time, kept a close watch on both the incoming fish and Jake's actions with the paddle. After a brief struggle, the large northern pike surged and broke the surface three boat lengths from the bow. It threw itself into the air, spun end-for-end, and wrenched the lure free from its jaw.

Izzy used more of the swear words Rick had taught her.

"You need to set it hard, then pull with steady force. If it wants to run, let it go a bit. Don't jerk it after it's been set. You'll tear right through the skin."

"I know. I've fished before. A lot," Izzy muttered.

Another half-truth. She had *watched* Rick fish a lot. She reeled the line in and recast the lure into the lake. The line tightened as Jake resumed paddling.

"Look." She pointed north. The opposite shore emerged from the haze. "Should we be able to see that? Shouldn't we have found the river by now?"

"Yeah. The river must have been to the east, not the west."

"I thought you said you knew where you were," she growled. *Where was he taking her?*

"I did. I mean, I do. Crossing a lake this size without a map and a good idea of where you started from isn't an accurate business."

"So we've got to go all the way back?"

"Yep." Jake set the paddle down across his legs and pulled the map from his pack. "Unless you want to try to go up fifty klicks of the Churchill. We could head for South Indian Lake."

"Is that doable?"

Jake shook his head. "Not really. Not for us. The Churchill is big. And fast. We'd have to portage the whole way. Better to turn back around and head for Laroque."

"You sure you know the way?"

"Yes. I know the way," he snapped. "We must have just missed the river by a couple of klicks to the east. Bad luck. That's all it was."

Jake stowed the map and picked the paddle up.

Izzy turned away from his glare. Jake swept the canoe into a tight turn, throwing the bow directly over her line. Izzy reeled it in as quickly as she could, so it wouldn't get caught on his paddle.

"Watch my line!" she warned as he accelerated faster than she could pull in the slack.

"Just reel it in."

"I am." Izzy spun the crank. The line snagged on the keel and before she knew it, it snapped. The lure disappeared into the depths.

"Damn it! Look what you made me do," Izzy said.

"Me? You're the one who broke the line." Jake leaned forward and snatched the rod from her hands. "That was my best lure."

"I didn't do it on purpose. You turned without looking where I was." This scrawny boy who had just got them lost was accusing *her* of not knowing what she was doing?

Jake examined the rod and let out a frustrated sigh. He shook his head, but did not meet her gaze. He reeled in the excess line, then rethreaded the line back through the loops on the rod. From his pack he dug out another lure—a small silver spoon with a single treble hook on the end. He tied it with nimble fingers, bit the extra line from the knot, and pressed two small lead weights an arm's length from the lure. He reluctantly handed the rod back to her.

"You still trust me with your precious fishing rod?" Izzy asked.

"We need lunch, and I need to paddle. Be careful. We lose that lure and we'll be using our hands."

Izzy waited until he realigned the canoe, now with the bow pointed east, then cast the line far out to the side. She glanced back at him only once. He was lost in thought, barely paying any attention to her. She let her emotions cool. Jake hadn't reacted to her words, not like Rick would have.

So maybe this boy wasn't quite the same as Rick. Still, Rick had been nice at first, too, and the day was still young. She peeked at the shore. Once they got back to land, she'd be able to make it on her own if she needed to.

Her stomach picked that moment to complain, as if to remind

her that as much as she wanted that to be true, it wasn't entirely true. Life in the bush, alone, was more than a little difficult.

Izzy returned her focus to the task at hand. Getting lunch was up to her.

CHAPTER 31

Jake

An hour later, Izzy hooked a pike that nearly sawed through the thin filament line. Jake grabbed the rod from her as soon as he realized how big the fish was. He couldn't afford to lose that last lure, and more importantly, if the line did break, he didn't want to have her to blame. Still, she didn't seem to take his help very well. She barely said a word as the fish cooked over a hastily built fire. For a while, it was like Jake was all alone again, only now with more responsibility.

They passed their previous night's camp around dinnertime, but Jake didn't even slow down. Two kilometers farther east, they found what they were looking for: the river snaked out of the forest, rippling and bubbling with runoff from recent rains. Jake put his left arm in the air, bent at the elbow to signal a right turn. Izzy didn't get the joke.

The lazy flow ran wide enough and deep enough to paddle. According to his map, less than two days' paddling and portaging remained until they would reach Laroque. Two rivers and two lakes stood between them and their goal.

They camped just a few kilometers from their previous night's location. Knowing where they were, and that the girl seemed capable of surviving the next two days, lifted Jake's spirits.

"You can have the tent and the sleeping bag," Jake said as they polished off the leftovers from lunch.

"You sure?" Izzy asked.

Jake lifted the canoe and propped it up against a log near the fire. "Yeah. I'll be fine out here." He grabbed his hatchet and hacked a few branches off a nearby cedar tree. He crammed the boughs under the canoe. "Sleeping on these branches won't be so bad. Done it before."

"Whatever." Izzy eyed the branches for a moment, then disappeared into the tent, zipping it closed.

Not even a thank you, Jake thought. *Whatever.* A little appreciation for all he had done—was doing—would have been nice.

Jake threw another hunk of wood on the fire and crawled under the canoe, pulling his clothes tight. The reflected heat from the fire made his cubby under the canoe bearable. He tried to force the expectation for her appreciation out of his head. This girl was not right. Whatever had happened to her had damaged her in a dozen ways. Everything he did to help her seemed to be grounds for suspicion. Everything he said was taken the wrong way. His journey home to this point had been exhausting. The last thirty hours with her had pushed him, and his patience, to the limit. When they got to Laroque, he'd be glad to be rid of her—to turn her over to the authorities, or whoever was left there.

He had his own issues to deal with.

•◆•

He paddled, and together they portaged the entire length of the river the next day. The distance wore down, five kilometers before lunch, four after, then three more after a quick break. The river drained an L-shaped lake so large they couldn't see one side from the other. He knew this lake though. He had seen it from the air a half dozen times. To the southwest loomed another large lake. On the western side of that lake, on a thin spit of land, was the town of Laroque.

Safety. Rescue.

The next river was a steeper, upriver run, requiring more portaging around rapids and shallows on marked trails used in the not-so-distant past. Jake swung the canoe up over his head on the portages, while Izzy carried his pack. At the end of the trailhead leading to the final lake, Jake set the canoe down and raised his aching arms over his head in victory.

"What?" Izzy asked as she halted her scan of the water ahead to look at the boy dancing a little jig.

"We made it!"

"Looks like another big lake."

"Sure. No more damn portages, though. We'll follow the shore all the way around to Laroque, and we're there."

"Can't we just go straight across?"

"Too far in this canoe. Wind gets bad out there. We'll hug the shore. Safer that way."

"Can we make it tonight?"

"Tomorrow, early, probably."

Izzy cracked a smile—the first smile she had made since he found her. He couldn't help but smile back. He did another silly dance to celebrate.

"Let's go before you embarrass yourself any further," Izzy said. Jake stopped dancing as she chuckled at his expense.

"We'll be home by this time tomorrow," he promised.

Izzy's smile faded. "We'll see."

They slipped into the canoe and paddled through the afternoon. Jake dug into his memories for the exact geography of the lake to avoid getting lost in some back channel. The sun had long disappeared when he finally pulled them up onto a narrow strip of beach, surrounded by thick jack pines and reeds. He made another small fire, ate another fish caught by the now-silent Izzy, and smiled. Nothing could stop them from reaching Laroque the next day, short of a massive storm. The weather seemed to be holding. Izzy did not seem to share his enthusiasm.

He tossed and turned that night. The anticipation of the end of the journey was too much to contain. He would paddle into Laroque, victorious—a survivor of an incredible trek—an accomplishment no one could ever deny.

As the night crawled by, his excitement was tempered by one other, unforgettable fact: tomorrow, for better or worse, he would also find out what had happened to his father. That issue forced doubt into his brain and stirred an uneasy stomach.

CHAPTER 32

Izzy

"Let's go." Jake pestered Izzy for the third time since his predawn shake of the tent. Izzy knelt by the lake and splashed water onto her face.

"Give me a minute," she mumbled. She stretched her back. Two days of lying in the bottom of the impossibly small canoe had crimped her like a staple. Her hamstrings had locked tight sometime during the brief night. She stood, made her way over to a nearby tree, and used that to lean against while she stretched her calves.

The first streaks of light lit the horizon to the east.

"What time is it?" Izzy switched legs.

"I don't know. Four, maybe. Let's go," Jake said.

"Just wait a second, would ya? I need to stretch." The night on the ground had been uniformly uncomfortable. Izzy longed for even the comfort of the old pine bough bed back at the cabin. She spat on the ground at the thought.

"What about breakfast?" Izzy asked as she finished her stretches.

"We'll catch something once we get moving. I don't want to waste any light today. We've got a long way to go."

"Want me to paddle for a bit? You can fish?"

"No, I'm fine."

Jake picked up the paddle from the canoe and held it close, as if he was worried Izzy might fight him for it. *Fine.* She rolled her eyes, then looked around the camp for something—anything—that would work as a paddle—a broken tree limb, or an old board washed up on shore. Her search was fruitless. She let out a sigh, checked to make sure they hadn't forgotten any of their gear, and hopped into the bow as Jake shoved off.

Jake paddled them into a mild chop and turned right a minute later. It was still so dark that Izzy could barely see the shore.

"You sure this is safe? Shouldn't we wait another fifteen minutes?"

"We'll be fine. I can hear the waves on the shore. The sun will be up shortly."

A slight breeze blew off the starboard quarter, forcing Jake to make occasional course corrections to prevent being blown out to the center of the lake. As the sun finally brightened the sky to the east, Izzy spotted whitecaps out on the center of the lake. Her stomach roiled at the thought of another day in a seesawing boat. The western shore blocked the wind though, and as long as they stayed in its lee, the waves seemed manageable.

Izzy dug out the fishing rod, checked the knot on the lure, and began the search for breakfast.

"Wouldn't want to be out there today," Jake said as he noticed the waves.

"No."

"When the wind really kicks up out here, the floatplanes can't land in Laroque. Hopefully they'll be there today."

Izzy snapped her head around.

"Jake, there won't be planes there. I told you. The flu. It was really bad. Everywhere."

"Someone will be there." Jake scanned the water ahead of them. Izzy knew better. If there was anyone there, they weren't likely to be friendly. She checked behind them. Still no sign of Rick. Had he given up? Let her go? Her hopes began the long, slow crawl up from the pit of despair she had lived in for so long. If Jake was right . . . and there were people in Laroque . . .

"What's that?" Jake's question broke her train of thought. He pointed forward to a long, dark mass just off the starboard bow. Izzy reeled in her line as Jake maneuvered around the half-submerged branches of a large log floating in their path.

"Just driftwood," Izzy said. She reached out, grabbed one of the broken limbs, and rolled the log over.

"My dad called logs like that 'keel wreckers.'" Jake said. "They can tear the bottom out of a speeding boat or the floats off a plane just like that." He snapped his fingers. "We"—he tapped the canoe with his fingers—"probably don't have to worry about that. Might dump us though. Let it go."

Izzy held on to the log for a moment. "It's burned." She pointed to a long black scar running up the side of the trunk.

"Campfire, maybe?" Jake disregarded her concern.

Something struck Izzy as odd about this log. The bottom was broken and splintered. The exposed wood had not yet been worn down by seasons of weather and waves. Izzy studied the log for a moment, then released it as Jake resumed their course southward.

The farther south they went, though, the more burned timbers they saw piled up on the shore, stacked by the waves like the walls of a fortress. Hundreds of others bobbed in the shallows. Broken pieces of fire-burned wood turned the shore black. A lump formed in Izzy's throat. Jake's face, which had, not so long ago, been filled with excitement, blanched. What they saw had but one explanation.

Jake pushed back in to the shore, slowly navigating the tangle of deadwood. They approached a small peninsula, where the logs in the water were so thick that Izzy could have walked across them like a logger riding a raft of timber down a river. As they passed the escarpment, the sight beyond took Izzy's breath away.

The trees were gone. A river, its southern shore darkened by a clog of burned sticks and charcoal, formed a barrier that had somehow held back the flames. To the north, the green that had become so familiar continued unabated. To the south lay a black-and-gray wasteland. Sooty mud separated misshapen, telephone-pole remnants of isolated trees.

A few humble patches of grass, somehow bypassed by the fire, floated in a sea of destruction. Izzy scanned the horizon for an end to the burn. More charred hulks of wood dotted the landscape to the west and to the south. In the gloom of an overcast sky, it was a moonscape on earth: a muddy, blackened moonscape.

Jake beached the canoe next to the river, slipped on his boots, and wandered into the burned-out forest. Izzy did not venture away from the shore. Dark mud, mixed with burned leaves, slivers of wood, and clumps of charcoal, clung to Jake's boots. After a few steps, the weight of his boots increased to the point where he had to strain to lift them. He turned around.

"What the hell happened?" he asked her, as if she would know.

Izzy shook her head. He wasn't asking what had destroyed the landscape. He was asking how it could have burned so much without someone stopping it. He was asking why people hadn't been there to stop it.

"The flu," she said finally.

Jake appeared not ready, or not able, to accept her story. He expected to arrive in Laroque, to be welcomed, and then to fly home. Izzy knew better. There had been a time right after her parents had died, when denial had taken over. It had taken days for the reality to sink in. Weeks even. She, however, had seen the flu happen. She'd been through it. She'd seen the dead. Every time they went into a house to salvage something, the dead had been there, a reminder of a dream that wasn't. When the food ran out, reality became the only thing that mattered. Starvation destroyed everything, including hope.

Jake had not been through that. He would have to see it with his own eyes to believe it.

Jake picked his way through the mud to a small patch of grass a few meters from shore. He bent down to pluck the bloom off a ground-hugging wildflower. Izzy stayed on the gravel, stepping carefully over more of the downed timber. There were other signs of life here—deer tracks, bird footprints, and the peculiar drag of turtle carapaces carved into the mud. But the forest was gone.

Izzy followed the shore, avoiding the worst of the mud.

"You think it's still burning?" Izzy asked.

"Doubt it. Looks like this happened last year. See these plants with the little flowers? They only grow in the spring. They'd have burned off if this had happened this year. Besides, it's been too wet this year for this to burn. Way too wet."

"Oh." She and Rick had been on the far side of the lake on their trek north. They had seen none of this. All they had seen was snow and ice, in every direction.

She walked a little farther down the barren beach and stared inland. A small red fox tracked her progress from behind a fallen tree, a short distance away. Grime coated its fur. It stood with its head low, suspicious of any sudden movement and ready to scurry off should Izzy approach.

Izzy headed back to the canoe, meeting up with Jake just short of the bow. Jake dislodged the mud from his boots by slamming the soles together. The fox jumped at the sound, bolting westward with its tail between its legs. It stopped twice to see if it was being pursued. Izzy lost sight of it as soon as she clambered back into the canoe.

Only a few kilometers separated them from Laroque. With each stroke of Jake's paddle, Izzy's fears of what they would or wouldn't find there grew. She kept those fears to herself. There was no point in worrying Jake any further.

CHAPTER 33

◄○►

Jake

Jake's eyes darted back to the shore after every stroke, searching for an end to the destruction. Around every rocky outcrop, he expected to see the return of the green forest, but upon rounding each corner, they discovered only a greater expanse of charred land.

Twice they pulled in to shore: once to cook and eat a small whitefish Izzy caught, and once for a bathroom break. Each time, Jake climbed to the top of the tallest object around—a rock or a half-destroyed tree—and scanned the distance. Each time he was rewarded with an unending panorama of blackened mud.

Twenty kilometers of rough shoreline and bobbing driftwood passed before Jake spotted the first signs of civilization. A concrete slab with a stone hearth and a few mangled pieces of tin roofing poked out of the dirt where a cabin had once been. On one edge of the slab were the burned and rusted remains of a mattress, box spring, and metal frame. A stainless-steel sink and melted copper pipes lay on another part of the slab. Jake didn't stop to investigate.

A little farther, beyond a group of charred stumps, the scene repeated. This cabin still had one rock wall standing, and behind it was an old cooking stove, the outside oxidized by fire and weather. Three more lots near that one were equally destroyed. A tricycle lay on its side near the water, the rubber burned off its wheels, its melted plastic seat draped over the seat post in a ghoulish form.

The shore turned east and formed the familiar man-made breakwall, over which Jake had flown so many times on his way to various hunting camps. A road ran along the shore, protected by a break wall of tar-covered wooden pilings and rocks. Another stack of scorched logs buried the outermost rocks. Jake worked the canoe around the spit. The docks for Laroque hid from the northerlies on the southern shore. Jake ground his teeth as they rounded the tip and the village came into view.

There were no planes tied up to the dock. There wasn't even so much as a rowboat there.

The burn stopped at the road that encircled the downtown— stopped, or had been fought off, he wasn't sure. Splintered stumps bracketed the small community. The buildings farthest from the village center were scorched, their paint blistered and peeling. Fire had destroyed the roof of one building, but the rest of the town center remained standing. A lone pine tree between two preserved buildings was all that remained of a once-thick forest.

Jake let their momentum take them alongside the dock. He fended off a direct hit with the blade of his paddle.

"Tie us off," he instructed as Izzy jumped up from the bow onto the dock. She grabbed an old rope from a post, looped it around one of the canoe's struts, then secured it to a rusted cleat. Jake tossed Izzy his pack and hopped up after it.

He stood slowly and surveyed the area. The silence of the downtown crawled under Jake's skin. To his right was the gas station that serviced the boats, floatplanes, and vehicles that normally crowded the dock. Thick black shrouds covering the pumps crackled in the morning breeze. A white sign with blocky red lettering hung nearby: GAS'N'FLY. The lower portion of the y threatened to snap off in the next big gale.

"This can't be real," he said.

A little more than a year ago, this small town had bustled with hunters and fishermen every summer day. Floatplanes pulled up to the docks at fifteen-minute intervals from dawn to dusk on the weekends. The counter at the small diner never stopped serving breakfast. The smell of frying bacon filled the air, creating a lineup that went out the door on busy weekends. Today, the only smell was of wet soot and churned lake water. The only sounds were their footsteps.

Jake drifted toward the general store. Izzy followed a short distance behind. Outside, the door of a large ice cooler hung open. Dirt, leaves, and a puddle of stagnant water filled the cooler instead of ice. The metal cage for propane tanks stood unlocked and empty. The window of the store's entrance door had been smashed, the glass left in a billion pieces that crunched underfoot. Jake swung the door open and peered inside.

The store stank of urine and scat. The few man-made items left had been flung about the floor. Shredded cardboard boxes had become nests for mice and rats and whatever else had called this place home the last few months. Anything edible or organic had already been eaten by the animals. Pressure built in Jake's chest. He backed out of the store and moved on down the road.

The rest of the businesses—a hair salon, the diner called the Fisherman's Grill, and a hardware/bait-and-tackle store—were in similar states of disrepair. Thick black dust covered the tables and the counter in the restaurant. A few of the chairs had been tipped over or pushed aside. The pantry was empty. Not even a sugar packet remained behind the counter where Geri, the ever-present waitress, had worn the linoleum thin with her constant back-and-forth shuffle. Whenever Jake had passed through town, Geri had always given him a fresh-baked oatmeal cookie. Jake looked at the empty counter, salivated at the thought of a cookie, then slid back through the door.

The hulk of an old bulldozer squatted a hundred meters from the docks. The fire had destroyed a tree just a few meters away, but not even the rubber hydraulic hoses were burned on the yellow machine. Just beyond the dozer, scorched remnants of the forest continued as far as Jake could see to the west, north, and south. A few more concrete slabs lifted out of the mud like tipped gravestones. Chimneys, hearths, and rusted stoves formed silhouettes against the gray sky.

But it wasn't the bulldozer that drew his attention. To the south, a cluster of wooden crosses stood guard over a depression in the soil. Dread rose through his spine as he approached. He slowly counted them. Thirty-five. The sight of the crosses pulled the visions of the graves he had dug for his mother and grandfather to the forefront of his mind. He checked the names scrawled onto the crosses in black marker. Chuck Red Eagle, the owner of the Fisherman's Grill, and his wife, Linda. Tom Hudson, and two of his kids. Years before, Jake had played hide-and-seek with those kids, while waiting for his dad at the store. At the end of the line was Geri Denny. Jake closed his eyes. The pressure in his chest flared and burned. He remembered Geri's always-smiling face, her blond bouffant hairdo, and her raspy smoker's voice. His stomach twisted and his fingers tingled. Thirty-five graves. None had been here when he had flown out to the cabin. He turned back to look at the town, covering his mouth with his hand.

This was not how his journey was supposed to end, standing before a row of grave markers. His father was nowhere to be seen. The village of Laroque was abandoned, scraped clean of human life. Fifty people had lived here once. Now there were only thirty-five crosses, with the names of the dead already faded by the weather.

A cramp tore across his stomach. Jake doubled over in pain as bile flowed from some deep reservoir. He coughed and spat onto the ground.

This was not how it was supposed to end.

This was how it had started.

Jake sank to his knees, and for the first time since Amos had died, the tears fell.

"Jake—" Izzy began talking, but Jake heard none of it.

Until that moment, his trek had a beginning and an end. As tough as the intervening days and weeks had been, he had thought it would be over once he reached this village. Everything—months of planning, months of watching Amos fade away—had had a purpose. Weeks of freezing days and colder nights had been warmed by his determination that he would make it this far. He had never considered the possibility that this wouldn't be far enough.

Jake abruptly jumped to his feet and ran from marker to marker. His father, he confirmed, was not buried there.

The houses. Maybe he was in a house? They hadn't *all* burned.

He spat more bile out of his mouth, away from the graves, and ran for the first house.

"Jake!" Izzy protested.

He ignored her. The door stood open, the hinge busted. A broken two-by-four from the railing of the small porch rested across the entrance. He hurdled over the wood and entered the cottage.

"Dad?"

The smell hit him. Scat and urine again, but tinged with something else he could not quite recognize—something sweeter, not overwhelming, but powerful enough to make him cough on the first whiff. The smell grew stronger. A chill kneaded his spine as he worked his way through a living room full of torn furniture and into a kitchen that had been professionally ransacked. His eyes watered. Mice scurried ahead of his footfalls, their squeaks of alarm warning others that a stranger approached. He pulled his hands closer to his sides and stepped around the piles of mouse dung littering the floor.

A closed door on his right opened into a small bedroom. Faded wallpaper drooped from water-stained wallboard. A bed stood against the south wall, raised up on red milk crates to provide more storage underneath. A small white desk took up part of the west wall. The smell was even more pungent here. Jake covered his mouth and nose with his dirty sleeve. It took a moment for him to recognize the child-sized lump curled into a fetal position atop the stained bedsheets. Trickles of black hair ran across a pillow crusted with remnants of the slowly decomposing body. The hair danced as the breeze from opening the door moved through what had been still air. A shudder crawled through Jake's body.

He recoiled and bumped into the door frame. Dust dropped from the ceiling as the force of his impact shook the thin walls.

Part of him wanted to run out of this place of death. Part of him needed to know how someone could leave a child to die alone in her bed. His feet moved him to an open door further down the hall. A queen-sized bed held another body, this one also curled up, but larger and partially consumed by some kind of animal. The rank odor matched the gruesome scene, and Jake could no longer hold in the meager contents of his stomach. What he hadn't lost at the grave, he vomited on the floor by the door. He ran from the house, wiping his mouth on his sleeve, and nearly tripped over the two-by-four as he vaulted off the porch.

"Jake—Jake, we need supplies," Izzy said as he sped past her.

He sprinted back to the canoe as fast as he could. He had no desire to inspect the remaining houses. Laroque was a ghost town, empty of everything but trouble. He could feel the spirits he had disturbed chasing him, and he wanted only to be far away from this place.

Jake was back in the canoe and ready to release the mooring before Izzy reached the dock.

"Jake—"

"We have to go. Now." Jake reached for the cleat securing the canoe to the dock.

"We can't, Jake. We need supplies."

"Get in the canoe." He didn't have time to argue with her. If she wasn't going to leave with him, he would leave on his own. He couldn't spend another moment in this place. Jake's shaking fingers struggled to release the knot.

"No," Izzy said. Then she did something Jake absolutely did not see coming.

She stole his paddle.

CHAPTER 34

Izzy

"Give that back. We need to get out of here."

Jake reached for the paddle, but Izzy stepped back from the edge of the dock and held the paddle away from him.

"No! There are things here we can use—things we need. Clothes. Another paddle. Another sleeping bag. Blankets."

"We'll just go. We can't stay here."

Jake's hair had broken free from its ponytail during his run. It fell forward, partially obscuring his face, but it could not hide his desperation.

"Go where? Where are we going, Jake? What's the plan?"

From the moment she had stepped onto the dock, Izzy had known what they would find in the village. It had been the same when she and Angie and Rick had returned to Thompson. But this place, she knew, was truly deserted. No one could have stayed here. Not with the forest gone. Without the trees, the winter wind would have been unstoppable. Only the dead would have wintered over here.

"I don't know. Away from here. Away from this." Jake's face fell to his hands. He moaned and pounded a fist on the canoe.

"You can't run from this, Jake. Not from this." She waved an arm toward the main street. "This is what things are like now. You have to learn to survive in this. Out there, once we're out of this damn forest, this is what you're going to have to deal with."

"My dad—"

"Isn't here—"

Izzy stopped. In a perfect world, Jake's dad was somewhere just ahead, but Izzy knew the odds were far better that he was dead. If Jake hadn't realized that already, it would soon dawn on him. And when it did, he'd be useless. She needed him to stay coherent until they got somewhere else. They couldn't stay here. That wasn't an option. They weren't nearly far enough away from Rick yet. She glanced back at the lake. He'd be coming. The black hole in her soul knew that to be true.

"He's gotta be up ahead, then . . . somewhere." Jake scanned the lake to the south, then looked to Izzy as if she would know the answer to that question.

"We need supplies. It'll only take a few minutes." Izzy set the paddle on the dock, but not close enough for Jake to grab it without getting out of the canoe.

Jake's eyes drifted to the village core. "I can't go back in there."

Izzy nodded. "Fine. Just help me carry stuff and figure out what we need. I'll do the searching. Can you do that?"

Jake remained motionless for a moment, then pulled himself out of the canoe and joined her on the dock.

"Let's make it fast, okay?"

Walking into the town the second time raised the hackles on her neck more than the first time. The dead had been disturbed here now. Jake's run through town seemed to have awoken more of the ghosts. In Thompson, every house had felt that way upon their return. Back then, Angie had been there to help Izzy fight them. Jake wasn't ready for that fight.

Izzy covered her mouth and nose as she stepped into the general store. Jake stood in the center of the road, nervously glancing up and down the street like an Old West gunfighter, scared of his own shadow. Izzy ignored him and carefully picked her way between piles of scat and shredded cardboard.

Her list ran through her head. Food, of course, though she expected to find none of that. This place had been ransacked long before they arrived. Perhaps a sleeping bag had been left behind—or blankets at the very least. Another paddle. A second tent. A compass. A knife. Clothes that fit her. New shoes. Something she could use as a sling.

She paused at the second aisle. A small glass showcase had been shattered there. The display of fillet knives and multi-tools had been cleaned out. Around the corner from there, the mice had done a nice job of chewing into a plastic-wrapped rain poncho. Izzy grabbed it, peeled off the remains of the outer wrapper, and draped the green poncho over her arm. It would be nice to be somewhat dry during the next rainstorm.

Her scavenging complete in the store, Izzy left and presented her find to Jake.

"That's it?" he said after inspecting the damaged garment.

"It's better than nothing."

"Sure," Jake said. He turned back to the docks.

"We're not done yet." Izzy grabbed his arm. "We need to check everything."

She tugged him back toward the bait-and-tackle shop. "I need your help." She didn't—not really. She could search every building on her own. In his current state of mind though, if he headed for the docks without her, it would take only a minute for him to *leave* without her. That was a chance she couldn't afford to take.

In the bait shop, she found the paddle she needed. She also salvaged a loop of nylon twine—perfect for making a new sling—and a piece of plastic that would, in a pinch, do as a pouch. It wasn't quite as flexible or as durable as the rawhide she had used at the cabin, but until she had something better, it would work. She presented her finds to Jake, who admired the paddle but looked at the other scraps with disdain.

"What are those for?"

"You'll see."

She dashed across the road to the diner. In the kitchen there, she searched until she found a collection of knives. The big ones had already been taken, but there were plenty of paring knives and steak knives. She'd lived for months with just a kitchen knife. These, all professionally sharpened, would do just fine. She also grabbed a good pair of scissors, almost dancing as she rounded up the supplies. This kitchen was a gold mine. She wrapped two knives and the scissors in a towel and dumped the collection into a plastic garbage bag. She grabbed a few extra bags as well. They could keep her dry while paddling. She added another item to her mental shopping list: a backpack to carry her stuff.

Jake was still standing in the street right where she had left him when she emerged from the diner. She waved him forward to the houses that remained on the southern side of the street. Jake shook his head. "I'm not going back there."

"Then stay. Right there." She pointed at the ground as if instructing a disobedient puppy and raced forward to the second house, skipping whatever it was Jake had seen in the first one. He hadn't said what he had seen, but she could guess.

A pit of burned mud surrounded the second house. Scorched siding peeled off on one corner, but the structure itself seemed intact. She hopped from dry area to dry area, trying to keep the borrowed shoes on her feet somewhat clean. She tripped as her foot slid forward in the loose-fitting sneaker and fell to one knee.

"You okay?" Jake called out from his place of safety down the street.

"I'm fine." She pushed her way back to her feet, then stopped. Near where she'd slipped in the mud was a fresh boot print, leading into the house. She glanced back at Jake. He hadn't come anywhere close to this house. And the print was large—much larger than his boot. A chill worked its way down her spine.

She stood and took a step back.

"What's wrong?" Jake asked. Izzy held up her hand and took another step away from the house. A second later, she turned and sprinted back the way she'd come, grabbing him by the sleeve.

"We gotta—we gotta go," she stammered.

"Why?" he asked, jogging with her.

"Footprints."

"There are people here?" Jake slowed and turned back to the house. Izzy slid to a stop, reached behind him, and grabbed his arm again.

"They're Rick's."

"You sure?"

Izzy nodded.

She didn't hold him back this time when Jake bolted for the canoe. She followed, right on his heels.

CHAPTER 35

Jake

After twenty minutes of hard paddling, Jake's adrenaline rush subsided, leaving him weak and dehydrated. The paddle now felt heavy and rough, like a log instead of a precision-made tool. He rested it across his lap and buried his head in his hands.

The images of those bodies and those graves were too close to recent memories. He had helped his grandfather lower his mother into her grave. He had thrown dirt onto her, watched the sheet they had swathed her in become muddy and wet. The bear fur had protected his grandfather, but the dead had a smell that was not easily forgotten. The smell of the bodies in the bungalow in Laroque still clung to his clothes. The canoe rocked with the oncoming waves and added to the frothing sadness rolling through his chest.

"Dad! Where are you?" he screamed into the sky. He stood in the canoe and screamed again.

"Jake!" Izzy grabbed the sides of the canoe.

The next wave nearly tipped them over. The sensation of falling broke him from his momentary loss of control. He thumped back down into his seat and hung his head.

"Jake? You okay?" Izzy shifted backward in the canoe.

"I want my dad."

"Maybe he's up ahead."

"What if he's not?"

"What if he is?"

"I can't—I can't keep going—I just want to stop. I'm tired. I'm hungry. I miss them. My mom. My dad. My grandpa. I miss them so much."

"I know. God, I know, Jake. But we can't stop. Rick will find us. If we stop, he'll kill us."

Jake looked behind them. There was no sign of Rick, either in a canoe or on the land.

"You sure it was him?"

He didn't really need to ask. He knew Rick would follow them.

She nodded. "Big print. Fresh. I don't know how he got here ahead of us, but he did."

"We lost a day when we went the wrong way," Jake replied.

That was his fault. He should have paid more attention to time and distance when crossing the lake. It had been the best he could do under the circumstances. There had been no time to get a fix on their position, and so little time to take compass readings when the waves kept coming. They had made it across the lake alive, and that, at the start of the crossing, between Rick shooting at them and the weather, had been long odds indeed.

He could do better now. He pushed his hair back from his face and pulled the map from his bag.

Seventy kilometers to the west was the village of South Indian Lake. It might as well have been a thousand. Seventy kilometers of burned mud—sticky, heavy and impassable, with no cover, and little wildlife to hunt. The few roads that existed wound around the features of the landscape, so that the actual distance would have been closer to double. His eyes followed a blue line through the forest, across a few more lakes, up a few rivers, across another section of forest, and then down another watershed to a road. Once on that road, it was but a few kilometers to Thompson.

He knew parts of the route, especially those closer to Thompson. His family had fished those rivers and lakes dozens of times. They had paddled the river and run its rapids. He had never done it without his father, but he knew the area.

First, however, they needed food and clean water. And he needed sleep. A shiver rolled through him as the wind spun the canoe. A low-hanging cloud draped across the sky beyond Laroque. Jake watched it and noted its dark gray color. Another storm was brewing.

Jake picked up his paddle.

"Where are we going?" Izzy asked.

"Home," Jake replied.

"How far?"

"Does it matter?" Jake asked.

"No. It really doesn't," Izzy replied.

CHAPTER 36
◄○►

Izzy

"God, I'm hungry. And this is *not* cutting it." Izzy tossed a half-chewed cattail stem aside in disgust.

"Catch another fish, and we can eat something else," Jake said from behind her as they fought their way through the brush. "Or get that sling out again and show me what you can do with it. Until then, stop complaining. Doesn't do any good."

Izzy didn't bother to look back and didn't bother to argue with him. The sling she had made with the twine and plastic was okay, but it wasn't anything like the one she had built the previous winter. The rocks she fired with it refused to fly in a straight line. Jake had taken a brief interest in it when she had first put it together. Now it was a source of aggravation for her, and something he used to dig at her with when he was grumpy. He had been plenty grumpy these last few days.

On the lakes, the fish had been easy to catch. In the thick bush, food was whatever plants they could find. They had left the last lake behind three days before, and they hadn't had a solid meal since. The constant bushwhacking, chopping away at undergrowth with the machete, and fighting off the bugs sucked up Izzy's energy like a sponge.

Still, it was better than the alternative, she reminded herself. When she made this trek during the winter, there hadn't even been cattails to eat. All there had been then was an unending, hip-deep layer of snow. At least that was gone now, replaced by hip-high stinging nettles and downed trees. They had tried to boil the roots of the nettles—Jake said his grandfather said they were edible. That meal had been a complete disaster and left them both sick to their stomachs.

Izzy's eyes focused on following the old trail. Jake had called it a portage, but this path hadn't been used in years. Either that, or they had lost the trail—again. Twice in the past two days, they had been forced to turn around and backtrack a significant distance after finding themselves stuck deep in some swamp too wet to cross on foot, and too choked with weeds to paddle. Each time they had turned around, Jake had reminded her to pay more attention. He couldn't—not with the canoe on his shoulders. She had, after all, told him that she was very good at orienteering.

It wasn't her fault that he believed her.

They had given up on paddling the rivers. A constant rain had soaked them for over a week since leaving Laroque. The flows ran high and fast, and paddling into the current took ten times the effort it would have later in the year. Instead, Jake carried the canoe and his gun through the bush, while Izzy slogged the pack with the weight of all their gear. Her back hurt. Her feet had blistered in three spots from the ill-fitting shoes.

But she knew it was even worse for Jake. He hadn't been sleeping much. She had offered to let him use the tent, and she would sleep under the canoe. He had refused. Without food and without sleep, the boy carrying the canoe behind her should have been just inches away from death. Yet somehow, on a few cattails and pigweed leaves, he kept going.

They reached the shore of the next big lake just as a torrential downpour dropped out of the sky. Izzy's ragged poncho protected her somewhat, but as they pushed off into the lake, she wondered whether this leg of the trip would involve more time bailing out the canoe than paddling.

"Shouldn't we wait this out?" Izzy asked as the wind drove spray from a breaking wave directly into her face. A check of Jake's face showed his determination to continue. Within a few minutes, the shore disappeared from view, hidden by pelting rain and waves. Izzy's empty stomach lurched with each sudden drop. A particularly large wave hit her flush in the chest, nearly knocking her overboard. The bottom of the canoe filled with water.

"It'll be better once we get around the point." Jake dipped his head toward a dark shape on the horizon, impossibly far away.

"If we live that long." The wind stole Izzy's reply and blew it away from Jake's ears—not that he would have listened to her if he had heard. Izzy checked behind her one more time. Jake's look had not changed.

Izzy dug her paddle into the oncoming wave. The small canoe teetered on the brink as the wave rolled past. She timed her next paddle stroke and leaned back as the next wave slammed into them.

"Jake, it's not safe! We have to head in." Another wave slid them sideways.

"We'll make it. Just paddle!"

Izzy tightened her grip on the paddle. Arguing with Rick had never worked either. *They always have to have their own way. If they'd just listen to me once in a while, life would be so much easier.* Izzy muttered a curse and pulled her paddle through the next wave and the one after that.

Almost imperceptibly, the peninsula grew larger in the distance. Izzy's arms and back screamed for relief. The gray-green mass in the distance resolved into individual trees. Izzy pushed the bow toward the shore.

"No!" Jake ordered. "Go right! Hard."

"What?" Going right meant going back into the middle of the lake.

"Go right!"

"Why?" Izzy shouted.

"Look. To the left of that big cedar. In the bush."

Izzy tried to find the big cedar in a multitude of trees. One looked slightly larger than the rest. Her eyes dropped to its base, then tracked left. A large bush—some kind of half-dead juniper by the looks of it—sat just where Jake had pointed.

A slight movement caught her eye. She stopped paddling while her eyes determined what it was that she saw. Slightly blinded by the continuous fog of rain over the past hour, it took a moment for her vision to adjust. Then the rain slackened, and Izzy once again spied the movement on the shore.

Most of the land was green with a thick layer of pine needles. But there, among the bushes, a slightly darker area stood out, and a patch of brown moved. Some of the sticks in the bush were, in fact, antlers. A buck. Izzy gulped the cold air. Now that she saw the animal, she could see nothing else.

Izzy glanced back at Jake. The grin on his face told her all she needed to know. That deer would be their dinner. And their breakfast. And all the food they would need to reach Thompson.

Yet Jake hadn't reached for his gun.

"You want me to take a shot?" Izzy shifted in the canoe to reach for the gun.

"God, no." Jake shook his head. "I'll take it, but not from here. We'll go around the point, then I'll hike back." He pointed slightly to the right. "Keep paddling. I'll tell you when to turn."

Izzy slid her paddle back into the water. Her eyes split time between watching for the next oncoming wave and checking to make sure the deer did not suddenly spook and run. They rounded the point, well out of reach of its rocky bottom and whitecapped breakers. As Jake had predicted, the water beyond the point, out of the wind, lay nearly flat. He steered them neatly in to a sheltered strip of gravel. Izzy bounded from the canoe and onto the beach, ready to head out on the hunt.

Jake dragged the canoe clear of the water. He shook the rain from his clothes and dumped the lake water from his boots. He removed the rifle from its case.

"Come on. Let's go," Izzy urged.

"You're not coming. You don't have a gun, and neither of us have vests. I don't want to get separated and end up shooting you."

"I'll stay close. What if you need help?"

"I won't. Stay here. Dump the canoe. Check the gear. See if you can get a fire going."

Jake checked the gun for load, and his belt for his knife.

A second later, all Izzy could see were the moving branches where he had disappeared into the brush. *Left behind again. Just like with Rick.*

She shook the rain from her poncho and kicked the ground.

CHAPTER 37

Jake

The grind across the lake had been too long and too dangerous. Jake had known that as soon as they set into the water, but admitting defeat by going back would have been a kill shot to his hopes of getting out alive. His arms and back had nearly buckled under the pressure of trying to keep the canoe upright and on track. Izzy had been correct to question the decision. Again, his impatience had forced a mistake. His grandfather's voice chirped up. Jake shushed it. Now wasn't the time for a lecture. If he could get this buck, the risk would have all been worth it.

Water dripped from every branch and every leaf. Jake took long, careful strides, making as little noise as possible. His pace slowed as he closed on his target. His eyes scanned the shore, looking for the familiar cedar. The new angle rendered his memory of the deer's position nearly useless. Everything looked different. He took his time. In this thick brush, he would get only one shot. Their lives depended on it being a good one.

The whistle of the wind and the crash of waves obscured any sounds of his prey. The smell of the churned-up lake disguised any animal odors. All he could smell was fish, and he wasn't sure any longer if that smell was the lake or his own fragrance.

He paused and checked for the slightly darker area in the brush. He was close. The hair stood up on his neck. He stepped forward, waited a heartbeat, and repeated. He had seen hunters walk right by deer hidden in grass next to them and laughed as the deer scampered away once behind them.

He flexed his stiff trigger finger. It barely moved. Slowly, he removed his hand from the trigger guard and stretched it three times. His skin was white with cold. He blew warm air into his hand.

Five meters ahead and to his right, the deer bolted from its cover.

Jake's fingers fumbled back to the trigger as he pressed the gun to his shoulder. The deer rocketed away, heading northeast from the lake, already at a full run by the time Jake was ready to shoot. The thick brush obscured a clear view of the animal as it fled. Jake hastily lined up the rifle, led the animal slightly, took a quick breath, and squeezed off a shot.

CHAPTER 38

Izzy

The sound of the rifle made Izzy jump. She stared in the direction of the shot, wondering if Jake would come back with the deer in tow, or, more likely, empty-handed. A little gloating would have felt *so* good right then—but not as good as a full stomach.

He should've let her take the shot from the boat. She could have made it. *Easy.*

She knew that was a lie. She'd shot a real gun exactly twice in her life, both times from a prone position with her arms well braced, not from a boat on a frothing lake.

Still, he should have let her go with him. Two sets of hands were always better than one.

She picked up a rock and tossed it into the waves. A heavy drop of rain smacked her directly between the eyes. She wiped it away with the back of her hand. She wanted to scream—wanted to scream at the weather—it was supposed to be summer and warm, not this cold rain that never ended. She wanted to scream at the lake—lakes were supposed to be easy to paddle on. Every stroke out there had been murderous. She wanted to scream at Jake for treating her like a little girl. He went out and did the hunting, and she was supposed to what? Cook? Clean? Get a fire going? Her anger fizzled. A fire. They needed a fire to boil water and to dry their clothes, if that was even possible out here.

Reluctantly, she turned for their beached canoe and set about doing what needed to be done. She put the pack and their supplies on the beach and dumped the water out. Another twenty minutes on those waves and the water would have been up to the cross braces. She shook the canoe in every direction possible, until the only trickles of water were from the rain still hitting it.

She dug the flint and striker from Jake's pack, intent on building a small fire on the gravel. After five minutes of fruitless searching, she gave up on finding dry tinder and put the flint back in the exact place it had been. Once, she had put it in the wrong place and Jake had completely flipped out. Not a Rick-level flip out—he had only sworn once—but he had looked at her with suspicious eyes and didn't seem satisfied until she dug it out of the bottom of the pack and handed it to him.

She glanced at the fishing rod and then at the lake. With the rain and the waves and the wind, the shallows would be filled with churned-up silt. The fish would be off in the deep water waiting for the weather to subside. She left the pole in its case and instead pulled the sling from her pocket. Rocks on this beach were plentiful, and she needed the practice.

She launched one, then another, and another, in the direction of a washed-up stump to the southeast. Her arms, exhausted from paddling, balked at the strain. She fought through the pain and whipped the rocks overhead. One out of ten flew close to where she wanted it to go. With her salvaged scissors, she trimmed the plastic pouch down so the corners were a little smoother. The next rock flew a little better. The one after that nearly hit the target. Another adjustment and the sling felt almost right. It still wasn't as good as the first one she had made and learned with, but in a pinch, it might just work.

She hurled the stones at the stump until her arm felt like it would come loose from its socket. She turned back to where Jake had disappeared into the bush so long before. Worry crept into her mind.

He should have returned by now.

What if something had happened to him?

What if he'd gotten hurt?

She pocketed the sling and set off through the bush to follow him.

It didn't take long to reach the opposite side of the peninsula. There was no sign of Jake. The spot by the cedar tree was vacant, but a multitude of hoofprints in the area suggested it was a popular hangout for the antlered kind. On a nearby leaf, a spot of blood proved that Jake had at least grazed the deer—unless it was Jake's blood. Izzy shook the thought from her head.

Izzy's view drifted out over the water, where the waves still rolled and broke, though the rain seemed to have slackened, and the wind calmed. She could almost see to where they had set in just a few hours before.

In the distance, a shadow broke over the crest of a wave. Izzy strained to make it out. It disappeared into the next trough, then reappeared a moment later, riding the next crest.

In the instant before it vanished back into the gap between the waves, Izzy knew exactly what—or rather *who*—it was. Her stomach lurched. Sweat formed beads on her forehead. A knot lodged in her throat. She watched a moment longer, then turned and sprinted back to the canoe.

CHAPTER 39

Jake

The recoil from the rifle stung Jake's fingers and jarred his shoulder. He chambered another round as the expended cartridge spun off into the leaves. The deer disappeared behind a cluster of trees.

"Damn it!" Jake raced off in pursuit as fast as his aching legs could carry him.

The layer of disturbed mud on the ground tracked the animal's direction. Jake charged after it, his quiet stalking replaced by a full-out sprint. The hooves of the deer churned up pine needles as it worked itself deeper into the brush. The buck crashed through the forest, knocking more water from branches as it ran.

Jake paused at the spot where the deer had been when he had taken the shot. A thin mist of blood had settled onto the leaves. Jake's hopes soared. Had he missed altogether, the chase might have ended right there.

He turned to call to Izzy, then stopped. Every moment he wasted waiting for her was another moment he might lose track of the deer. The chase was already on. He turned back to the trail of hoofprints. A drop of blood on a branch and blood spatter on the ground gave the first indications that the bullet had more than just scratched the deer. Jake climbed over the trunk of a downed tree that the animal had hurdled without slowing.

The deeper he went into the trees, the harder the ground became. The tracks disappeared. Only the blood trail—a few drops here and a few drops there—allowed him to follow the injured beast's progress. The trees thinned as he climbed a small ridge. He temporarily lost sight of the trail as it crossed a creek. A few minutes of frantic searching picked up a large pool of blood where the deer had paused for a moment. He was back on the trail.

He fought to keep his bearings as he worked his way farther inland. He checked his compass frequently and paid careful attention to possible landmarks: dead trees, unusual rocks, and creek beds. Even so, after a while, it all began to look the same. Without a pencil and paper, getting back to exactly where he'd started would be a crapshoot. The fear of becoming lost this close to home blossomed in the back of his mind. He wished he had brought his backpack. His thoughts drifted back to Izzy. He hoped she would stay put. It would be hard enough to find her as it was.

The blood trail thickened. More than once the buck had stumbled and left smears on the rocky ground. Jake slowed his pace. His legs were not used to running. His energy reserve dwindled. Only the adrenaline—the thrill of the kill—kept him going.

The metallic smell of blood infused the air. To the starving hunter, it was divine. He hopped over another downed tree. A long streak of red ran across a layer of moss partially torn free from the log by a wayward hoof.

The buck lay next to a small bush just ahead of him, panting and wheezing. A thick froth of blood and foam dripped from its mouth and nose. A bullet wound pierced its side halfway down its back, just above the bottom of the ribs. Blood coursed down its hide. It moved as if to stand, but its weakened body could not obey. Jake knew that feeling—had felt it every day since this unending trip had begun. He also knew that his life—Izzy's life—depended on this animal's sacrifice. He put the gun to his shoulder and dispatched the injured buck with a second shot, this one to its head.

He took a moment to catch his breath and to assess the deer. The buck had done quite well for itself in feeding this year. There were seven points on the antlers, all with little damage done through either fighting or sparring with trees. It was early in the season, and the animal had been strong and healthy. Jake didn't have tobacco to sprinkle, but he did speak the words of thanks to the spirit of the deer as his grandfather had taught him, and asked for its strength to be imparted to Izzy and him.

Jake cleared the chamber on his gun by pulling another round into place. He allowed himself only a moment to celebrate. Bears and wolves could smell blood in the air better than he could. The chase had left a long trail of it leading to this spot.

Jake set the gun against a tree and removed his sweater. He studied the buck for a moment, then removed his T-shirt and pulled his knife from his belt. The damp chill attacked him while he was without his gear, but the last thing he wanted was to smear blood all over his clothes. Blood was impossible to remove in the bush. It would eventually harden to a crust, but it would always smell like blood, fresh or not.

With a series of quick motions, he field dressed the deer. He saved the heart, liver, and kidneys. Those would be their first meal as soon as they had a safe camp and a fire. His mouth watered constantly as he thought of cooking up the meat. He wanted to build a large fire, to warm up, and to feast on his kill, but he could not do it right there and then. Izzy needed food, too. The pile of discarded guts steamed in the cool air, turning the ground into a red morass of leaves, dirt, and blood. He stuffed the edible organs back into the carcass and tied the gut closed with his belt.

The timer in Jake's head ticked at a furious rate. He guessed that a kill this big, in these woods, with this much blood, meant he could have as little as half an hour before the uninvited guests began to arrive; a half hour to return to his canoe before he would be forced to defend his dinner. And the chase had taken at least that long. He wanted to start the clock from the time the final kill had been made, but as soon as blood had been spilled, the race against the clock had started.

Jake cursed himself for not remembering to bring everything he needed to finish the field-dressing process. If he'd taken his time, he would have remembered to bring the machete to cut off the antlers, and rope to use to tie the forelegs together. Instead, he pulled the laces out of one of his boots and lashed the legs to the antlers. The antlers would do as a drag line. Jake wiped his hands off on the moss, donned his shirt and sweater, then grabbed ahold of the antlers. The gun he looped over his shoulder.

The deer weighed perhaps fifty-five kilos—not huge by the area's standards. He'd seen many bucks closer to eighty. On wet, even ground, the deer slid easily. The trail, however, was littered with downed trees and brush that forced Jake to lift the carcass in order to pass by. The points on the antlers snagged on everything and poked him every time he pulled them free from an obstacle. Lifting the deer was easy at first, but with each downed log the deer grew heavier, until it felt like a ship's anchor, needing a winch to drag. Jake muscled it over each deadfall, straining with every move.

He followed, where he could, the blood trail left behind by the fleeing deer. It would have been faster to take a more direct route and to avoid the existing trail altogether, except he wasn't familiar with this area. The lake lay somewhere to the southeast and the canoe was hidden on a little unremarkable bay along the shore. The closer he could aim for the canoe on the first try, the better.

It took concentration to stay on the trail. The blood track had soaked into the ground and darkened on wood to look just like another knot. Jake put his head down and pulled the carcass as fast as his wasted body would allow. The jackhammer pounding of his heart blocked out the background noise of the forest. His hands hurt from gripping the antlers. A misplaced step sent him sprawling onto the ground, cracking his knee on the root of a nearby tree. Getting up dug deeper into his faltering reserves.

He smelled the water long before he saw it. Through the thick brush, Jake finally picked up sight of the breaking whitecaps. He left the carcass and hopped into the shallows, ignoring the impact of the cold water. He waded in deeper for a better view of the shore. His pulse quickened when he failed to see the canoe to his right, where he had guessed it would be. Then relief flooded his body as he found the large cedar where the chase had started, a hundred meters to his left.

In the forest, close behind him, a wolf howled. Two others responded. He jumped back onto the shore, grabbed the deer, and dragged it along the forest floor, in the direction of where he had left Izzy and the canoe.

It took less than three minutes to cross back to the beach where they had landed. When he arrived, the beach was deserted and the canoe gone.

Jake spun in a quick circle. Everything was gone. He had left her with the canoe and his gear, and she had taken it all.

Jake checked behind him, panicked. The wolves would be coming soon. He rubbed his bloodstained hands together. He'd be lucky if they only took the deer and didn't kill him, too.

"Izzy!" Jake called out over the water. The wind had abated in the time it took him to track and kill the deer, but the surface was still far too rough for an inexperienced paddler like her to make it on her own.

"Jake!" came a whispered voice from behind a fallen maple. Izzy's head popped up from behind the log.

"What the hell are you doing?" Jake yelled. "We gotta go." He dropped the antlers and raced forward.

"We can't, Jake. Look!" Izzy pointed southeast, along the shore. Jake's head snapped around. It took only a moment to see what had spooked Izzy.

There on the water, perhaps a kilometer ahead of them, was a large silver canoe, paddled by a single, large man.

CHAPTER 40

Izzy

Jake hunched down, as if to hide, then glanced backward. Izzy kept her eyes locked on the lone man in the canoe.

"He passed by here maybe ten minutes ago," Izzy said from behind the log. Every word she whispered still seemed like a bull-horn alert sent out to Rick. The silver canoe twisted momentarily, the bow sent shoreward by the ebb and flow of the wind-driven water. Izzy ducked lower.

"Grab the stuff. We have to go," Jake whispered back.

"We can't go. Not with Rick out there," Izzy protested.

"We have to. In a couple of minutes, we're going to have company here. And I'm not hanging around to see how big this party is going to get."

For the first time, Izzy noticed the dead deer on the ground.

She raised her hand for a high five, which Jake shook off.

"We gotta go. Now."

Jake vaulted over the log and grabbed the canoe, which was stashed behind it.

"Where are we going? Back into that?"

"Across it," Jake said. "If we can get across, we'll be safe."

"If?"

"*If* is all I got right now. I'll guarantee you though, that if we don't get moving now, we are not going to be safe *here* in two minutes."

Jake tipped the canoe up and over his head and ran for the water, nearly stumbling due to a boot missing its laces. Izzy grabbed the paddles, then made a second trip back for the pack. Jake scrambled back to the deer and dragged it across the gravel to the waiting canoe.

"Tilt the canoe so I can roll this thing in. I can't lift it all at once."

"Is it going to fit?"

"We'll make it fit."

Izzy did as ordered. In the distance, Rick paddled farther away, working his way southeast. He hadn't noticed their movements, their efforts drowned out by the crashing waves, pattering rain, and noise of the wind in the branches. Still, Izzy had trouble prying her eyes away from him. *How had he not seen her?*

Jake slid the deer into the center of the canoe. The hind quarters practically sat on Jake's stern seat. The antlers were so large that they rose up directly behind Izzy's bow seat. If she leaned back suddenly, they'd puncture her kidneys.

"That's not safe." Izzy pointed to the rack.

"Just get in. We'll fix it once we're on the water."

Izzy tossed the pack in on top of the deer and jammed Jake's paddle in next to his seat. Jake shoved the laden canoe deeper into the water. Izzy had to run through the shallows to catch up. The freezing water soaked her loose pants all the way to her hips, threatening to pull them down to her knees with every step. She jumped into the canoe as a wave lifted the bow. Jake joined her a second later.

Izzy turned to adjust the deer's antlers, but stopped.

A wolf launched itself down the bank and into the shallows where Jake had been just seconds before. It stopped as the cold water reached its shoulders. Jake grabbed his paddle, then dropped two quick strokes into the water to widen the distance.

One gray eye and one yellow eye tracked them as they sped away from the beach. The growl came a few seconds later. Izzy nearly dropped her paddle, and a bow-on wave threatened to capsize their overloaded boat. Jake corrected their lean.

"You gotta keep paddling," he urged. "We're going to ride a lot lower in the water with this thing in here. I can't get us across on my own."

Izzy adjusted her grip and pulled the paddle through the next whitecap.

Izzy glanced back at the shore. The wolf had retreated from the water. It watched them for another moment, its eyes locked with hers. The wolf growled once more, then turned and dashed back up the bank, into the woods. Izzy shivered as she turned and paddled into the wind.

"You sure we can make it?" she asked, eyeing the onslaught of rollers headed their way.

She knew what Jake's silence meant.

They didn't have a choice.

CHAPTER 41

Izzy

They reached the opposite shore half an hour before dusk. Izzy collapsed over the bow as Jake drove the canoe into a gap between the roots of willow trees crowding the shore. The fight across the lake had nearly killed them. The waves and the rain had come perilously close to swamping their small craft a dozen times. She had stopped bailing and paddled for all she was worth once the land actually seemed reachable. Her feet sat in ankle-deep water.

Now the wolves were on the other side of the lake, and Rick had not—to the best of their knowledge—seen them.

"I'm so cold," Jake moaned from behind her. He dragged himself from his seat, tripped over the gunwale, and fell into the water, face first. He coughed and sputtered as he knelt in the surf. Izzy resisted the urge to laugh at him. Jake had spent everything he had left to get them across the water. He looked broken.

"Come on, Jake. We need to get you dry."

Izzy forced herself out of the boat. Her legs wobbled on the slick rocks. She looped an arm under Jake's chest and lifted him to a standing position.

"I know, Dad. Shelter. Fire. Water. Food. I'll do it," Jake babbled. Izzy stumbled under his weight.

"Right."

She sat him down against a nearby log while she searched the area for a decent campsite. She settled on a small gap under a large white ash tree. It wasn't perfect—it sloped far more than she would have liked—but it was drier, not as rocky as the rest of the area, and hidden from the water. She dug the tent from the pack, set it up, threw the sleeping bag in, and dragged Jake to his feet again.

"Need to butcher the deer."

"I know how to do it. Just rest. I'll call you if I need you."

Izzy pushed him into the tent, then pulled his soaking-wet sweater and shirt off him. He did little to help—or to object. His waterlogged pants would have to be wrung out before they would be dry enough to wear again. He began to shiver.

"I can't sleep now."

"Yes, you can." She pushed him into the sleeping bag, ignoring his final protests, zipped the bag closed, and left the tent.

Outside, under the thick canopy of branches, the wind barely registered. Izzy ran back to the canoe and slid it clear of the beach. She would hide it as soon as she could empty it out. She stared at the deer that had accompanied her across the water, butchering it with her eyes, imagining where the best cuts were and what they would eat first. She spat a mouthful of saliva onto the ground.

"Shelter. Fire. Water. Food." She echoed Jake's mantra.

Starting the fire took every skill she had learned in her time in the bush. She peeled bark from a birch tree and plucked pillowy fluff from an old cattail. She grabbed the smallest twigs from a downed tree and removed the wet bark, tossing it aside. She pulled grass stems from a patch of foxtail on the gravel. She piled everything she needed well away from the lake, between two deadfalls that would hide the light of the fire from any passersby. Only when she had gathered everything she needed to start the fire and keep it going did she try to light it. Even then, it took five minutes of diligent effort to get a spark from the flint to catch in the cattail fluff. She cupped the ember and blew on it gently until the collection burst into a brief, intense flame. She added the oily birch bark, then the grass and the twigs. Soon, flames engulfed the small pile. She added larger pieces of wood in a small pyramid, letting the heat from the first flames dry the bigger pieces out before the weight of water within them could extinguish the fire. She admired her handiwork. Even Rick couldn't criticize those results.

She dug the water pot from the pack, filled it from the lake, and hung it over the fire on a sturdy branch rigged over the two dead logs beside the fire before turning her attention to the deer. Inside, she found the heart and the liver where Jake had stowed them. She cut the organs into thin slices, tossed them into the frying pan, and waited for them to cook. The smell of sautéing meat wafted through the air, intoxicating her.

Jake emerged from the tent, wrapped in only his wet sweater, just as the meat finished cooking.

"Get back in the tent. I'll bring it to you," Izzy ordered.

"I'm fine."

"God, you're stubborn. Get back in the damn tent. Now." Izzy stood, careful not to drop the frying pan. "I'll have food for you in a minute."

Jake looked like he was going to object again, but turned and crawled back into the tent. In the light from the fire, Izzy caught her first glimpse of his emaciated legs—as thin as matchsticks. She wondered just how they had brought him this far—and how much farther they could go. She looked back at the deer, then scanned the darkened forest around them. With the wolves on the other side of the lake and Rick ahead of them, this seemed as good a place as any to hole up for a few days and recover. They had shelter, fire, water, and food aplenty, now that they had the deer. A week, or even a few days, would allow them to smoke some of the meat, and that would make the final push to Thompson so much easier. She didn't let her mind go to what would happen when they got there. There were things that needed doing here first.

She slipped into the tent with a large plate of hot food and a cup of tea. Jake lay curled up in the bag, shaking like a leaf, looking almost delirious with exhaustion.

"Here, try some tea."

She pulled him to a sitting position and set the cup against his lips. His hair fell over his face. She pushed it back, looping it over his ears. He drank slowly. She handed him a thin slice of the venison heart. He stuffed it into his mouth with his fingers, then reached for a second piece.

"One at a time. Chew it well. Let your stomach adjust."

She pulled the plate back from him and ate a piece of her own. The rich meat slid down her throat like liquid gold. The temptation to gorge was almost too much, but she remembered the lesson learned after Rick got that first deer at the cabin and forced herself—and Jake—into a sensible pace.

They ate in silence until the plate was empty.

"You need to sleep now," she said.

"What about the deer?" he asked.

"I'll take care of it. I've done it before. Plenty of times."

"Okay."

Jake burrowed back into the sleeping bag. Izzy left the tent and stretched in the cool evening air. The rain had finally stopped. The trees still dripped and the wind still blew up above the forest, but in that little hollow, on the side of that lake, they were fed, and they were safe.

CHAPTER 42

Jake

"You sure you're ready for this?" Izzy asked again as they loaded the last of their gear into the canoe.

"The weather's good. The water's flat. We've got food. We've been sitting around on our asses for three days. It's time to get going."

Jake set the bear canister, now completely stuffed with jerky, into the center of the canoe. Every container and piece of plastic they could find had been filled with thin slices of meat smoked over their campfire. They had eaten almost continuously since waking the second day. Still, nearly half the deer would go to waste—it wouldn't keep long raw, not with temperatures suddenly spiking into what counted as balmy weather in the North. Jake split the remainder into three piles, scattered about the woods. The scavengers would feast well tonight.

"Thompson?" Izzy stood beside the canoe, hesitating before getting in.

"Not like we have a choice. It's a big town. We'll sneak in. See what things are like. Maybe they're better now."

"What about Rick?"

"He's got three days on us. He's probably already there. Not much we can do about that."

They stood, an uncomfortable silence falling between them. As much as Jake wanted to get back to Thompson, if only to see if everything Izzy had told him was true, he didn't know what he would do once they got back there. Rick's existence didn't make things any easier.

"He's not going to give up," Izzy stated.

"No. Probably not. I just—I just don't know what else to do, where else to go. Maybe my dad is there. He'll know what to do."

Izzy's facial expression did little to build his confidence that what he said was possible. She didn't let the look linger, though.

"Maybe," she said, forcing a smile onto her face. Jake tried to return the gesture.

"Hop in. We're wasting daylight," he said as he put his best reassuring face back on. She stepped carefully into the bow. Jake checked behind him one final time for any gear, then pushed the canoe into the lake.

On the flat water, the distance flew by. Only the ripples spurred by a flock of geese disturbed by their presence broke the refection of the mirrored surface. With Izzy paddling in perfect rhythm with him, they sped onward to their next goal. Beyond the southern edge of this lake was a portage over a ridge—a ridge that separated the Churchill watershed from the Odei. Beyond that ridge, all the rivers ran downhill to Thompson. Across a few lakes and down a few rivers—all of which he knew well enough to navigate without a map—then they would be home.

They spoke little. Even while camped, gorging themselves on food, they didn't spend much time together. With just one sleeping bag, a campfire to keep going, and meat to smoke, they hot-bunked; one climbed in after the other left, but before the bag got cold. For the short periods they were both awake, they always seemed to find things to do, away from each other, like gathering firewood or searching for edible plants to enrich their diet. They were avoiding each other, and both knew it. Talking would inevitably lead to discussion of what lay ahead. With empty stomachs, the conversation had always revolved around the next meal or the next portage. Now, with full stomachs, the immediacy of their predicament had abated somewhat, and they could look beyond the few days it would take to return to civilization.

Once out on the water, with pleasant, almost enjoyable paddling finally possible, the silence became too much for Jake to bear.

"Izzy?"

"Yeah?" She jumped at the sound of her name.

"What do you want to do when we get back to town?"

They both stopped paddling. The canoe coasted across the open water.

"Do?"

"I mean, do you want to stay in Thompson? Or go somewhere else? Do you have relatives anywhere around? Outside of the city? South?"

"No. Not nearby. I have a couple of uncles who lived out in Alberta—they were working up by the tar sands. But I don't know if they're still there . . . or alive. You?"

"It was just me and my folks, and my grandpa, here. My mom's folks live out in BC somewhere. But I've never met them. And like you said, I don't know if they made it either."

"You've never met your other grandparents?"

"They didn't like my dad much. My mom was white. My dad was—" He pointed to himself.

"Ojibway?"

"Cree."

"Oh. That's a shame."

"What?"

"Not that you're Cree—that you never met your grandparents. My mom's parents lived in Winnipeg. My dad's dad lived in town.

He died in the flu. My dad's mom moved back east a long time ago. Couldn't get ahold of her after it all started. My mom's folks didn't answer the phone after the first week."

Jake shook his head and returned to paddling. Izzy's ability to list off the dead and the presumed dead without so much as a grimace still stunned him.

"So what do you want to do?" Jake asked.

She shrugged. "What do you want to do?"

"Don't know."

"Are we . . . sticking together?" she asked.

"If you want to."

"I think so."

"Good. Me, too." Jake relaxed a touch. As much trouble as she had been in the first days after he rescued her, having someone else around made this trek so much more bearable. The work of setting up camp and watching the fire didn't seem so relentless. Paddling, and especially portaging, was a breeze with two compared to one. Having someone to talk with, besides his memories, buoyed his spirits even more.

They paddled on and reached the portage shortly after noon.

"One more climb, and it's all downhill after that," Jake said.

"Yep. Ready?"

Jake lifted the canoe over his head and adjusted his grip.

"Let's go."

CHAPTER 43

Jake

Two nights later, they camped by the base of a set of rapids on the upper reaches of the Odei. Downstream from the white water, mist draped the riverbanks like sheets covering old furniture. They alternated shifts in the tent through the night. By sunrise, they had each slept about six hours. Jake felt at least partially refreshed when Izzy cajoled him out of the tent as the sun rose.

Izzy cooked more venison and filled them both full of tea while Jake broke camp. Twenty minutes later, they set in downstream from the last set of rapids.

Jake kept a wary eye out for the portage markers. He spotted the first one two hours after entering the flow. They were out of the boat and ready to haul their gear downstream as soon as the boat touched shore.

"Jake . . ." Izzy led the way, scouting the trail. Jake had pinned his hopes on this one being easy. Using an old trail was usually better than breaking a new one. The closer they traveled to civilization, the better the old trails became.

"Yeah?"

"You need to see this." She stood two boat lengths ahead of him, about to cross the grassy boundary between the shore and the trail. Jake barely had time to grip the center cross-brace on the canoe.

"What is it?" He ambled over while stretching his back.

She pointed to a shallow depression in the dirt. A track of footprints veered off the trail from the river. A broken branch here and a bent sapling there led to a campsite partially hidden from the trailhead. A small fire pit, circled with rocks, still radiated warmth.

"It's fresh. From this morning."

"Rick." Izzy spat.

"Probably." Jake shook his head. He circled the fire in ever greater circles, looking for telltales that would prove the fire builder's identity. A flattened cluster of weeds betrayed where a tent had been. Jake tested one of the leaves from a crushed plant with his fingers. "This was probably standing yesterday. So he wasn't here more than a night. Two at the most."

"So he's waiting for us?"

"He should be all the way to town by now, Izzy. And as far as he knows, we're ahead of him. So why wouldn't he keep going? Maybe he got tired."

"If he wasn't finding our camps, he'd know we were behind him."

"We could have camped anywhere. The odds of him finding our camps would be so small."

"He knows we'd have to come through here, right? He knows we'd be on the river and on these portages. He knows these woods."

"If he knew, this would have been the place to wait for us. He didn't."

Jake could tell by her sour expression that she wasn't buying it. He wasn't either.

"Can we hike it?"

"I'd rather not. Not with the shoes you've got on. I'd have to carry you half the way."

Izzy smirked and shook her head. "How far ahead of us is he?"

"Assuming he got moving around sunrise, too, he's got an hour, maybe two on us. Depends on how hard he's pushing today."

And on whether or not he stopped and is waiting for us.

"How long is this portage?"

"Not long, I think. Then there's an open stretch, and another branch of the river joins in after that. There's a set of falls a little way past the confluence. Big ones. Water gets real fast, real quick."

"So we keep going?"

"We don't have a choice."

"What if he finds us?"

"We'll just have to find him first, and avoid him."

Easier said than done.

Jake walked back to the canoe. He had hoped Rick would have given up the chase by now. Rick had a fully stocked cabin, and Jake had taken nothing but Bill's canoe and Izzy. Hell, she had almost taken herself. Except here, almost two weeks later, he was still chasing them. He spun back to Izzy as he reached the canoe.

"Izzy?"

"Yeah?" She turned her attention from the trailhead back to Jake.

"Izzy, I have to ask. Why does he want you back so bad? You're *not* his daughter, right?"

"No. I told you my dad died from the flu," she snapped as Jake walked closer to her. "He was a neighbor."

"Why then? Why does he keep following us?"

"I *don't* know," Izzy said. She couldn't meet Jake's eyes when she said it, and Jake knew he had to press further.

The man had shot at him. He had killed Bill Six Rivers. And the more Jake thought about it, the more convinced he was that Rick had molested Izzy. Something else nagged at him. She had left something out—something critical. He stopped, glanced back at the river, then up to the sky as he searched for the words. When all this was said and done, and the blood had been spilled—and it seemed Rick had already decided there *would* be blood spilled—Jake needed to know that there had been no other options. If he ever saw his father again, he needed to be able to tell him that. His father's words echoed in his mind.

Do what needs to be done.

"I need to know who I'm dealing with, Iz. Because I'm going to need to take this gun out of its case."

She turned her eyes to Jake. Her face bore a pained expression. The words came in a burst that nearly knocked Jake off his feet.

"Rick didn't just kill Bill, Jake," she said. "He also killed my sister."

CHAPTER 44

Izzy

"He killed her?" Jake took a step backward.

"That's why I had to run. He killed her and blamed it on the gangs. They took Angie, and they raped her. But *he* was already raping her, and when they did what they did, he killed them all. He said she was damaged . . . *spoiled*." Tremors rippled through her voice. "He doesn't want me spoiled like she was. He couldn't deal with the fact that someone else did that to *his* woman. Now he wants me for his wife." Tears slid down her cheeks. "I'm fourteen, Jake! I'm *not* going back to him. *Ever*. He took *everything* from me. Everything I had left, he took, and he destroyed. He killed Angie. He took me up there and he . . . he . . . he's insane, Jake. Just insane."

Jake swore. But he didn't question her story. The look of doubt that had so often crossed his face had vanished, replaced by rage, then pity.

"I'm so sorry, Izzy. I don't—I can't imagine . . . what you went through. I can't—I'm so sorry." He slouched forward as if to give her a hug. Izzy retreated, albeit involuntarily. Jake stopped and squeezed his eyes shut.

"Jake—" She moved forward, but Jake had already spun away. "Jake, thank you."

"Thank you?" He turned back to her.

"Yes. Thank you. For saving me. That day. In the lake. I couldn't keep . . . I couldn't stay there any longer. I wanted to die. And then you came along and pulled me out. I've never thanked you for that. Because I didn't know for sure that I really wanted to live. There's just so much . . . in here"—she thumped her chest with her fists—"that I couldn't let go. Can't let go. It's so hard . . ."

She took two big steps and wrapped her arms around him. Jake paused, then hugged her back, his long arms wrapping her tight. The hug lasted long enough for Izzy to catch her breath and halt the sobs that shook her to her toes.

Jake gave her a moment to collect herself before speaking again.

"Izzy, we're going to have to be quiet. We're going to have to watch for him, and be ready to run if he gets close. If we get separated, just head south." He pulled the compass from the carabiner and gave it to her. "I know this area well enough. As long as a blizzard doesn't drop out of the sky, I'm pretty certain I can make it back to Thompson without that now. Just take care of it."

Izzy took the compass and clipped it to the cord holding up her pants.

Jake removed the gun from its case, chambered a round, and checked the safety. He hung it over his shoulder.

"You okay with the pack?" They hadn't made a dent in the venison yet. The pack, along with the bear canister, probably outweighed her.

"I'll make it. Let's go."

Jake hurried back to the canoe, flipped it over his shoulders, and regained his balance.

"Let me know if you need to stop."

"Just go. I'll deal."

The canoe scraped every low-hanging branch, creating a screech Izzy was certain could be heard all the way to Thompson. Izzy tried to walk even more quietly to make up for the racket Jake made. Rick was close. She could feel it. Around the next corner, or around the next bend in the river, he would be waiting.

• ◆ •

Low clouds arrived around noon, but seemed reluctant to drop any rain upon them that day. Jake pulled them out above a section of flat water for lunch. Starting a fire would take too long. Besides, if Rick was close, he'd smell the smoke. Instead, they ate the dried venison cold.

"We're making good time," Izzy offered. She sliced off a bite-sized piece of the jerky and pushed it into her mouth. It almost took more energy to chew the tough meat than what she'd get out of it in return.

"Yeah. Pretty good." Jake picked at his food.

They would have made better time had they not been constantly on the lookout for Rick.

"What's up ahead?" Izzy asked. She wandered over to a cluster of cattails, plucked two, ate one, and handed the other to Jake, who ate it without taking his eyes off the river.

"Pretty smooth for a couple more klicks, at least until the branch joins up from the left. Then the falls, if I remember correctly. After the falls, a long run of fast water down to the bridge at the Narrows. We'll hop out there and go on foot to Thompson. It should be pretty quick and easy after the portage. All roads. No more trails to clear. No canoe to carry."

"And if you don't?"

"Don't what?"

"Remember correctly—where the falls are." She smiled and gnawed on a piece of the deer meat.

"Then we're gonna get really wet," Jake said with a nervous chuckle.

They finished their meal and repacked their gear. Izzy paused as she dropped the food pack into the canoe. The river moved past their picnic spot at a decent speed. They'd barely done any paddling the last hour before lunch. Jake had steered while Izzy watched for rocks, downed trees, and Rick.

"You think he's still out there?" she asked.

"I don't know." Jake shrugged. He pushed the canoe closer to the water. Izzy did not move.

"I should have that." Izzy pointed to the gun still looped over Jake's shoulder. "I can shoot."

Jake shook his head.

Izzy stared into his eyes. "You still don't trust me? After all this? You still don't trust me?"

"I do trust you, Izzy." He scuffed his feet in the dirt. "But this isn't just about trust. This gun is more gun than you've ever fired. The kickback will knock you out of the boat or break your shoulder if you're holding it wrong." He tapped the butt of the rifle. His eyes broke her stare and dipped toward the water. "Even if you could handle this gun, shooting a man is not like shooting a deer, Iz."

"How do you know? Have you ever done it?" Izzy crossed her arms.

"No. No, I haven't." His face fell. "And I don't want to, either." He wiped his brow with his hand, chasing away a mosquito. "But if we have to, I gotta think that our chances would be better if I were the one to take the shot. My father gave me this gun, Iz. I've been shooting it for years. If someone has to pull the trigger on *this* gun, it has to be me. I'm sorry. I'm not trying to be rude or mean or anything, but if it comes to it, *I* have to be the one."

Izzy took a breath. Five days ago, before the deer, his words would have sent her into a frothing rage, but today she understood. She understood Jake's tenuous tie to his past. She had nothing left of her parents, and only tortured memories left of her sister. She would have done anything to have a single prized possession that held some sort of memory.

"What are you going to do?"

He shrugged at that one. "Hope I don't have to do anything. He's gotta think we're in town by now."

Izzy didn't share his hope. Rick would be waiting, somewhere.

Jake put the canoe in the water. Izzy looked at him with an *Are you sure?* expression. Jake nodded, hopped in after her, and pushed them into the flow.

CHAPTER 45

Jake

Below the confluence, everything did run faster. The second river entered from their left. Remnant snowmelt and the recent rains pushed the water into a gigantic standing wave as the two flows crashed into each other.

"Dig! Hard!" Jake shouted at Izzy as the river threatened to spin them end for end. Jake flipped the paddle from one side to the other, not so much paddling as using the paddle as a lever against the side to correct the path of the out-of-control canoe. He should have gotten out and scouted the approach. The voice in his head was no longer his grandfather's. It was his own.

"Which side?" Izzy yelled. Ahead, mist thrown into the air betrayed the location of the falls. They seemed much bigger than he remembered.

The right side seemed so much closer—calmer. An outcrop of rock created a swirling eddy that would allow them safe access to the shore. On the left, the water ran straight and fast. They'd have only one chance to cross it before plunging over the edge. The right side would have been the sensible choice—the easy choice. If he could see that, then Rick would have seen that, too.

"Go left!"

"Left?" Izzy glanced back at Jake as if he were crazy.

"Left. Hard! Now!"

He slammed the paddle against the stern. Izzy reached over the port gunwale, stuck the paddle into the water, and pulled. The canoe barely moved to the side. Panic seized him. He had waited too long. Jake rammed the paddle deeper into the current, nearly breaking it trying to lever the keel over.

"Paddle!" Jake ordered.

The port side dug into the water. White foam splashed over both of them. Jake thrust the paddle in again. The bow crashed through another standing wave. He ripped the paddle back out of the water and dug in again, prying the craft forward. He jerked the paddle out at the finish of the stroke and slammed it back in again. The exhausting process lasted perhaps a full minute. His shoulders burned from the exertion. His hands went numb from his grip on the paddle.

Izzy hopped out as they reached the pullout and yanked the bow onto a narrow strip of exposed rock that offered the slightest protection from the swift water. Jake rolled out after her, gasping for air and latching one hand on to the canoe to stop it from pinwheeling away from the bank and over the falls.

"How far?" Izzy said, her voice dropping to a whisper.

"A few hundred meters," Jake croaked. His lungs burned. He put his head on his knees to catch a full breath.

"I don't see any sign of Rick."

"Good." Jake had counted on Rick taking the easy side, not because Rick couldn't paddle across, but because Rick wouldn't have believed Jake could power the canoe across that flow. Jake had almost proved him right. If it hadn't been for Izzy's help, he never would have made it.

Jake rested a moment to let the lactic acid leave his shoulders while Izzy held tight to the canoe. Izzy grunted with effort.

"On three," he said. "One . . . two . . . three."

Jake began to haul the canoe from the water. A bloodcurdling scream from across the river stopped him mid-lift.

"Isabelle!"

Jake nearly lost his grip on the thwart. The hull was half-in, half-out of the water, with the bow clear and the stern still half a meter below his feet. Jake's eyes jumped to the other side of the river. Rick stood there, with the big silver canoe on his shoulders, the bow tipped up so he could see them. With a single, impossibly quick motion, he tossed the canoe from his shoulders and threw it to the ground. Thirty meters of roiling water separated them from one another. Even over the sound of the waterfall, the thud of the aluminum canoe hitting the ground rang clear.

"You son of a bitch!" Rick aimed his words at Jake this time. "You little bastard!"

Jake fumbled with his pack as it dropped to the ground. His frozen fingers slid on the wet gunwale. The tug of the current wrenched the canoe toward the falls. He leaned back without taking his eyes off Rick and wrenched the canoe onto the rocks.

"Go home, Rick!" Izzy shouted in a much more powerful voice than Jake would have expected from her. She let go of the canoe as it tumbled onto the rock.

Rick pulled something from the side of his pack.

It took Jake just a fraction of a second to realize what it was. He turned to Izzy, still standing defiantly behind him. His left hand held the center brace of the canoe, which now lay in his lap. He used his right to grab Izzy's tunic. With a sharp tug, he jerked her to the ground next to him. The shot from the shotgun reached them at the same time as the retort shook the water off the nearby trees. Steel pellets ripped through the side of the canoe and into the trees behind him. Jake pulled his feet back from under the canoe and pushed Izzy behind a large cluster of roots. Another shot echoed as he dove after her. Splinters of wood and droplets of sap coated his back.

"Are you freaking nuts?" Jake shouted across the water. He rolled deeper into the trees and pulled Izzy with him.

"Are you okay?"

"Yeah." She rubbed a scrape on her knuckle. A drop of blood ran down her finger. Jake checked her as quickly as he could. The trail disappeared to their left. He held her close to the ground.

"When I say go, I want you to run down the trail about fifty meters. Wait for me there. If I'm not there in five minutes, head south. Follow the river until you come to a bridge. Follow that south, and you'll come to a highway. Head east. That'll take you to Thompson. Just keep going."

"What are you going to do?"

"I'll be there in five minutes."

He slowly moved to the right of one of the rocks for a better look at Rick, who popped two spent shells from the broken-open shotgun. He stood in plain sight on the bank, one leg slightly ahead of the other, his jacket hitched on the knife sheath on his right hip. Even in the distance, he loomed large and frightening.

Jake removed the loop of strap holding his gun to his shoulder and checked the weapon for damage. A piece of shot had pitted the stock. He winced and ran his finger over the chipped wood. The shock of being a target passed, and then anger overwhelmed him. He hadn't been hit, but his prized possession had. The only thing he had left that his father had given him.

Jake slid farther forward until a small gap in the rocks allowed him to aim his gun.

"Ready?" he asked Izzy.

"Yes." She paused. "Are you going to kill him?"

Until that moment, Jake hadn't decided. *If you leave a bear wounded, it only comes back angry. And an angry bear does a lot more damage than a dead one.* His father's words held true, even in this case.

Jake nodded. "Go."

Rick caught sight of Izzy's movement in the trees and lifted his gun. Jake raised his own to his shoulder, lining up Rick's chest in the crosshairs—and pressed the trigger.

CHAPTER 46

Jake

Nothing happened. The trigger would not budge.

Rick snapped his barrel into place. Jake's eyes widened. He pulled his head back from his gun. It took him a moment to realize why it hadn't fired. He hadn't disengaged the safety. He watched in horror as Rick raised his gun into the firing position. Jake released his safety at the same time. He put his shoulder back against the butt plate of the stock just as the shotgun reached Rick's shoulder. The shots were simultaneous, and both off-target.

Jake cringed as more buckshot flew over his head and pinged off the rocks around him. Leaves sputtered off branches and dropped onto his neck. The retort of his own gun roared in his ears, drowning out the sound of the river. He checked down the path. Izzy had disappeared from sight. Rick had vanished as well. Jake crawled forward. Little cover protected Rick's side of the river—just a few flat rocks, an old stump, and the silver canoe. Jake ejected the spent cartridge from the chamber and slid another one into place. There were only two places Rick could have hidden, if he had not already fled back down the trail. If he was behind the stump, anything short of a .50 caliber round wouldn't punch through it, and Jake wasn't about to wait for him to poke his head back out. However, there was another way to slow him down. Jake lined up the gunsight on the keel of the canoe.

"Let's see you keep up with us now," Jake said with a grimace.

Jake fired. The canoe shuddered and jerked. A large hole, about the size of a golf ball, appeared where the bullet pierced the aluminum. Jake ratcheted back the bolt and put another hole through the bottom. Four seconds later, he added a third one for good measure, slightly forward on the bow. Rick did not return fire.

Jake waited thirty seconds, cranked his bolt back, and slid another round into the breach. With his eyes still on the opposite bank, he moved toward his canoe. His pack, his tent, and their food were all still in there. Hidden by the rocks, he crawled back, stopping every few seconds to check for Rick. Only the holed bottom of the canoe looked out of place. The last shot had cracked the center of the keel, and any weight at all would cause it to fully collapse. Rick's canoe was out of commission. Jake hoped Bill's had fared better.

There weren't three holes in Bill's canoe. There were a dozen pinpoints of light coming through its port side, and half a dozen deep scratches from ricochets along the side as well. Jake crawled from cover to cover to grab his pack. He tossed it down the trail without drawing more fire, scrambled closer to grab the food canister, and rolled it down the trail as well. Still nothing moved on the opposite bank. Jake repositioned his body parallel to the overturned boat.

With no way to right the boat without exposing himself to fire from Rick, Jake weighed the pros and cons. Ten kilometers of bushwhacking versus ten klicks in a leaky boat. He slowly raised his hand to the top of the keel near the bow. He kept as low as he could, lifted up onto his knees, and yanked on the keel with his right hand while holding the gunwale steady against the ground with his left hand. He rocked it twice before it began to slowly tip over.

The shot ripped into the bow as the boat hung on the verge of completing the roll. Pellets smashed into the bottom of the boat. A random pattern of dots emerged in the fiberglass. A steel ball the size of a BB lodged into the heel of Jake's boot. His arm had already been coming down to let the boat complete its rotation, saving Jake from serious injury. Shards of rock ripped into Jake's clothing. Pinpricks of blood, like nicks from a dull razor, marked his cheek. Jake dropped back down behind the canoe and the shelf of rocks. A second shot ripped into the canoe right where he had been just a few seconds earlier. His feet drove him into a low running position, knowing it would take Rick a few seconds to reload. He didn't stop to return fire. He grabbed the pack and the canister and ran after Izzy as fast as his legs could carry him down the trail.

They would have to make it out on foot. Rick was on the southern side of the river—the side they would have to reach for safety. Jake knew of only one spot to cross over, and if Jake knew it, he was sure someone like Rick knew it, too. It would be an all-out sprint to that spot.

They couldn't afford to lose this race.

CHAPTER 47

Izzy

Izzy ran down the trail, flinching with each shot, counting her steps until she figured she had gone far enough. An outcrop of granite blocked her view of the river. Two shots, almost simultaneous, reached her ears. The woods went silent, as if every bird and animal were watching, waiting to see what would happen next. The rock she leaned against hummed with the vibration of the falls, but the falls no longer seemed to make noise.

She wanted to call out to Jake, to see if he was all right. She opened her mouth to speak. Another blast cut her off. More shots followed in quick succession. The shots blended into a single volley. The last time she had heard so many shots, her sister had been killed. Now she feared the same for Jake.

A crashing noise on the trail broke her from her memory. She grabbed for a stick, ready to fight Rick off with her bare hands if he had somehow crossed the river. Instead, she released a huge sigh of relief and dropped the stick as Jake appeared, coming for her at a dead run. He skidded to a stop next to her. He adjusted his pack and secured the canister to the top of the pack frame.

"Is he dead?"

Jake shook his head. "We've got to go, and go fast. We've got to get to the bridge at the Narrows before Rick does."

"How far?" she asked.

"Ten klicks, maybe twelve. We'll follow the river, but we gotta stay far enough away that Rick can't see us."

"I heard a lot of shots." She looked at his face. "Are you hurt?" She wiped some blood from next to his right eye. He pushed her hand away and wiped the back of his hand across his face. It came away smeared with blood.

"I'm fine."

She looked back toward the falls.

"Don't worry about that. Just watch where you're going. We'll go as long as we can tonight. Keep the river on your right. Stay away from the edge. Let me know if you have trouble keeping up." He looked at her shoes. She reached down and pulled them off. She handed them to him.

"Barefoot? You sure?"

She wasn't sure, but the blisters on her feet from the shoes were only going to get worse if she continued to wear them. Her feet had toughened considerably in the last year. She flexed her toes in the soft dirt of the forest while he stowed the shoes. The cool soil almost felt welcoming—healing. "I'll manage. Wish I had my mocs, though."

Jake stuffed the shoes into the pack, then led them past the falls and into the forest.

She had no trouble keeping up. Jake had trouble staying ahead of her. He carried the pack with the canister strapped to the top and the gun in his hand. He struggled as the pack slid from side to side, forcing him to grab trees to keep his balance. After a few minutes of running, she spoke up.

"Slow down," she said.

"You tired already?" He wiped his hand across his brow.

"No, you're going to run yourself into the ground before we get halfway there. Trust me, I'm a runner. Slow the pace. We'll make it farther and faster," she said, remembering the advice her mother had given her when she had first started training.

"I'm fine," he growled.

Izzy shook her head. He didn't want to show weakness, and she understood that. He started off again, running. After ten minutes, he stopped and took a sip from his canteen.

"Another couple of hours and we'll bed down for the night." Jake stood with his hands on his knees, taking deep, shuddering breaths.

"Sure." Izzy's hands rested on her hips.

"You used to run?" Jake asked.

"Yeah. I won the city cross-country meet for my age right before the flu. Mom and I used to run half marathons twice a year."

"You're only fourteen."

"I'll be fifteen in November," she said, annoyed. "I've always been small for my age. We started running 5Ks when I was six. I've run the Manitoba Half-Marathon three times. We were going to do the full marathon this year." She paused. "So when I talk about pacing yourself, you should probably listen to me. I know what I'm talking about."

"Oh."

"Running barefoot isn't quite the same, though." She pointed to her feet. "And I'm not in great shape anymore, so slowing down a bit wouldn't be a bad thing for me either."

"Sure." He rubbed his side. "We'll slow a bit."

"Thanks." She shook her head as he turned back to the east.

"Ready?" he asked.

"Yep."

Jake slowed their pace to a fast walk and kept it up for almost three full hours with just a short break for water. Darkness engulfed the forest. With a thick layer of low clouds and no moon, they wouldn't be able to see well enough in the night to make any time once the sun completely disappeared.

Their only consolation? Rick likely wouldn't be able to travel then either.

CHAPTER 48
◄○►

Jake

Sleep that night consisted of a series of alternating short naps interspersed with moments of sheer panic. Jake jumped at every sound during his watch. Every wind-caused rustle of leaves put his hands on his rifle. During Izzy's shifts, every creak of a branch had her tapping him to warn of Rick's impending approach. Up well before dawn, they moved swiftly as the first glow in the eastern sky brightened their patch of the woods. They snacked on pieces of venison roasted during the night, and they jogged through the gloom. They talked little.

Sometime around noon, they stumbled through a shallow, water-filled ditch and clambered up the side of a rutted winter road, heading in roughly their desired direction. They reached the bridge an hour later. They paused before making the final run across.

"Do you see him?"

"No." Jake removed the lens covers from his rifle scope and meticulously scanned the opposite shore. Weeds covered the aging box girder bridge. Spots of peeling olive-green paint remained on the steel, but brown rust overwhelmed the structure. Steam rose off the river, filling the area the locals called the Narrows with mist. Overhead, the clouds fled the scene. The next night, Jake guessed, would be cold.

"Do we go?"

"Give me a minute." They hid behind a downed tree that neatly blocked the road two hundred meters from the river. The far side of the river, another fifty or seventy-five meters away, disappeared and reemerged from a veil of mist as if someone were towing a train of clouds down the river. Jake completed two more scans, then nodded.

"Let's go."

He clamped the butt of the rifle against his shoulder as they moved out from their hiding spot. He hoped that they had made better time than Rick. The distance was about equal. Jake and Izzy had used every minute of daylight to gain an advantage. *Rick probably did the same*, Jake thought. He didn't say it aloud.

They walked as quickly as their aching feet would allow. Extended time walking had forced Jake to make more room in his cramped boots for his toes so as to avoid blisters of his own. By the light of the campfire, he had finally cut the toe caps off his boots with his knife. Now, instead of being blistered, his toes were wet, cold, and numb. His boots filled with water and mud from puddles, streams, and creeks too numerous to count. On the other side of the bridge, they still had a few more kilometers to hike to the outskirts of town. He hoped his feet wouldn't fall off from trench foot before then.

The road rose to the broken concrete approach to the bridge. At one time, logging trucks had rolled over this one-lane structure on an hourly basis. Spring floods had left the framework under the roadbed impaled by dozens of broken trees. High water had slammed the footings and washed out large sections of the embankment. It was just a matter of time before all support was lost and the bridge fell into the churning rapids below. Jake couldn't help but notice that no one had come out to repair the damage.

Every step they took put them farther into the open. Jake measured the distance to the first steel girder. His grip on the gun relaxed. His eyes searched the opposite shore for any signs of movement.

At fifty meters from the bridge, he shouted a quick order to Izzy: "Run, Izzy! Run!"

They sprinted toward the steel frame and slid in behind it. The forty-meter-long bridge hung over the water on trestles that appeared ready to fail at any moment. Long sections of rusted rebar poked through the fractured concrete deck. The sides of the bridge would protect them from shots from upriver or downriver, but if Rick were close enough to appear at the far end of the bridge before they finished the crossing, he could fill the roadway with shotgun pellets. Jake's heart drummed in his chest, only partially from exertion.

"Okay, let's go, fast as you can. Watch for the potholes. If you see Rick, duck behind one of the girders. When we get all the way across, get into the trees on the left as fast as you can, okay?"

"Yep."

Jake led the way, gun pinned to his shoulder. The safety was off this time; he had checked it three times before they started the initial run, and verified again at the last stop. He weaved around a large hole in the deck that fell straight through to the water. He counted the distance in his head. Fifty meters. Forty. Thirty. Twenty. A movement to his right caught his attention. He slowed slightly, turned the gun toward the motion, and fired. His finger flew off the trigger as his arm reached behind him. Izzy ran hard, right on his heels. Her tunic hit his hand. He grabbed at it. His left foot slid on loose pebbles. His hand redirected Izzy's momentum down and to the concrete curb. She tripped and slid to a jarring stop. The blast of Rick's gun echoed through the trestle as the ping of shotgun pellets rang off the steel beams. Jake spun as he dropped to the deck. The gun slid from his grip as he protected his face from impact with the ground. His chin slammed into the rubble. Stars danced in his eyes.

The feeling of liquid running across his back broke him from the impact-induced fog. He arched his back and searched with his hand to determine where he had been hit. After searching fruitlessly for three or four seconds, he pulled his hand back and checked it for blood. It took a moment for him to realize that the liquid was not warm; it was cold. A pellet had punctured one of the water bottles strapped to his pack. He almost let out a laugh, but the ache in his chin squelched it short. There *was* blood there, and plenty of it.

"Izzy?"

Izzy groaned.

She lay wedged into the gap between the curb and the bottom of the bridge railing. Jake pulled her down into the gutter and crawled forward on the deck until he was even with her. Her eyes were closed. A large scrape crossed her forehead and terminated near her right eye. A circular knot there had already swelled to the size of a Ping-Pong ball. Blood gushed from a laceration along her temple. She tried to raise her head, but Jake held it down.

Approaching footsteps forced Jake to delay any further inspection of her condition. He brought his rifle forward, cranked the bolt, and shoved a new round into the chamber. With his finger on the trigger, he assumed a prone firing position, raising his head barely above the gutter's edge.

Jake slowly lifted the gun over the concrete lip to locate his target. Rick had been hiding behind a thick pile of stumps to the right of the road for his first shot. He now closed the distance to the bridge at a full run. Jake aimed between the bridge supports, caught a brief glimpse of Rick's legs, and fired. With a quick pull on the bolt, he slid another round home. He had had six rounds in the clip when he started. Four remained. He fired again. Three.

The footsteps slowed and hesitated. Jake had a bad angle on Rick through a thin slot in the ironwork. He lined up another shot and took it. The bullet grazed one of Rick's legs. The response was a howl of pain and anger, and a vengeful return volley from the shotgun.

Two. Jake ducked below the curb as he cranked another bullet into the chamber. He popped his head up and fired another shot as Rick retreated back to his pile of stumps. One.

"You ain't getting off that bridge alive, boy!" Rick taunted as soon as he reached cover, a slight hint of pain in his voice. Jake slid the last bullet into the chamber. He checked Izzy's head and rubbed her face.

"Izzy? Izzy, you okay?"

Izzy's hand came up to her forehead, gently touching the swelling lump. She groaned again, and coughed.

"It hurts." She curled into a ball, both hands clasped to her head, knees pulled to her chest.

He couldn't lift himself up far enough to examine her—not that he would have been able to do anything if she was injured beyond a scrape or a splinter. He had no medical training, or even a spare bandage. His own blood ran down the outside of his throat from the cut on his chin. He set his chin on his arm to staunch the flow.

He evaluated his options. They had fifteen meters to go before they were off the bridge. Rick was below them and to their right, behind a wall of stumps. Even after the bridge, forty or fifty meters remained to reach the tree line. To Jake's left, a shallow ditch, half full of water, ran along the edge of road. Jake could crouch and run, fire his last shot, and hope that kept Rick's head down long enough for him to find better cover. Doing that, however, would leave Izzy alone on the bridge.

They could stay and try to out-wait Rick, but the concrete deck sponged heat from their bodies at an alarming rate. The drenching fog above the river only made it worse. In an hour, they would be too stiff to walk. In a few hours, without moving and without a fire, they'd be dead from hypothermia. They were both soaked in sweat, and with the punctured bottle having drained across his back, his vital organs would soon be wrapped in a cold towel. Neither of them had the reserves to wait it out. Jake had no option but to move.

With just one shot left, he had to reload. He released his pack, rolling it to the top of the curb. His movement drew more fire. The bag moved backward. Pellets ricocheted around the girders. Izzy twitched at the sound and let out a short shriek. Jake reached into the bag, trying to find the plastic box with his spare bullets. Instead, his hand felt something colder, and harder.

It took a moment for Jake to recognize what it was. His heart jumped as he pulled his grandfather's army .45 out of the bag. The green dishcloth he had carefully wrapped around it clung to the barrel sight. He plucked the cloth free and wrapped his fingers around the grip. The gun was heavy—almost heavier than his rifle. He remembered back to the first time he had shot it. His heart had pumped a million beats an hour then too, but for different reasons. His grandfather had hauled this gun around a half dozen countries, though according to Amos, it had never actually seen combat. That was about to change. Jake pulled the slide back, chambered a round, and set his rifle on the bridge deck next to Izzy.

"Izzy, can you hear me?"

She nodded slowly.

"I'm going to try to make a run for it. See if I can't pull him away from here."

"Jake . . . don't leave. Take me with you."

Jake held her down with one hand. "Stay here until I come back, or until the shooting stops. Then run for the trees on the left, okay?"

"No, Jake. I want to go, too. Don't leave me here."

"I'll leave the rifle. It's right here. If you see him coming, you use it, okay? It's got one shot left."

He pushed the rifle in front of her and ran his hand over her head. Her blood-ringed eyes lodged one last protest, but he could wait no longer.

"I'll come back. I promise."

He began to move.

CHAPTER 49

Izzy

Izzy grabbed for Jake's pant leg as he slithered forward. Her ears rang from the blasts of his rifle. Blood coursed down her cheek. She objected one last time, but it was too late. Jake was gone.

Panic surged through her body and she began to tremble. From cold. From fear. The broken concrete seemed to latch on to her, anchoring her body to the ground. She took a deep breath to settle her nerves. The smell of gun smoke and pine and blood mingled into a bewildering mix. The river rumbled beneath the bridge, humming through its superstructure as if an army marched nearby.

She was alone.

The pounding in her head slowed just enough to form one coherent thought.

I can't stay here. I have to move.

She reached forward and touched the rifle. Jake had said there was one shot left. One shot with a gun that would probably break her shoulder the first time she fired it. She lifted her head above the concrete edge. Jake disappeared to the left. Rick was somewhere to the right. *Where exactly?* She pulled the gun closer. It was so much heavier than the .22—too heavy for her to manage.

Jake had told her to stay put.

She couldn't stay there. Not with Rick out there. He'd be coming. He'd kill Jake, and then he'd come back for her. But she couldn't go back the way they had come. She wouldn't go back there, ever.

She moved the only way that made sense. Forward.

CHAPTER 50

Jake

On his elbows, Jake crawled five meters, rested, then another five. At any time, Rick could bolt from his cover and catch him without an angle on the stump pile. As Jake scooted forward, he gained a better view of the ground ahead of him. The ditch to his left followed the road closely. Forty meters from the bridge, the sight of a concrete abutment caught his attention.

Rick had a better gun at this range—one that could make up for poor aim—and better cover from which to use it. The only thing Jake could do was try to keep Rick's head down as he ran, so Rick couldn't get off a shot while Jake was exposed.

Jake jumped from the prone position to standing as fast as his fatigued legs could manage, using the last angular bridge beam to cover his move. His left hand braced his right hand. He fired at the pile of brush. The .45 boomed like a cannon. His arms drifted upward with the recoil. He re-aimed the barrel at the corner of the stumps where Rick had disappeared, then sprinted down the short embankment to the left and slid into the ditch. A twig near the pile moved. Jake fired again.

The ditch was deeper than Jake originally thought. The bottom held a reservoir of fast-moving water. Jake ignored the discomfort of cold water running through his open boots in favor of the safety of concealment.

The stumps still protected Rick from Jake, but the berm of the road would prevent them from seeing each other if they moved. Their current positions led to a stalemate, but in time, Jake—and Izzy—would lose. Jake had but three rounds left in his gun. Rick's supply of shot seemed inexhaustible.

Jake worked his way south toward the abutment, careful to stay concealed by the road. He monitored the approach to the bridge. If Rick made a run for Izzy, Jake would have a good line of sight only once Rick reached the road. He wanted to poke his head up to check on Rick, but it would mean giving away his position. The longer Jake stayed concealed, the more places Rick had to watch to figure out where Jake was.

The roar of the river running through the debris below the bridge disguised any noise Jake made as he moved. Still, he moved quietly, as if he were stalking a wounded animal. To Jake, that was what he was doing. He couldn't think about it any other way. He covered the ground to the abutment at a fast jog. A short tunnel made of a double layer of creosote-covered railroad ties supported the road over a creek that fed the ditch. He plunged into the darkness. If Rick was waiting on the other side, there would be no retreat—Jake would be penned into this wooden crypt, likely for all eternity. Frigid water rushed into his pant legs, nearly up to his groin. He stifled a cry of pain. With one hand, he pulled himself along using the underside of the trestle deck as a guide.

A copse of dry grass hid the exit from Rick's view—not that he was looking in that direction. Jake's speed and quick decisions had put him behind and to the right of Rick. The barrel of his gun led the way through the grass, separating the stalks with barely a shimmer. Ahead, a dozen meters away, Rick crouched behind his pile of stumps, eyes fixed on the road where Jake had disappeared just a minute before.

The shot was clear and easy. And at that moment, Jake was glad he didn't have his rifle and its scope. Even without the scope, he saw something he didn't want to see: a human being. Rick was no animal. Maybe in behavior, but not in form. Rick grimaced and pressed down on the top of a thin streak of blood on his leg where the bullet had nicked him. He wiped his nose with the back of his hand, then rose slowly, scanning the far side of the road. These weren't the actions of an animal. This was a man, made too human in Jake's eyes by the close range.

Five seconds passed. Jake began to lose the feeling in his still-submerged legs. Five more minutes and he'd be too cold to walk. He had a pair of semi-dry pants in his pack. That was a lifetime away. Jake hesitated ten seconds longer, hoping that Rick would do something—anything—that would justify taking the shot. Rick didn't move.

"Drop the gun!" Jake shouted from his hiding spot. It wasn't his most commanding voice. It shivered with fear and cold and came out more of a cry than an order. Rick's head spun around. His gun came up at an incredible speed.

Jake's heart thudded. In a flash, he was back in the clearing with the bear. The bear had run when Jake stood tall. Rick wouldn't run. The expression on Rick's face morphed into that of the bear. His teeth were long and sharp. His nostrils flared. His eyes locked onto Jake's position. He roared in anger.

Jake squeezed the trigger.

The .45's recoil knocked him off balance. Jake's shot missed high and to the right. His left foot lost its grip on the bank, sending him sliding backward.

Rick fired as Jake toppled into the creek. The shot scythed through where Jake had stood just a second before. Blades of grass spun through the air. Water funneled into the neck of Jake's sweater. He gasped and tried to pull himself back to the bank. The .45 slipped from his grip and dropped to the muddy creek bed, out of his sight and out of his reach.

"You stupid kid." Rick appeared over the edge of the creek. His shotgun pointed directly at Jake. It could not miss from there. "You should have never taken her. She was mine." His hand tightened on the trigger. Jake raised his arms to protect his face.

The rock hit Rick flush in the temple. Rick's eyes bulged as his head snapped sideways. His gun discharged harmlessly over Jake's head. The sound of the shot rolled like artillery under the trestle while the shotgun pinwheeled off to his left. The force of impact threw him into the creek. Rick's head bounced off a large river rock before sliding face-first into the water. He did not move again.

Jake's eyes fogged. He dove under the water to retrieve the Colt and came up with it aimed at Rick. Jake kicked Rick's back, but he was dead.

Water cascaded from his clothes as Jake scrambled out of the creek. The slight breeze felt like a gale as it chilled his body even further.

There, on the berm of the road, stood Izzy, her sling dangling from her right hand. She wiped her face with her left hand. Blood from the cut on her temple created a mask of red on one side of her face.

"I told you I was good with this thing," she said.

Jake glanced back at Rick. Water built up around the new obstruction in the creek and flowed over the top. Jake swerved and skittered up the muddy embankment, trying to gain traction toward the road and Izzy.

She slowly drooped to the ground, her face suddenly pallid and lifeless.

"Izzy!" Jake dashed to her, grabbing her as her knees hit the ground. "Oh, Jesus."

Her skin was cold to the touch. He laid her gently on the ground. She was so cold. *Fire.* We need fire. *Shelter. Fire. Water. Food.* Jake just had to keep moving until they had those things.

He raced to the bridge, grabbed his pack and his rifle, and ran back. He stripped off his wet pants and shirt and pulled out his last remaining pair. The wet ones he left where they fell. The dry pants weren't as thick as his others, but the suck of heat from his skin slowed. He discarded his socks for a somewhat drier pair, though just as rank. His boots he dumped out and then put back on.

He needed fire and warmth. Izzy needed immediate medical care—more and better care than he could give her. His fingers fumbled with the rifle, added a half dozen rounds into the magazine, just in case. The Colt he safed and dropped back into his bag. He shouldered his bag and looked at Izzy. He would have to carry her. It took him a moment to figure out how to do it. He slid the pack down his back slightly and threw Izzy over his shoulder in a fireman's hold.

He took five steps and froze in his tracks.

"Stop. Right. There." The voice came from down the road. It took him a second to recognize that it wasn't the same crazed voice he had heard just minutes before.

There were actually two people: a middle-aged man in a blue jacket carrying a .22 rifle, and another man, somewhat younger and leaner, carrying a Remington similar to Jake's. The .22 was aimed at the creek to Jake's right, where Rick lay motionless. The Remington was pointed squarely at Jake's chest. Even in the hands of a rank amateur, the gun couldn't miss from that range, and this man looked like he knew stock from barrel just fine.

"What the hell is going on here?" the older man in the blue jacket questioned. Jake took a quick glance at the body in the creek. Izzy spasmed in his grip.

"He was trying to kill us!" Jake explained.

"Looked like you had the same intentions," the man said.

Jake nodded. "Yes, sir. But not by choice." The weight of Izzy and the pack began to tip him backward. He shuffle-stepped to keep his balance.

"What's your name?" the man asked.

"Jake. Jake Clarke."

"Where you from?"

"Thompson."

"Ain't seen you around."

"I've been in the bush a while." Jake shifted his feet again. Izzy convulsed in his arms.

"Sir, can you check on—my friend? I can't hold on, and she's hurt, bad."

He adjusted his grip on Izzy as she started to slide off his shoulder. He had no choice but to trust these two, despite the fact that one still pointed a gun directly at him. The older man gave a tip of his head to the younger one, changing positions while the younger man cautiously approached Jake from the side.

"How long have you lived in Thompson?"

"All my life, till the last year or so. My dad and grandfather ran Clarke Excursions." The man's expression changed slightly at the name. "You know it?"

"You're Leland's boy?" The man's gun dropped lower. The younger man arrived and slowly pulled the hair back from Izzy's face while keeping his distance from Jake.

"Yes, sir." Jake's eyes welled up at the mention of his father's name. He clenched his jaw. "Have you seen him?"

His chest locked up. He dreaded the answer. The younger man reached over and grabbed Izzy off Jake's shoulders as though she were a feather-stuffed pillow.

"I'm sorry, no. Not since before the flu."

The barrel of his gun now pointed at the ground. Jake's spine could no longer support him, and he fell forward on his knees. Drops of blood fell from his chin onto the gravel. The enormity of his journey landed squarely on his exhausted body.

"Davis, she's conscious, but barely. Exposure for sure. Maybe hypothermic. A concussion, too, probably."

Jake turned his head to Izzy. The younger man held the inert girl with one arm while examining her with the other. She was limp and gray, her hair matted with blood and mud.

"Take her back to the camp, Eddie. Get her warmed up."

Davis waved Eddie south, then stepped forward to Jake, who had barely moved from his bowed position on the ground. Davis reached down and lifted Jake to a standing position. He held his shoulder with one hand to help him maintain his balance. Eddie was in motion before Jake could try to follow.

"Who's the girl, Jake? I don't remember Leland having a daughter."

"Her name's Izzy. She was with Rick in a cabin out there. She— she asked me to help her. I think he kidnapped her, but I'm not sure," Jake said. Davis's eyes went wide with familiarity.

"Eddie, that's Izzy—Izzy Chamberlain," Davis called out. Eddie stopped in his tracks. He looked back down at Izzy's damaged face.

"Is that Rick?" Eddie asked. He pointed to the body in the creek. Eddie's face flashed with an anger that made Jake shiver. Jake nodded. They knew who she was. And they knew Rick.

Eddie gave Jake a nod of his head that conveyed more respect than he had ever before felt, then headed off down the road at a near run with Izzy carefully cradled in his arms. Jake looked down at Rick's body, then back to Davis.

"We didn't want to kill him. He just kept coming. He was going to kill us."

Jake closed his eyes and tried not to remember the image of Rick standing over him with the gun. Izzy had saved him. Another second and it would have been all over. He rubbed his face with his hands.

"I know, Jake. We know about Rick. You done good. Your dad would be so proud. You done real good."

"It was Izzy. She saved me," Jake admitted.

"Looks more like you saved each other, son." Davis removed his hand from Jake's shoulder. Jake swayed, but then steadied himself.

Jake gazed back into the trees to the north, as if he could see all the way to the cabin, back to a boy standing on a dock, ready to start an impossible journey. A lifetime had passed since that last morning on the dock, yet he could see back into that boy's eyes. That boy had not been ready for the trip. Yet here he was.

Davis gave Jake a moment to catch his breath. "Come on. We've got a long walk ahead of us. It'll be dark in a couple of hours, and I don't want to be out here then. It can get pretty nasty without the right gear." He took a brief glance at Jake's boots and shook his head.

Jake nodded and flexed his mud-encrusted toes.

"We'll find you new ones when we get back to town, unless you want his, now." Davis pointed at the boots on Rick's lifeless feet. Jake looked at them for a moment, then back at his own. He couldn't bring himself to do it.

"No thanks. I'll make it." Jake picked up his gun and adjusted his pack. Davis retrieved Rick's shotgun, pulled the fired rounds from the barrel, and draped the broken-open gun over his arm.

"You ready to go home?"

"Yes, sir," Jake said, taking a long breath. "But I'm not sure where home is these days."

He took a final glance at Rick, and then a long look past the bridge and into the deep woods.

He had made it. He hadn't done it alone. Amos had pulled him through the winter and passed on the knowledge of his ancestors. Izzy had saved him more than once. Still, he knew, without a doubt, that Davis was right. His father would have been so proud.

EPILOGUE
◄○►

Izzy

The world bounced up and down. Left, then right. Something wrapped around Izzy's forehead.

"Jake?"

"He's right behind us."

"Who are you?" The contents of Izzy's stomach gurgled and threatened to erupt.

"I'm Eddie."

"Where's Jake?"

"He's coming. We're taking you home."

"I want to see Jake!" Izzy threw her left elbow backward to try to break the man's hold on her. He stopped walking and adjusted his grip on her, turning so she could see back up the road. Two figures walked side by side in the distance. One waved.

Jake!

"See. You're safe."

Izzy coughed and tasted blood and dirt. She raised her hand to her lips. Her face felt taut and swollen, her eyes heavy.

"Where's Rick?"

"He can't hurt you any more, hon. You're safe now," Eddie said as he resumed walking.

"Where are we going?" she asked.

"To our camp. Then to Thompson. We'll have you home by nightfall. She's going to be so happy."

"She?"

"Angie. Your sister. She's been looking everywhere for you. She never stopped."

Eddie picked up his pace.

Her vision began to bounce. Her head spun.

"*Angie's alive?*" *Rick hadn't killed Angie? How? Why?*

It didn't matter. Angie was *alive*. That was all that mattered.

"Yes. You rest now, okay? You're going home."

The bouncing faded into the background. Her vision narrowed. A single word echoed through her mind as the blackness settled in.

Home. She could finally stop running. Her sister was alive. Rick was dead. She and Jake were safe. The cold left her bones, and warmth wrapped her chest. She slept.

Author's Note

This is a work of fiction, and while the city of Thompson is real, the village of Laroque has been pulled out of the ether. Any resemblance to other villages in the area is completely coincidental and unintentional. Description of Jake's route and the land of the North is based on my best research efforts from afar. I can only hope to have come close to describing one of the wildest places left on Earth and interweaving what I think is a gripping story. I would enjoy hearing from local residents and experts on where I went wrong and where I was right.

◄○►

Acknowledgments

The first draft of this book, completed in 2008, exceeded 139,000 words. Fewer than 10,000 of those original words remain, and most of those are now in a different order. While I did write the words on my own, the difference between the length of that version and what you have just read, and the quality of that version and what you have just read, is a tribute to the many people involved in this journey to publication.

I subjected far too many of my friends and relatives to the trials of reading that first draft. To those who endured what must have been a painful read, I am truly grateful. Without your feedback, I never would have continued pursuing my dream. To those readers, including Mike Barsoski (friend and fellow Canuck), Eric Briggs (my hunting and parenting consultant), Morgan Briggs (my YA reader and someone I am sure will have far more writing success than I ever will), Marcia Briggs (my mother-in-law and second hunting advisor), Carolyn Coene (my aunt who never says good-bye without a tear in her eye), and Teri Towne (fellow author and office distraction), I thank you so much for your help.

For Benjamin Newland, with whom I formed a two-person critique group, I hope to someday read your work again. Thanks for helping me to stay enthusiastic about writing during the tough times. Who knew priests could be so damn cool?

Jason Black did a wonderful job of steering me through the earliest days of editing. His services (and friendship) proved invaluable in getting to the meat of the story and working through the hitches in the plot. Had it not been for his guidance and assistance, I most certainly would still be buried on the slush pile somewhere.

For my Aunt Anne Stratton, who snapped the photo that adorned my early website's version of the book, thank you for setting the tone of the book through that image. It let my mind settle into the story each time I looked at it.

I also want to thank Jerome Pettys for helping to do the original cover art and website image design, and Jen Sanders, who did my headshots—you both made me look far better than I appear in the mirror.

Cherie Dimaline also gets credit for advising me on First Nations life, history, and beliefs. I'm so thankful you were able to set me straight where it mattered.

Greg Tabor did a wonderful job with the cover for the first edition. Hopefully it helped you to take a chance on a writer you've never heard of.

Now I need to thank two very special people who changed the course of my life.

First, Mrs. Ruth Ann Jensen, who was my teacher in seventh grade and my English teacher in eighth and twelfth grades. I would not have my love for writing and creating stories had you not encouraged my talents at an early age. I will never forget that "being outspoken isn't always a bad thing."

Second, Pam Binder, president of the Pacific Northwest Writers Association. Had it not been for her pulling me aside when I was at the lowest of my low points after getting rejected by agents at my first PNWA conference in 2009, I would never have continued to write, and I never would have made the hard decision to cut this book in half and start over. Always with a smile on her face and an extraordinary ability to listen, even in the busiest of times, Pam pushed me to be a professional and never let me doubt my ability to persevere.

Of course, any writer who gets this far must have a fantastic team on the business and editing side as well. My agent, Sally Harding, always carries a velvet hammer, and uses it often to get me doing what I need to be doing. She took a chance on a manuscript that needed "a lot" of work because she thought I had the "chops" for telling stories. I can only hope I have proved her right. Along with Sally, I must credit her crack team at the Cooke Agency for keeping things going, especially Rachel Letofsky, who helps with just about everything, from paperwork to story ideas, and always with a smile and an infectious laugh.

Over at HarperCollins Canada, Hadley Dyer probably had no idea what she was getting herself into when she bought this book. But she stuck with me from one personal disaster to another, and helped me to learn about the ropes I didn't even know existed. She was right when she said there would be days when I would curse her name after getting another round of edits back. But she was almost always correct in her editing suggestions, and the story is so much better because of her efforts and patience. Maria Golikova and her team got the book ready for production, and made it shine.

Finally, I need to say thank you to my direct family: my mother, Simone, who taught me there was little better in the world than sitting down on a cold winter day with a good book, and my father, Tony, who taught me that nothing good ever comes easy. I hope I have done it right.

For my son, Reece, and my daughter, Lorelai, thank you for putting up with me every time I disappeared into my office to write. You bring such joy to my life that I miss you even when we're just one room apart.

And to Lisa, my wife and partner in life, thank you so much for being there through all of this. You listened to me go on about stories, read who-knows-how-many drafts, and kept the fire going even when winter never seemed to end. It's been a long journey to get here, and I'm so glad we get to travel this road together. Luv u.